POD

LALINE PAULL

corsair

CORSAIR

First published in the UK in 2022 by Corsair
This paperback edition published in 2023

1 3 5 7 9 10 8 6 4 2

A CIP catalogue record for this book is available from the British Library.

ISBN: 978-1-4721-5662-4

Printed and bound in Great Britain by Clays Ltd, Elcograf S.p.A.
Typeset in Garamond Three by M Rules

Papers used by Corsair are from well-managed forests and other responsible sources.

FSC
www.fsc.org
MIX
Paper from responsible sources
FSC® C104740

Corsair
An imprint of
Little, Brown Book Group
Carmelite House
50 Victoria Embankment
London EC4Y 0DZ

An Hachette UK Company
www.hachette.co.uk

www.littlebrown.co.uk

For India Rose

i want to go home,
but home is the mouth of a shark
home is the barrel of the gun
and no one would leave home
unless home chased you to the shore

WARSAN SHIRE,
'Home'

It is not down in any map; true places never are.

HERMAN MELVILLE,
Moby-Dick

Prologue

Half-dreaming at the surface, Ea wakes in an instant, her reflexes always on high alert. But it is only a wild and lusty chase. The young couple leap, splash back down and then, twirling in their bubbles, join together belly to belly. Ea admires their dance. Some things never change.

Others do. Within three generations, this pod has racially blended into a new tribe that mixes spinner grace with bottlenose strength. Like all the old, Ea finds the young more beautiful every day, but she would not go back. Time goes so fast now anyway, calves barely weaned and now mating, dusks and dawns racing each other as if the whole ocean has accelerated to a new rhythm. She does not mind, because it means reunion comes closer, with the ocean and with one whose heart still beats in hers. Since the seasons blurred, the moons lost their meaning and it is not for her to dictate the spawning of fish or coral. It is odd, at this time of her life, to miss the rituals she so resisted when she was young. Perhaps none of this would have happened if she had not. Everything broke apart, but Ea no longer blames herself. What happened was bigger than any fault of hers.

*

Ea watches the amorous young couple, now drawing an excited throng. If she and her dwindling cohort of elders find the younger generations shallow and lacking in curiosity, they keep it to themselves. They avoid nostalgia and unless some rare youngster makes reference to it, they even forget they are of different races. Ea is the last spinner dolphin of the remote and peaceful Longi tribe. The other elders are bottlenose dolphins, of the once notorious Tursiops megapod. Hard to believe how once they clung to those identities.

Ea tries to live in the moment, knowing each peaceful day is a gift. Even if she can never quite relax. Some nebulous feeling, some old vigilance wakes her in the deep of the afternoon, when the rest of the pod is asleep. Then she listens to the ocean with all her attention, but there is nothing unusual to hear. No grinding horrors, no cries of pain. Sometimes one of her fellow elders wakes shrieking, dreaming in red water. Ea is glad to be there to give comfort. It is over. This is a different place.

Sometimes Ea wants to share her story so that people know what it cost to be here. But kind and respectful to the elders as they are, the young dislike their painful tales. Ea understands. She was once the same.

The truth is hard to believe, harder to bear.

1

Pelagic, of the Sea

Just below the equator, somewhere in the Indian Ocean, is a curving archipelago almost four hundred miles long. The biggest and most easterly island starts the chain which dwindles to the west, terminating in three tiny atolls. There is a gap in the chain where, in the latter part of the twentieth century, one atoll was completely vaporised during nuclear testing.

These troubled waters shelter broken nations, refugees and ghosts, but this is the story of two estranged cetacean tribes, cousins with a painful past. The first are the Longi people, a tiny pod of *Stenella longirostris*, or spinner dolphins. The second is the megapod of common bottlenose dolphins, or *Tursiops truncatus*, who drove the Longi from their home and took it for themselves.

Each pod has pride and virtue, each feels above the other. They do not know they share one fatal flaw: they think they know this ocean.

2

Unnatural Child

The glow of dawn marked sea from sky as the silver Longi pod streamed back from another successful night hunt. Young Ea was ready to put her plan into action, edging out of the throng coming up the wide channel back into the safety of the lagoon homewater. As soon as she was in she peeled off to the side, subtly so she would not be seen leaving the group, but determined not to get caught up again in the daily lovemaking.

Ea was indignant and upset that because she rejected every suitor, she was the one considered to have the problem. She was neither tired nor unwell, she just did not want to have sex and she did not care how healthy a pastime it was. Coming of age was something she had secretly looked forward to for quite another reason, and it was a colossal and bitter disappointment. Her hearing did not improve, the music of the ocean did not miraculously burst into her mind. Instead, the ugly frightening sounds continued that even her own mother suggested might be in her imagination. Ea alone suffered them, furious and ashamed that somehow she might have brought that pain and fear on herself.

She knew she was valued for being a good hunter, but what Ea craved was to be normal. To spin like everyone else was the key to fitting in, and if she could only hear the music of the ocean like everyone else, she too would be able to tune in and do it. She was fast, healthy and wanted so badly to succeed – but she had never heard the music. Spinning was the Longi's art form, it was dance, athleticism, most commonly just for entertainment and sport, but it also held a spiritual element. It was union with the ocean itself and everyone who experienced that state even once, shone with authentic Longi joy. Calves learned by puberty, but by maturity, Ea knew her attempts were empty technique with graceless result.

There was no explanation for Ea's peculiar acoustic disability, which caused her to suddenly start in fear at disturbing noises in the water. Perhaps she was too sensitive, even by Longi standards. The sounds came unpredictably, straight into her sonar melon and painful enough to send her whirling off course to avoid them. At those times people encouraged Ea to spin to transcend her fear, but that only resulted in her greater frustration and headaches that lasted for days.

Obsessed and envious about other people's spinning, not a day passed when Ea did not secretly try, one last time, to hear that healing music – but the ocean continued to withold that gift. Anger became her way of coping. If she could not have it, she did not want it. She could hunt, that would have to be enough. She was an outsider with a reputation for being difficult, and only her mother knew how badly she grieved, and how much she hated pity.

Sexual maturity was a disappointment and a shock. Disappointment that her hearing did not improve, and shock that, despite her awkwardness, she was inundated with suitors. Ea assumed that her ugly inner world of bad thoughts and cravings and resentments meant her outer self would match – but that was far from the case. All the Longi people were beautiful, but she was exceptional.

In Ea, the grace of her people was exaggerated, from the long black lines around her eyes, to the flashing pearly belly marked with long glittery dashes increasing the impression of her considerable speed. The Longi had exquisitely shaped pectoral fins and tail flukes and in this Ea was no different, but her face set her apart. Her long rostrum, or beak, was slightly more elongated than usual, and the rounding of the bone above the eyes, a little wider. Her eyes were more precisely slanted in the outer corners, and the black line around them, a little thicker. To swim with her on the hunt was to experience her natural grace in motion, and it was very hard to believe that she could not spin. That was why even though people knew about her hearing, they still infuriated her by urging her to keep trying.

There was no music. That part of life was not for her. Ea practised acceptance.

Now she was out of the throng, swimming silently across the lagoon, slow enough not to cause a wake and draw attention to herself, but fast enough to get beyond where they would spot her and call her back. She was going to her refuge, the black coral wall where lived an ancient moray colony. It was a dark forbidding place where the water had a different texture, and Ea was the only person who ever went there. The adult Longi respected the morays but could not help their aversion to their unattractive faces, while the calves shuddered at the sound of those vicious neighbours on the far side of the lagoon.

She had found the wall by accident, searching for a remote place to sulk. She came upon them with such a shock she almost opened her blowhole. The great eels swayed halfway out from their crevices, staring at her with hot little yellow eyes. Fascinated, Ea saw a sophisticated intelligence in their wicked faces and was no longer frightened. When they stopped glaring and returned to mysterious inner contemplation, she correctly took it for tolerance of her presence and felt flattered. The moray wall became her secret refuge, and her mother kept that knowledge to herself.

Ea was almost there when the sun lit the horizon and she passed over the colourful coral plaza of the lagoon floor. Behind her in the water were the sounds of the pod at play, the adult trills of pleasure, the shouts of the calves in the nursery area. She could pick out the gossipy clicking and buzzing of the post-hunt discussions, and it gave her some satisfaction to know she and her mother had once again excelled. They had their own silent language that her mother had taught her when she realised Ea was different; it was their secret.

Today the morays were expecting her, swaying halfway out of their holes, some holding themselves in shafts of light as if to show off their elaborate patterns. There were her favourites, the huge dark blue and black one with the mottled brown spots, and the livid yellow and green one with the grey lines. Others remained in camouflage, thick shadows with yellow eyes. They made no attempt to be friendly and expected no courtesies and Ea was glad to see them. She had just taken a large diving breath to go down to visit, when a distant howl came through the water.

It was not one of the frightening noises deep in her head nor was there any pain in her sonar melon. It was a real sound from a living being, but coming from further away than a dolphin could click. There it was again, fine and distant and so precise that she knew it was not the cry of an attack or of being wounded, nor the music of the ocean, because no one would spin to that. Someone was sending that sound out across the vast. It was a message.

Ea positioned herself the better to receive it. She had an odd sensation in her heart, as if it were swollen and tender. The sound – and then silence. She listened with all her attention. There was nothing for so long she thought she might have imagined those new sounds, which would be an improvement – but then it came again. This time it was a cacophony of booms and slams, then silence, then one more howl. There was a pattern.

It was a whale, it had to be. Ea had never seen or heard one before but she knew they were distant cousin kin. Though she couldn't decipher the meaning, the sound pulsed in her blood. Was the whale singing in Old Pelagic? No one used it any more, but the Longi click derived from it, and she remembered her mother telling her it used silence as well as sound. Ea went to where the black wall was crumbling, the better to listen.

The distant whale boomed again like faraway thunder. Then as his great billows of sound were still travelling across the ocean, he wailed across the top of them in a harsh and soaring lament that filled Ea with sadness and rage. It faded away, and the silence that followed had a different quality. It was over. The whale had passed on, leaving Ea with the ache of relief that someone else understood loneliness and pain.

A hiss made her whirl round. The great eels were fully emerged from their holes, their hooked jaws beginning to open. They had been waiting for her, but in her excitement at the whale she had forgotten her normal respectful mode of arrival and had ignored them. Now they were offended. She knew it by their hard eyes and the way they raised their long serrated dorsal fins. The hiss was all around her in the water, growing stronger.

Go . . . go away . . .

Ea shook the whalesong from her mind and drew back from the morays. They were not her friends and they were expelling her. But she could not go back to the pod yet because she did not want to make love with anyone and she felt too raw from hearing the whale, to go back and be polite.

Without seeming to swim the morays had come closer, their dorsal fins rippling in a current only they could feel. They were staring at her, no longer tolerant. Panic flared in her. To move she would have to pass so close to those jaws; they could scar her so easily.

Come, Ea, this way, come now, my darling—

It was her mother's voice in her head, in their silent hunting language. Ea turned to see that she was there, and her relief was greater than her indignation at the intrusion.

She rushed closer, and big as she was, tucked herself in echelon position behind her mother's pectoral fin. Her mother shielded her in the turn and together they left the moray wall and ascended to breathe at a safe distance. They floated on the surface without speech and although Ea was upset her sanctuary had been discovered, curiosity overcame her sulk.

Who was the whale? she asked, not in their private language but in the Longi click.

A rorqual whale of some kind, her mother answered. *He passes this way sometimes.*

Why does he not visit us? I thought we were cousins.

Ea felt her mother's loving energy waver for a moment.

Distant. He travels on an old songpath of his people . . .

But why is he so sad?

Ea felt the water pause around them, then her mother resumed her soothing attention.

You understood his song?

He made me feel sad. That's all. I didn't understand. Was it Old Pelagic?

It was. That's clever of you to remember. How did you know?

You said it uses silence. Like when we hunt. What does he sing about? Ea felt her mother thinking too long about the answer, which meant she was hiding something. *Tell me!* she buzzed, rudely. *If I'm old enough to be forced to dance Exodus—*

Exodus is all of our responsibility, Ea, not just yours! It is our duty to those who helped us be here now! If you want to know so badly, the whale sings of pain and death. But he sings for his own people, not ours. Does that satisfy you?

We have to help him. Energy rushed through Ea as if she had swum through a shoal of jellyfish. She had understood him.

We can't. There's nothing we can do.

Ea stopped in complete surprise.

We? Does everyone hear him?

Her mother came close alongside, so that Ea could feel her warmth and love.

It does no good to hear pain, Ea. We choose to hear the music, we spin—

Well, I can't, and I hear pain! So I have to do something about it.

You can, my darling. Enjoy your life.

What good does that do?

Ea's mother did not answer, but went ahead a little way. They had crossed the lagoon and were almost back at the main group of the pod. The loving moil, that daily erotic gathering from which Ea fled, was over. The pod was ready for sleep. All was peace and beauty.

Ea forgot the confused and frightened parts of herself and instead felt the pleasant bodily fatigue from the hunt. For now, there would be no ardent suitors. When she tried to remember the whale's song, it was gone.

Shh . . . peace, darling. Her mother took her sleeping place with her friends, and rolled in the water to let her warmth curl out to Ea. It was the Longi invitation to sleep alongside one another, and Ea needed the comfort. As the sleeping pod rose and fell at the surface she sank into the group rhythm, first resting one eye and brain hemisphere and then the other, so that in synchronised vigilance, all were protected.

Beside Ea, her mother remained awake until her beloved, troubled daughter sank into sleep. Only then did she too enter the deep rest state.

3

Exodus

Beside her sleeping mother, Ea breathed carefully so as not to disturb her and lay at the surface fully awake, troubled by many things, new and old. New was the baffling information that perhaps the whole pod heard the whale in pain but said nothing about it, and old was the imminent matter of the dreaded Exodus. The thought fluttered Ea's heart like a wounded fish. The ritual dance was still two whole moon-cycles away from performance, which happened just at the rising of the great full moon of the summer. The pod loved to return home together just as the ocean spawned in an orgy of lust and release, and then they too would make love.

Ea now wondered if she was the only one anxious about it, because there was a rising tension in the pod as people started to practise for it. The most athletically and creatively talented spinners had been finessing their technique, while the less gifted went around reassuring themselves and others that everyone would rotate in from the outside in a fair and safe way, as the pod travelled during the ritual. Exodus could not be held in the safety of the lagoon because it required greater speed than the space allowed for the spins and leaps that were vital to expressing real fear, triumph, liberation and transcendence. For Ea, it was just another opportunity for humiliation and failure.

She knew and respected the fact that Exodus was the Longi people's kinetic prayer of thanks to the ocean for the survival of their pod. All calves learned the story of how the Longi had been forced out of their beautiful original homewater by the invasion of the cruel barbaric Tursiops tribe. Their passage across the ocean from that moment was perilous and marked with many losses. It was commemorated in this group dance of spinning, formal and spontaneous falls and splashes, which traced a large circular shape that took the pod from the safety of the lagoon out into the vulnerability of the vast where it reached its climax; then on safe return to the homewater, everyone could put the story behind them for another year.

Ea knew the story backward and forward. All the calves and youngsters grew up thrilled by the annual summer practice of the adults just beyond the lagoon. They could not wait to learn the dazzling travelling spins and astonishing percussive falls, and Ea's own mother often numbered more than seven revolutions. The spins linked to certain splashes and falls which also had meaning both in the sounds underwater to the whole pod, and in the effervescent lyrics they pulled down around them. But first you had to tune yourself, body and soul, to the music of the ocean. Watching her mother's silver form throw out sparkling spirals of water, awestruck little Ea had found it sublimely beautiful. Her mother's artistry left airy poetry trailing in the water behind her; her splashes and falls were rhymes of sound.

Now, years later, Ea only felt dread at the prospect of joining in. Spinning in Exodus could bring on a trance state, and she had many times witnessed her mother helping to restore the senses of those who had slipped into it and could not return alone. Sometimes people had visions and even channelled spirits of the ancestors. Sometimes they believed they had already joined the ocean and had to be called back so that they did not prematurely leave their bodies for good. Then other people would gather around the one who was alive but drifting in another ocean, and their touches and clicks would bring them back to the pod. Ea already had trouble with her imagination, and so the very last thing she wanted was a frightening vision or uncontrollable experience. The whalesong today was different. The tender sonic pains echoed in her mind. Someone, somewhere, was a kindred spirit.

4

The Singer

Though his painful song was sometimes heard – most recently by Ea – the anonymous whale only ever broadcast from far out in the vast. He had never been seen by any of the dolphins of the archipelago that was the centre of his great orbit, but by the carrying power of his huge baritone voice, he was from that mighty whale kin-group of rorquals. His noble lineage included the Blue, the Fin, the Minke, the Grey, the Right and the Humpback and he was of that last clan.

This singer was a mature male in his physical prime, weighing a ton for each of his thirty-two years, and with pectoral fins outstretched, measured fifty feet across. But despite his distinguished singer ancestors, the Rorqual was a lonely pariah. No one wanted to hear his new song, which was a radical departure from the popular and traditional power-ballads. Not one male of his ocean-wide kin had ever copied it in approbation, nor single female responded with her own mellifluous low of invitation. This song was his life's work and he had spent years developing it, from the smallest unit of sound to the finessing of every long movement. He had woven different themes with the uniting power of his chorus, until the whole song-cycle was complete and could take up to three sleepless sunrises. Even after this, the Rorqual continued developing his declamation, timbre and the transitions between his rolling bass-baritone that came from the depths of his huge body, and the higher voice he could issue like a sound beam from his head.

None of it made any difference. For years, the young passionate artist in the Rorqual kept experimenting, trying to find a better expression for his song in the hope that it would finally let him connect with the audience whose lives he was trying to save. Eventually the older, wiser, heartsick whale that he was years later consoled the artist within, with the truth he had long known. No one wanted pain, in song or any other form. They fled from it, but this was exactly why he sang: to warn them away from danger and guide them to safety.

Long before Ea was born, before the Longi had any need of Exodus and were still happy in their original homewater, the Rorqual and his whole extended family were joyfully en route from the far southern cold to the tropic breeding ground. Crowds of humpbacks travelled the same songpaths, eager to gather with friends and relatives and witness the sport of the young.

The Rorqual was now of age and had developed the beginnings of an armoury of sharp barnacles on his pectoral fins. He knew they were for mating battles, but he disliked conflict. Having witnessed the leviathan breaching clashes of the males, he wondered why they did not just sing better. A good song was what the females really liked, and from a young age he had enjoyed amusing those in his own family with his efforts. As his range increased with maturity while keeping his playful nature, they had high hopes for him being awarded Singer of the ocean. This was the annual honorific that went to the male of any race whose song-cycle was most emulated, and part of the fun of the songpaths was hearing each family's aspirant to the title take their moment to entertain the cavalcade.

The young Rorqual was working on his own version of a traditional aria when the family crossed the familiar currents that marked the start of the tropics. The breeding archipelago was now very close and the excitement was rising from the different groups: ready females at the front, jostling bachelors at the back and elders holding the middle. Trying to perfect a phrase but unable to hear himself properly in the din of the competing songs, the Rorqual swam aside to perfect it.

He felt the happiness in the water from the group of females up ahead, mothers and grandmothers gossiping as they reunited after a long year apart. He heard the breaching splashes of the young bucks practising, eager to make the heat run together for the receptive females, but it was still too noisy. He moved off further.

Then came an unfamiliar sound that swallowed all theirs, followed a moment later by a great push and shove in the water from one side of the songpath. Something huge was rushing upon them, heading directly across the crowded route. A high and faceless metal beast ploughed the surface toward them. While people were still turning to behold its colossal and terrifying size, it went straight into, then over them. Then it was gone.

The young Rorqual turned in the crimson gyre of the monster's wake. He swam in his family's blood. He looked for them, but the entire cavalcade had scattered. The Rorqual refused to believe his family were gone. He waited for a long time. He searched until the sharks came for the blood. Only then did he leave.

*

He wandered dazed, until his body felt the magnetism of another songpath. Automatically he turned to follow it, in the hope it led to more of his people. His song was stuck deep in his body, like the long metal spike still carried by one of his missing uncles.

The songpath was eerily silent but the Rorqual could detect with his sonar that up ahead was a peculiar gathering. Reaching out with his sonic beam he received the impression of some cetaceans, fish of different nations, a turtle – and bizarrely, a hammerhead shark. The image was detailed but had to be wrong, because there was no motion.

All were dead. As the Rorqual came closer, he saw them twisted in a deep, transparent veil that stretched horizontally out of sight. It was laid straight across the ancient route he was on, another that his people had always travelled. It too ran between the feeding and the breeding grounds, and here whales chose to sing certain songs over others, describing the currents, chasms and mountains of its different sea areas. There were verses about where the sharks had their own crossings and feast waters, and though no part of the ocean was ever completely safe, a good song could mitigate much danger.

The Rorqual felt himself choking. He forced himself to look at the small blue whale calf, the nylon filaments cutting into its skin where it pressed so hard against it. It was rotting and he guessed its mother had stayed beside her little one, until she could no longer bear it. Or the sharks came. And yet . . . there were also many sharks caught in the veil of death. The Rorqual was dazed with horror but forced himself to go on bearing witness. His mind beat with shock, he wished to roar with anguish but he was dumb. In the distance he heard that sound again, the metal monster. As he gazed at the hanging dead he felt the rage rise inside him, and he copied the monster's roar, so that he would remember it. He filled himself with the sound and the sight and the agony, into his throat, then his chest, then his heart, then his blood. He swallowed it all into himself, then he left.

The silent young Rorqual wandered in shock for several sleepless days and nights, not daring to stop. He did not know how to get back to the route his family always took to return to the southern ice, so he maintained his forward course. By the currents he was still in the tropics but an unfamiliar area, and when one day the jaunty song of some humpback bachelors came into his mind, at first he thought imagined it. The song was an old classic, but transmitted from somewhere nearby, and in hearty voice.

It came from merry group of young troubadours, naturalised equatorial laterals they proudly told him. What a wonderful place to live this was! The Rorqual could not tell if they were joking, but they warmly welcomed him into their group and he was grateful. They were relentlessly enthusiastic to repeat this one travelling ballad of the polar–tropic route, but they had adapted it to be about enjoying life and being content to stay put. When the Rorqual asked about their other kin, because there were no females, elders or calves, the troubadours only sang the louder. Half their song celebrated their many blessings of plentiful food and beautiful waters, and the other described how lustily they would compete for maidens in the next heat run.

The young Rorqual stayed with them, for he had no one else. But his voice remained stuck in his body so that he could no longer sing. To keep his place in their band, he managed to summon a great booming percussion from his body; though the volume made them wince, they understood he was trying to join in, and were supportive. He listened to falsetto harmonies more suited to their small home range, and found their music trite and sentimental. One day they finally asked him why he did not sing himself. He could not answer and only wished to keep booming his one monotonous part in their song, but they had made a decision.

Sing to us!

When he refused they made a childish song-round of their demand, which they found highly entertaining. The Rorqual felt something stirring deep within his body. The bachelors kept up their nagging until he feared his head would burst. Something was happening, something was rising inside him, choking him – bucking in his great gullet like a struggling squid – and then he knew what it was. A terrible song that had been incubating in his flesh and bones and blood. It trembled his lungs like a storm.

SING TO US! the troubadours cried. *Express yourself!*

Into the ocean, from the body and soul of the Rorqual, came a mighty torrent of sound. It was all the love and rage and grief he carried, booming and whooping louder than any whale had ever sung, carrying for hundreds of miles. His power shook their bones as the song drove into their minds so that they too felt the pain in his heart and could taste the blood in the water. The troubadours bellowed in panic, looking for the metal monster the Rorqual conjured with his song. When he stopped, they were furious.

The song was pure horror! He had traumatised them with his sick imagination. They were so sorry, but these were creative differences too great to resolve. They wished him well in his travels, and that he would take his song far away. If he wanted to return in a better frame of mind and join with them in some happy songs, he would be welcome. Meanwhile, they would continue to enjoy the bounty of life, refusing to worry.

Cast out by the troubadours, the Rorqual wandered again. He held to his anger and his truth: the beautiful ancient songs had led his whole family to destruction, and he would never sing them again. Nor would he return to polar seas but remain in this warm and fatal ocean filled with metal demons, who drank blood, spewed filth and whose song was sonic torture. The Rorqual was but one lone whale and his song no weapon against them – but it might yet be a beacon to safety, if people would only listen. When time and again he exhausted himself singing yet not a single person gave any sign they had heard, he descended to fierce meditation in the deep, and vowed to improve his song.

The years went by but he kept faith. He was the Singer. Loneliness was the price.

5

Tursiops, the Megapod

Two days' swim from the tiny Longi tribe at the far eastern end of the archipelago, the Tursiops megapod of over five hundred dolphins was not drowsing quietly in the midday sun, as was their custom after a hunt. Instead they were starting to panic. Never a quiet population, their anxiety rose to a racket through all the sleeping bays as they argued over the meaning of the latest rumbling noises. Yes the sky was dark, but was that thunder, or a new signal that the ocean demons were about to start up? And if that were the case, where was the signal for permission to rush to get a ration of sarpa fish, to dull the pain before it started? Who could say for sure that it was a storm? Everyone must of course wait for the click from the great lord Ku . . . but what if . . .

No one dared finish the thought. In the First Harem, the great lord Ku's First Wife, the imposing and beautiful Devi, knew the gossip. It was the foundation of her power. What people were saying was *what if he is wrong, what if he is now too old to tell the difference, what if he is sick—*

What if, what if?! Devi whirled around in anger and her co-wives shrank back in submission – not a click or pulse of disloyalty ever escaped them. If it did, or if Devi even suspected it, theirs would be the terrible fate of being sent to live as an unprotected peripheral in the filthy margin of the homewater. No one spoke.

Devi angled herself the better to make sense of the cacophonous jabber of the huge pod. She could hear the tension rising, in the form of water slaps and buzzes of anger. Physical disputes were common in the pod, especially when the effect of sarpa was fading. Behind her, Devi's co-wives murmured the possibility she might use her privilege and take them to the sarpa grove first. Storm or demons, they did not care; they were all addicted to the tranquillising fish, but did not let it get in the way of hunting and sexual tasks. Devi shut off her hearing selectively, a skill she finessed in order to eavesdrop more effectively, so that she could try to detect any sound of the ocean demons. These were the supernatural forces that had followed the Tursiops to this new homewater and who now fought each other out in the deep. With little warning, the ocean would be rent with agonising roars and bellows of rage and their violent acoustic fury could permanently deafen even a strong Tursiops male if he caught the full blast of it out in the vast. The sickening vibrations of the demons' combat caused daymares, hallucinations and could even shake calves loose from their mothers' wombs. The only remedy was to take what rocky shelter the bays provided, and to eat sarpa.

Sarpa salpa were the little silver fish with strange mirrored eyes and a tiny flash of yellow down their sides. The original inhabitants of this homewater, the effete and superstitious Longi, had shunned the shallow-living shoals as foulfish. But when the Longi had left and the demons began to shriek and roar, one of Devi's harem named Yaru had the idea of using it to purge. She hoped that vomiting might ease the pain in her head, but instead the fish sent her into a trance state. Observing that Yaru was now able to withstand the sound of the demons better than everyone else, Devi claimed credit for the discovery. After that everyone wanted it.

Though the powerful effect of the first time was never so good again, the anaesthetic property remained. The lord Ku ordered all those fish the property of the First Alliance, under strict rationing, and they were herded back into the narrow cove full of kelp forest where Yaru had first discovered them. In return for this discovery and boon to the pod, the lord Ku turned a blind eye to Devi's more frequent visits, though his second in command, the lord Split, did not. No one else dared enter the grove, because Tursiops discipline was martial. To breach it was to risk serious injury and become peripheral, or die.

Listening carefully to the ocean, Devi came to her conclusion. Not demons, but a very strong storm. The pod needed to muster in the vast while there was still time to get out of the bay, otherwise the waves might trap and batter them. She was desperate for her lord Ku to give the command, but she did not know where he was. Panic was spreading through the water, and if the pod grew too overwrought, it would be impossible to control them. In any case, they would not take instruction from a female. Exasperated by the clamouring of her co-wives for sarpa, Devi tail-slapped the nearest one then went out to settle the other harems in a similar fashion.

Returning to the First Harem, she could hear that her great sub-adult son Chit had resumed his loud, tuneless chanting. She knew he did it to soothe himself and on seeing her return, he squealed in delight and rushed to her to try to suckle – something Devi hated. Assiduous co-wives quickly took him away and tickled him into laughter and distraction, and Devi noted who was first – and last – to help her. Once again, Yaru, the youngest co-wife whose daughter was still suckling, was focused on her own child instead of the First Wife's needs. At least she had not had a son, because lord Ku was desperate for a better male issue than sweet-natured simpleton Chit, who refused to fight and could barely hunt.

Were not Devi his mother, he would long ago have died of age-appropriate bullying, and only in return for Devi's draconian grip on all the females did the lord Ku permit his rejected son's shameful seclusion in the First Harem. This was to the chagrin of the lord Split, the lord Ku's closest ally in the First Alliance and father to a boorish youth – as yet too unruly for warrior training. Though his warrior valour was equal to the lord Ku's, he was feared rather than loved by the pod, and everyone knew it. Split was so named for the deep pectoral fin wound he sustained fighting off a great white shark on the Crossing, which also nearly tore off the lord Ku's dorsal fin, now healed at a crooked angle. This made the lord Ku recognisable at a distance and was a prominent reminder of his extraordinary powers.

Devi feared Split on her son's behalf so took care to be highly deferential in his presence. She guessed hearing failure was the reason for his intolerance of frivolous chatter and noise, but she knew he enjoyed meting out discipline to those who transgressed, usually females and children. Devi also correctly intuited that Split resented her frequent presence by her lord's Ku's side. She wished he knew that, despite how her lord sometimes treated her in public, their private relationship was one of love and respect. But for the lord Ku to acknowledge that would be to weaken his status and, like every female in the pod, Devi knew her own status derived from his – as did her safety and that of her child.

Out on the edge of the homewater, the lord Ku, the lord Split, and the ten massive males who were the warrior commanders of the First Alliance and who each held their own harem, rode high waves to feel the wind, then went down into the muscular turbulence. They were gathered at the place of convergence, an area of seabed above which the nightly hunt departed, and from where they could most easily detect the first vibrations of the demons. So far, all they could feel was the great incoming swell and the riptide running hard.

The lord Ku let the waves lift him again so that he could feel the wind. It caught his twisted dorsal fin so hard he had to brace his spine against the force, and again he thanked the shark that caused it, which he and the First Alliance had then drowned. The wound was his power, unlike the white lesions spreading on his body. They had started around his genital patch but now were around his eyes. They made him ugly, he knew – he saw it in the expressions of the young females he took – but as he spasmed in pain from the gust of wind that pressed against a swollen eye, he knew they too were a gift. Never had he been so precisely sensitive to wind speed and direction. The demons roared and rumbled, but these unseasonal disturbances were either wind or tide. Another great storm was coming. The lord Ku gave the order: the pod will muster in the east, beyond the seamounts.

In the harems, every female was primed by Devi for this instruction. She would consider any premature action on their part as insubordination, likewise if by a single click any of them revealed that she had readied them. Pod orders were the sole prerogative of the lord Ku and alliance commanders, but Devi also knew the safety of the people was at stake. As the pod mobilised for the muster, other and more personal plans were also put into action. Devi had long wanted to remind one particular young co-wife of her harem of the need for greater respect. Elsewhere and at great social remove from Devi's sphere, four large sub-adult males, still considered too immature to train for entry to an alliance, had long resented this delay of their sexual privilege. Had Devi been aware of their secret plan, she would have reconsidered her strategy. But her information network only ran to females, and in any case, the storm was upon them.

6

The Shriving Moil

Ea slept through the louring storm clouds. By the time she awoke in the late afternoon the sky was once more clear limpid blue and the water was cooling. Her brain felt reset, no longer jangling from right to left hemispheres in the anxious shallow drowsing so familiar to her. Beside her mother she had entered the slow controlled alternation of the Longi sleepwaves which calves learned as young as possible. Once they could do this they could join the pod sleep pattern, a sign they were ready to start work on their diving capacity. Ready for another good night's hunting, Ea was about to cross the lagoon to go to the meeting area when she noticed the quiet. No one was practising for Exodus.

Not a single splash, no excited cries of triumph or exasperation. But there they all were, gathered together in a peculiar concentrated hush. Ea could hear her mother clicking softly, the only one. Her tone was unusual, as if something was wrong. Then she stopped, and someone else clicked, also in that strange tone. Ea turned around and scanned the lagoon – completely unnecessary to use sonar here, they all knew every stone and coral branch – and was reassured that it was as boring as ever. But the discussion between the adults was not. This was not the usual afternoon love-in.

Cautiously, Ea went to investigate. All the adults, including those like herself – newly of age – were there. Listening to one of the uncles, they made room for her without comment. Ea knew him as a great hunter, lover of many, and enthusiastic for Exodus. He often cheerfully encouraged her to put her fears aside and take part, but today she felt he was weighted down from within. She went closer, confused by what he was saying.

He wished to tell them of the bad feelings he still harboured toward the Tursiops, for what they had done to his people, his family. There were soft clicks of support and commiseration. Someone else then stuttered her own painful confession, an older aunt who was a good friend of Ea's mother. She confessed that she wanted vengeance upon them, for what they had done to her boy. They had beaten him to death for daring to try to protect her. Someone else then spoke, this time about their cousins the pilot whales. Immediately people began shrilling and buzzing, and Ea rushed to her mother's side in fear.

There are no pilot whales here, her mother said. *Not for a long time.*

Never again! clicked several people. *Never will we help them.*

Betrayers! others cried out. *We trusted them!*

Ea pressed against her mother's side, deeply unnerved. *Who are the pilots?*

More relatives, her mother said. *Very intelligent. But they cannot be trusted. They—*

She did not finish because the water trembled with stress and fear at whatever it was the pilots had done. Ea felt a pulsing against her skin that was coming out of the people themselves. Hot bursts of energy, chaotic and blinding.

Let it out, someone pulsed. *Let it out!* and someone else rattled it like a weak war cry. *ANGER!* buzzed someone, and the pod buzzed it again and again.

Never trust a Tursiops, never trust a pilot! Woe and suffering to them!

Ea had never heard anyone in her family – that is to say the whole small tribe of the Longi – wish harm to anything or anyone. They prayed to the ocean before they went out hunting and gave thanks to the prey when they returned. But for past injuries, they harboured feelings of revenge to the Tursiops, who everyone knew were barbarians, also to the pilots, a hitherto unknown branch of the family.

What about the whale who sings in pain? Ea suddenly cried out, her inhibitions lowered in the fervent atmosphere. *Have the humpbacks hurt us too? Is that why everyone pretends not to hear him?* It was as if she had not spoken.

There is so much to cleanse this year. Ea's mother pressed her fin. *It is more painful this year, maybe because of this passing storm. There was a storm when we wandered. Exodus—*

It's still too soon! Ea didn't want anything to bring Exodus closer. *We don't do this until the red anemones swell—* She stopped. She and her mother had swum over them this very afternoon. They were already fully swollen as if they were about to spawn.

There are other signs as well, someone else said softly. *Some of the coral is pulsing too hard already. Some is withered at the top, as if it has already spawned.*

Then came tense debate: synchrony was a law of the ocean, so no coral could possibly yet have spawned. But then how was it that the blue algae near the nursery was already gone, and still one moon to go before that time? The stock fish must have eaten it.

If the stock fish had eaten it all, they would then leave the lagoon in search of more; it was their favourite food. Which meant in turn, there would be no forage fish near the calves to learn hunting in safety – would they now have to leave the lagoon in search of more food? No mother would sanction this! Had they mistaken the signals and missed the Spawning Moon? What calamity would befall them, how could this have happened!

Realising the timbre was now at a painful pitch, the Longi stopped their noise. The fractious water pulsed down, then calmed. The people turned to each other with pacifying strokes, their hearts beating hard at the rise of conflict.

It is beginning, clicked Ea's mother to her, *will you stay?*

Ea felt awkward, because she was already there. But the Shriving Moil was one gathering of the tribe where arousal was not encouraged. It was purely about cleansing bad feelings. Ea decided she would.

The older adults began it, moving together at the centre. Now with group permission, everyone released their psychic distress, as a tangible burst of energy in the water. Ea had thought she was the only one in pain, but now she felt it coming into her body from her kin. She wanted to flee, at the same instant as she wanted to comfort them. She pressed her fins back against those people who reached theirs out to her, and were now twisting and clicking unselfconsciously. People were confessing terrible forbidden feelings: anger, resentment, rage, thoughts of revenge – it came choking out in ragged clicks and cries.

Some of the older adults were breathing erratically, big bursts of spray escaping from their blowholes as they lost control of their feelings. Other people moved in to comfort and stroke, and Ea felt fierce protective love running through her, colliding with twists of pain and shame and guilt. Everyone suffered in some way, she felt that now. She pushed herself deeper into the warmth and comfort of her people. Loneliness and shame were gone, there was no exhibitionism, no performance, no straining to be good and kind and never have a bad thought. For once Ea felt safe to be the difficult awkward angry envious person she was, and still be accepted. Every single person was confessing the ugly secrets of their mortal hearts.

Something bright went through the whole pod, as if the ocean itself was washing them clean and new and perfect. Ea felt the little jumps and shivers of the people around her and began to laugh. Everyone was laughing, in relief and gratitude to each other. The sound drew the calves, who came splashing and chirping from the nursery area, and the adults went forward to greet them and play. The lowering sun threw bright gold streamers across their shining backs, and excited calves splashed glittering sprays in their happiness at the adult joy.

Still amidst her family and kin, Ea felt light-headed with amazement. Nothing could be wrong if her family felt like this. If the anemones were blooming too soon, if the coral was dry, if the algae was gone, even if that whale sang his strange song and no one cared, what did that matter if everyone was happy?

7

An Ill Wind

Wind bit water, wave smashed rock. Above, the dark clouds curdled and burst, but deep below, the fast-travelling Tursiops pod were once again grateful for the wise leadership of their lord Ku. The storm was something they could fight with their strength, and better to battle the heavy surge out in the vast than to let it pulverise them in their homewater. But as the pod neared the seamounts beyond the white reef edge, everyone understood they were still not safe. Boulders rolled and crashed against the submarine slopes, and all about from different directions of the vast, heavy wave-trains ploughed shoreward and collided.

The harems strove to stay close together, bumping and huddling their calves into the centre, every mother trying to get hers to the best place of safety. Yaru, the young co-wife who had roused Devi's insecurities with her confidence and the pleasure the lord Ku took in her company, kept her little daughter close. Devi only disliked the child because she seemed to unconsciously sense the threat to her mother, so shrank from the First Wife – but that was yet another sign of disrespect. In her indirect but unmistakeable way, Devi had let all the co-wives know that sadly, and dangerously for all of them, Yaru was challenging her for dominance. Devi never considered she was being paranoid because, as chief consort of the lord Ku, she had observed him orchestrate many machinations for control of the highly fluid male alliances. Ever vigilant against plots from the lower alliances, the lord Ku had long and successfully practised Divide and Rule; his First Wife likewise. The safety of the pod rested in a stable hierarchy, for the harems no less than the alliances. Her co-wives understood that it would be a service to the whole pod if somehow, perhaps even in this storm, Yaru were reminded of her place in it.

Understanding this, and by no single co-wife's overt act, as the pod passed the seamounts and went on into the vast, Yaru and her calf fell behind as the First Harem sped away. She would be somewhere at the back, and when they finally mustered, she would find her way back to Devi's protection. After she had learned her lesson. All the other calves were older and faster and Yaru clicked a loud pulse-train to her harem to wait for her, but in the tumult of boulders below and the howling of the wind when they came up for breath, no one heard.

Without the propulsion of the pod, Yaru and her little daughter fell back and back, until to her dismay, they were in the straggling ranks of the peripherals. These were the people without alliances: the sick, the old, the weak, the wrong thinking, and the odd ones. United as best they could manage, they all struggled to keep up with the speeding crowd, but they could not do it. Yaru saw an old female with many scars on her face stop trying and get left behind. Then the weak male who had swum by her side also dropped back. There was a dull impact sound as if from a blow, and he was gone. Yaru hated to do it but nipped her crying calf to make her go faster. Even that did not work.

The male alliances were formed of the warrior caste of the *vira*, whose responsibility it was to post scouts at the edge of the pod whenever there was a big manoeuvre. She cried out to them now in her loudest voice, to come to her aid.

It was all the four sub-adult Tursiops males had been waiting for. Confident enough in their physical power to leave the body of the pod and ride the storm at its edge, they had witnessed the old female fall back, then something – surely only a young shark if it chose a weak Tursiops – had dragged the old male down. That meant the imminent danger of predators was less. Then they heard a privileged female voice calling out to the *vira* for help. She sounded young. They waited for a moment, checking if any scouts had heard.

Yaru chirped in relief as the four big young bucks arrived around her. One was Split's son; she knew him by his harsh voice, like his father's. To begin with, she kept bringing her calf back in by her side, thinking how dense they were not to see her. To begin with, she did not believe what was happening. When she did, she fought with all her strength to stay with her calf, but the little one was already exhausted. The storm tore the child away and the mother was beset.

Later, when the waters calmed, the Tursiops megapod gathered together and alliances and harems regrouped. They made all the noise they could to drive off any threat, and the count-click came back that there were two fewer peripherals, which did not matter, but that all pod members were present and unharmed – with the exception of a co-wife missing from the First Harem. This was exceptional gossip, with many people secretly hoping it was Devi, but of course it was not.

Poor Yaru, always so wilful, Devi quickly supplied to her shocked co-wives.

Very wilful, they gratefully responded, absolved of responsibility. Devi's version was always the truth.

You must have tried to help her keep up, Devi elaborated. *I'm certain I heard you.*

Definitely, definitely, but the storm! So wilful – so hard to help her in the storm—

And so, the co-wives overlaid and strengthened what had happened to poor Yaru and her calf, and felt great sorrow in their hearts that she had ignored them. The pod turned homeward in the gusty grey aftermath of the storm, and it was soon established by clicks between the different groups that it was the co-wife who was always difficult, and only Devi's kindness had kept her in the First Harem for so long.

The four sub-adult males who had slaked their sexual frustration under cover of the tempest, heard but said nothing. They went quietly back to their lowly place in the reserve group of young males waiting to compete in the vira games, the initiation procedure for the alliances. They dared not look at each other. They had thought that she was a peripheral, whom no one would miss. They would never have dared touch the property of the lord Ku, leader of the pod. Their hearts raged at her stupidity in leading them on, in being such a duplicitous temptation in the first place. At least now she was lost.

To their horror, she was not. As the pod approached the seamount and she came directly in their path, Yaru swam an endless circle, bearing her dead calf on her back like a newborn. Over and over she whistled her darling's calf-name, as if calling her in from play. As if the motionless little body would suddenly wriggle back to life and splash into the water again.

The pod slowed. Even Devi was speechless. She had not meant this to happen, but it was too late. Then the co-wives began to chatter in shock, their clicks incoherent, becoming a wail, a high terrible sound that spread through the pod. The water clung thick with grief.

The lord Ku came forward and Devi met him. The calf was his

and, with the exception of the failed male that was Chit, he loved all his children despite them being female. Devi saw Yaru's mind was broken, as well as the telling marks on her fins where teeth had grabbed her and held her in position. Yaru screeched when males came near her, and then still bearing her dead child on her back, turned and swam back out into the vast. No one called to her, because everyone knew what she chose, with the last of her wits. She would keep her darling with her until it was no longer possible to go on.

Devi felt something terrible in her own heart but there was nothing now to be done for Yaru. The lord Ku was doubly incensed, not just at the death of one of his own calves, but at the rape of a co-wife. No honourable member of an alliance would ever do this, and the act was an outrage to the entire patriarchy. The offenders would be found, and dealt with. To forget this terrible thing, he granted Devi and the First Harem the immediate right to sarpa and let no one look askance on that. Devi made her most graceful obeisance to her lord. She took them to the grove for dreamfish, but before she let them eat it, she made her harem swear an oath: they would never mention Yaru again.

8

The Veteran

By the time it left the archipelago, the storm was a whirling dark core racing across ninety miles of open water. A nub of land lay in its path, a highly strategic outcrop and disputed possession of a large terrestrial nation, inhabited only by its military and their prisoners. The meteorological station had just enough time to raise the warning so that planes were secured in hangars and the airstrip cleared, and then the cyclone hit.

The deep-water port was currently empty of ships, but on the further side of the island, the shallower and now-defunct fishing port took the brunt. Chained to its harbour wall, six large dirty white plastic tanks rose and fell in the surge. Each could hold two beluga whales, one orca or six dolphins (albeit in crowded conditions), but five were currently empty, awaiting live seasonal goods for export. The sixth held a newly arrived bottlenose dolphin, heavily drugged for his injuries and not expected to survive another day.

He was not the only young male on this island kept in solitary confinement, in poor mental and physical condition yet still of value to his captors, but he was the only cetacean. He was a sixteen-year-old *Tursiops truncatus* and Marine Mammal Asset Mark XV, or MMA, and had been injured in the campaign that killed his handler. Born in captivity in the military, he was the consistently highest scoring animal of the program, so it was not just the sentimental force of his handler's dying wish he be saved, but hard economics. Hundreds of thousands of military dollars had been put into his training. If there was a way to recoup them by returning him to active duty, it must be done.

The military vet took receipt of this cetacean Tutankhamun, in his titanium travelling case. He had never seen a living dolphin with such burn wounds. He gave the animal a mercifully large dose of fentanyl to ease him into the marine hereafter and did not bother to make a visit on the day of the cyclone. When it had passed, he would excise and return the animal's biochip transponder and close the file. The remains would make excellent shark bait, the favourite sport at the base. A few people looked in on this high value animal, which had arrived from the Gulf on a military transport and survived a disastrous costly action many human personnel had not. His case was marked with his fifteen-digit alpha-numeric MMA reference and also scrawled with his nickname: Google.

On the other side of the world in San Diego, in the naval base of his captive birth, they had started to call him this when they realised he could find anything they asked of him, and would go on searching until he did. This young bottlenose dolphin had a phenomenal work ethic, was highly intelligent to the point they imagined he was even trying to emulate human speech. As he grew older, he put data together for himself. He could identify a range of military toys in the water and report them accurately via the infantile picture and sound games they still made him play.

He could match acoustic vibration to direction and even engine size, pairing digital recordings to what he had learned from his sorties into the ocean, from which he, like every other cetacean in the program, always returned. The MMAs, or Advanced Biological Weapons Systems, always came back to Base because their natural instinct needed a homewater. With no other dolphins to teach them otherwise, their tanks were their sustenance and security, both physical and emotional. Bonds between serving cetaceans were prevented and broken by separation or combat-game training if they began to form. The only bond the animal was encouraged to make was with its handler, for whom, when properly trained, it would do anything – not that it would be aware of the nuances. As for the ocean, it was merely the workplace.

Google performed all his tasks to one hundred per cent satisfaction, staying out as long as it took. His young trainer took huge pride in his animal's scholarship and, with no family of his own save the military, felt they were brothers. He guessed this was why the one game Google always failed on was human interdiction. Whether in the water or on boats, Google always marred his perfect record by refusing one task. The animal was willing to attach a marker to a diver's wetsuit, but never to jab the spike on his head harness into the chest. He did not mind tagging a float to a scuba tank because it would return the diver to the surface, but he refused to weight them down to drown, let alone use his own mouth to do it. Nor would he use his tail fluke to knock the diver unconscious, or fight with his own kind for dominance in the tank. It was as if he did not care about them, only his beloved handler, who correctly intuited that because Google identified humans as his natural kin, he could not hurt them. His young handler was proud of this one rule his animal could not break. He knew it meant love.

In his white plastic tank, still in the sling that kept his inflamed and ointment-smeared blowhole above the waterline, Google's huge body hung heavy as death. Large areas of his skin showed livid red where it had peeled away as he swam the flaming sea back to Base, the ship in the Gulf from which he and his cohort had left in their loaded nylon harnesses. He was the only one to return, shrieking out his signal so persistently that they were forced to bring him in, despite the horror of his condition and the listing ship. This MMA had completed his mission, but defied the suicide that was its inbuilt conclusion.

Mercifully far from his body, Google's mind swam freely in the opioid waters of the past. He was returning to Base, where he felt the anticipation of the boy – his anthrops was younger than the others – who waited for him. Google was bringing a number of markers retrieved from toys floating from weights, including those that other MMAs had missed. As he saw his boy waiting for him, Google felt answering joy in his own heart. Food was never his reward, but he craved this feeling that he got when they looked in each other's eyes. Yet afterwards, when Google was alone again in his tank, some strange grief surged deep within him. He wondered if that was why others in the tanks beat their heads against the sides, to share what they felt in the reverberations. Though the cetaceans were kept physically separated, and in any case shared only the most rudimentary common language because all their mental energy went into trying to understand what their anthrops wanted, they still transmitted feeling into the water. Google felt the pain around him and longed for the return of his handler in the mornings, to block out the confusion in his heart. He also welcomed the tiny stings they gave him into the veins of his right pectoral fin, which made him alert and single minded and tireless. Those too came in the morning, because had the cetaceans lived naturally, they would have been resting in the day. Then he and his young anthrops would go to work, surging with happiness. That was what Google lived for. That shared joyful feeling.

*

The memory was slipping, changing; it was now ugly and frightening, stronger with each bump and swell of his still-beating heart. His nervous system was surfacing as the fentanyl wore off; they had not given him his usual cocktail to suppress all his other anxieties – and now consciousness came searing back into his brain. The surging water heaved him high in the sling, then slapped him hard on his burns, wiping the salve with it.

A lash of pain tore Google screaming from his dream. Base was gone, his anthrops's face was gone, the drugs were gone and he was in a filthy tank that crashed against the concrete harbour wall. In the outward suck of the wave, the heavy anchoring chains pulled loose from their rusted plaques so that it tipped on its side. Google spilled from his sling and came thrashing to the surface as the water went into his blowhole. He spat a great shriek as he cleared it and instinct made him breathe and dive, just as the rest of the tanks tore away from the harbour wall and piled up in a swinging mass. A car came skidding down the slope to the jetty and landed in the water on top of them, pushing them down.

Google's belly, the only part of him not burned, hit the sludged and littered bottom of the harbour seabed, then the outward surge pulled him beyond the groynes of jagged boulders and into the safety of deeper water. Then he was in it, colliding waves punching him awake and swinging his pain at him from all sides. But when his fluke caught on a whirling timber he swam for his life; when his lungs forced him up for air and the world howled terror into his brain, his training saved him. He blocked the fear with recall, the first rule he ever learned: *Find Base.*

And if that place behind him was not Base, it could only be ahead: somewhere across the immensity of the workplace. The cyclone chose his path and pushed him on. The effort of swimming blinded him with pain, then he accepted it.

Stop Work.

Find Base.

9

Company

Ea was angry with herself. She had entered into the tangled painful spirit of the Shriving Moil and even enjoyed it, because that was her everyday state and, for once, other people were relatable. But now all the bad things were out, everyone reverted to loving kindness and relentless enthusiasm to get back to practising for Exodus. The relief was over. It was her own fault for joining in; she knew one moil was never going to change anything, but just for a moment she had left her own small and hurting self, and become part of something larger.

Swimming morosely on the edge of a group of her peers, Ea occasionally joined in some of the more cathartic moves, like the tail-slaps to the water. Perhaps she could make herself be happy and laugh like they did – but how could they possibly enjoy preparing for this hideously frightening thing? Her mother had told her that if she would just attempt things in the right spirit, the result might surprise her. Instead, Ea surprised everyone else with her forced cackle of laughter, her way of trying to be part of the general hilarity. Only people who succeeded could afford to laugh at their failures and imperfections. People like Ea, who lived the repeated humiliation of failure, turned and swam away.

She did not wish to go out beyond the drop-off, where the more confident young people were going to practise. The lagoon was getting too crowded, and the nearer it came to sunset, the more chance there was of attracting the hungry attention of the Residents. These were the shark gods of the near deep, whose habits were known. Though they were rightly feared, the Longi respected them and knew their habits. But beyond the local range of Residents were the Transients. These were the unknowable sharks of the deep pelagic and a source of terror to the Longi on their long journey of exile from their original homewater. In Exodus, they were described in a passage of desperate racing leaps.

Ea watched her peer group swim into the channel that led to the drop-off, and then, rather gratifyingly to her, circle around and return. It was too late to be safe. She could hear them clicking, agreeing that tomorrow before hunting they would help each other learn the first movement of the climax. The full sequence was never rehearsed because, for full catharsis, the pod must truly feel the terror of that past journey. Then their huge chaotic leaps of escape and falls of panic would be the truth, and likewise their gratitude for survival.

Ea retreated to the nursery area on the pretext of helping with the calves. She hoped she might find one like herself, withdrawn and intimidated by all the boisterous goings on in the lagoon. If she did, she would console them and, if they were old enough not to be too frightened, share with them the secret treat of a trip to the moray wall. She might even retrieve her hidden sponge, that she used to protect her rostrum when she dug in the sandy seabed for fish. She had the unusual urge to share, but the nursery area was empty. The calves were out at play and Ea was still alone. She heard her mother's click, amused and affectionate, helping other people excel at their practice.

Before she knew it, Ea was flashing across the plaza of the lagoon for the relief of speed, so that she did not have to think or feel. Beneath her, red anemones flared bright. They had proliferated around the entrance to the wide channel out to the drop-off, many more than she remembered. Some kind of curious black lace rippled over them, the effect made from large numbers of thin-legged black seastars, newcomers to the lagoon. The tide must have brought them, and they struggled to escape as the anemones ate them alive.

Ea went down to watch. The red anemones were spawning early and changing their diet. She was thinking she might mention it to her mother, when she felt her skin tingling as if she had been stung, but it was not painful. The feeling moved deeper into her body, so that she felt all her fins, and the muscles that moved them. It was a pleasant sensation, an intense slowing down and awareness of how she moved. Ea undulated to enjoy it more, then left the anemones behind as she swam further out into the channel, where the incoming tide rippled her skin and the breeze touched the sensitive circle of her blowhole. As she slowed at the surface, she let the golden shimmer from the vast pull her forward. She loved the moment of sunset, the beautiful warning of change, when those from the day hurried to safety and those of the night began to stir.

Ea felt a distant splash – or a series of splashes. Some new energy travelled through the water and flared against her skin. In sudden excitement she knew these creatures were not dolphins, nor any kin to them, nor were they sharks. They were fast approaching the Longi homewater on the ebb tide, so they must be very powerful. Ea stared – and the slow-sparkling water flickered back to normal. The wave of light was made by many bodies lifting from the surface on great triangular wings, the upper dark and lower bright. The splashes were distinct for a moment and then changed into a rushing sound in Ea's head, as she saw the wonder of shining wings flying like birds above the surface, then falling back into the ocean. This could only be the famed pilgrimage of the mantas, the deep pelagic giants of whom Ea had only heard in the old Longi stories. None of her generation had ever seen them, nor really believed they existed.

She gazed in wonder, unaware she was hovering at the end of the channel, right above the drop-off. The mantas were going to pass by the lagoon and she wanted to call to the pod to tell them, but awe took her speech. The only thing she could do was call out her own calf-name, and at once her mother called back.

Stay, Ea, don't be afraid, keep watching – we're coming!

The giant manta rays were dreamlike creatures from the time when the ocean teemed with friendly cousin-tribes – the Spotted, the Striped and the Longi – and all had shared the ancestral homewater in peace and harmony. That was ancient history, but here were the mantas again, sending waves of their own energy into the lagoon as greeting. The gathered Longi were amazed into silence at the numbers of the mantas, their colossal size, and the way their own bodies felt suspended, even as their hearts beat stronger. All newly ordained hunters in the Longi pod knew, if they ever saw the mantas out in the vast, to beware enchantment like this, because then they might become lost or worse. But here in their homewater there was no danger, and as the mantas came still closer, the pod relaxed. Their heartbeats synchronised and slowed to the hypnotic beat of the rays' wings.

Ea felt a great rising joy at the flash of understanding – the mantas were spirit kin to both birds and sharks, joining water and air, and this visit was a great blessing. Out on the hunt, everyone secretly yearned to be the one to see them. Even back in the homewater, if someone even dreamed of them, their energy rose to a higher vibration and everyone wanted to sleep beside them the following day. The elders knew that the mantas could also gift hyperconsciousness to those who saw them, and then the pod must protect that person until it had passed, which could take some time. Afterwards that person had to seek their gift, which might be exaltation in the spin, or extended sonic range, or subtlety on the hunt. But their mind took time to settle, which was why it was dangerous to see them out on the hunt. The mantas were beloved by the Longi because they had helped them end their terrible wandering in exile, showing the exhausted and heartsick tribe where to cross the migratory path of the white sharks, feared and worshipped by all. The tribe were almost all across, when a colossal female, the White Goddess, appeared in all her terrifying beauty and claimed her tithe.

This too was part of Exodus and Ea jerked in the water, the image whirling in her mind. Almost as fast, she felt the reassuring press of her mother – her real flesh-and-blood mother – there by her side. Ea's mind cleared; she knew what had happened. It was another moment of the Exodus ritual, the part when one of the tribe must swim out alone, in tribute to that Longi hero who willingly gave himself to the White Goddess, to spare the rest. Ea dreaded being that person.

Now she and her mother were pushed forward, the excited cheering Longi people suddenly released from their awe and crowding out through the channel. On the surface and below, they rushed out into the vast to greet the manta train. This visit in the holy month before the Spawning Moon must be reassurance that all would be well. Relief and happiness burst out of them in ecstatic whistles. The lowering sun touched all the manta wings with gold and then the leading manta went below the surface, and all the rest followed. For a moment the Longi felt a plunge of disappointment – they could not go so soon – but the winged gods had not left.

The great rays were curving around to swim a circle in the near vast. Ea was at the front, unable to make a sound because of the profound joy in her heart. The train of mantas beating their wings caught the sun, made ripples of light, became a giant gyre of smooth bright energy. The Longi could not help themselves, they went out further, the elders to the forefront to hold the rest back and protect their minds. Ea felt the mantas so strongly; they were such beautiful beings and their circling motion sent waves of bliss through her.

All at once, her hearing changed. The grunt and whine she struggled to ignore was gone, and for a moment the ocean sang in every cell of her body. All she saw were the black manta wings, every one different on the undersides. Then she saw the mantas' faces, their kind wise eyes, their steady gaze meeting hers.

Ea had not heard people calling to her to stop, nor realised that she had broken through the line of elders and raced out. She had not meant to dive deep and come up in the centre of the great manta circle, where she now found herself.

Wise and kind, amused and interested, the mantas gazed at Ea as they circled and held her in the dream. Her pulse so slow she barely used any oxygen, she saw their male and female faces, their white shoulders and black chevrons, each ray a uniquely different person. The wall of smooth gliding wings revolved around her, black and white, black and white. She became aware of a pattern repeating. And then she understood. *A message.*

Her lungs burning, Ea burst to the surface for air. Beneath her she felt the pulling current of the mantas leaving. She was gasping from her blowhole and could not see or hear but only feel her mother beside her. The water slapped around them as those who understood what had happened made a cordon to keep the curious back from Ea, who had to be assisted to remain at the surface. Her mind was still with the mantas, but she gradually became aware of the slackwater, and knew she was being guided back into the channel to the lagoon. With a shock that made her jerk, she understood the message.

Shh, wait, Ea's mother thought to her, close and speaking as if she were still a calf. *Wait, my love, don't speak yet.*

Ea felt her mother taking her to the nursery area, then the simple sweet calf energy around them. She could not see and could barely hear. She felt her mother's fin go over her, and tuck her, great girl that she was, into echelon position beside her. Ea let her mother support her at the surface and, though she breathed, she did not move. She did not want to return to consciousness because she did not want to remember the message the mantas gave her. She wanted to stay in that slow circling bliss, before it had flashed into her mind, clearer than any click. Only someone very bad would be given this impossible, wicked command.

BREAK THE POD.

Ea had the strong instinct she must keep it secret. To share it, even with her mother, felt too dangerous to risk. The Longi taught their calves that secrets and lies were like poison, and the pod must stay clean. But Ea had never been like others. She would hold the poison.

10

Comedown

Still dreaming manta energy, Ea stayed in the homewater and slept through the night hunt. Her mother stayed beside her until dawn, synchronising her breathing with her daughter's and feeling the new strength of Ea's theta brainwaves. She had also noticed something else, a very unwelcome physical change, but she herself needed to eat and restore her strength before she could help Ea deal with it. As the first wave of new mothers returned from the vast, ready again to suckle their calves, Ea's mother dashed out to catch the last chance of her own day's food.

Ea slept on, her beautiful body tilting in soft rhythm above and below the waterline as her blowhole dilated and contracted. The little calves were fascinated by this big grown female in their midst and they bobbed and swam around her, hoping she would wake. Everyone in the pod was deeply affected by what had happened to her, and there were some tokens of goodwill for her to find when she woke. Someone had left a sponge floating nearby, someone else a bright green seaweed sash that was part of the most popular game of the moment. It had drifted down to the white sand floor where it curled like a snake in Ea's swaying shadow.

Finally she woke in full bright of day, disoriented to find herself in the nursery area. For a long moment she could not remember why. Then she overheard the click of her name, spoken softly and at a distance. The mantas. She remembered, though not when it had happened. Her belly felt empty but she was not hungry. She remembered someone saying that the person who saw the mantas then led the hunt, which made her laugh.

Obviously not you, in this state, said a snide little voice very close by. *Everyone would starve. Hello jellyfish, hello larvae. Hello emaciation.*

Ea spun around with a splash, her balance unsteady. The voice was not that of any calf, and in any case, they had all now retreated.

Ooee! Bit closer!

Ea felt something on the right side of her head, behind her eye and her tiny earhole. A clenching tightness on the skin that made her want to vomit. She knew what it was.

Oh now, said the foot-long remora fish that was stuck there and was the cause of the sensation, *is that any way to start a beautiful friendship?*

Ea screeched in disgust and shook herself from side to side until she was dizzy and the water was churning. She grazed her face on the sandy seabed trying to scrape the creature off. From all sides of the lagoon, mothers rushed to see what disturbed the nursery – and saw Ea alone, as if being attacked by an invisible foe. Her mother went to her side.

Filthy parasite! Ea wailed, her body now surging with cortisol and adrenaline.

Ouch. The Remora moved to under her throat. Its sharp sucker plate on the top of its head dug into her soft skin, and it pressed itself harder. *I prefer commensal to parasite and names do matter, but we'll get to that later. We've got time! Dreary old Ma, she'll tell you.* Ea looked to her mother in horror. The Longi considered Remora the foulest fish in the ocean.

You're welcome, said the Remora, *and I take it as a massive compliment.*

STOP, PLEASE! Ea's mother clicked to the Remora in Old Pelagic.

Nice move, the Remora murmured to Ea. *She's showing respect.*

Ea's mother came alongside her daughter, level with the creature. *Please accept me as a substitute host. I will not attempt to—*

Ea bucked and shrieked as the Remora clenched harder and shuddered with tiny laughter. *Ew! Dreary old thing thinks I'm stupid, Ea! Eh-ahhh . . . EH-AHHH!*

Nothing could nauseate the pure and kindly Longi pod more than this creature in their midst, mocking their chief dancer and besmirching the beautiful Ea. She might be difficult but no one deserved this pollution.

Sorry, old dear, said the Remora to Ea's mother, its voice suddenly cold. *Cunning thing that you are, slipping closer and closer. If you try any tricks, guess who'll suffer?*

Ea threw herself up in an ungainly breach as the Remora bit her, to make its point. It seemed to be speaking directly out of her own jaw, like being possessed by an evil spirit.

Ooh, more compliments, it said to her. *We're communicating really well, this is impressive! Normally it takes a while, but this means we're already fast friends. Please stop and listen or I'll have to bite you again.*

Trembling, her eyes wild with shock, Ea stopped. Her consciousness was concentrated into the skin under her jaw where the Remora's sucker plate was attached, and from where it could wriggle its body against her throat. It made her want to retch.

Stop that. The Remora slapped its tail against her. *And cheer up because this is already working brilliantly, and you could actually learn a lot from me. We, the Remora, are actually very cool, or temperate if you prefer, and you should be celebrating our new union. Ey-aahh? Are you paying attention? By the way, I'm starving. Very much looking forward to when you need to relieve yourself. That'll be a treat.*

I BEG YOU—Ea's mother swam underneath her daughter, exposing her whole white underbelly to the Remora. It shuddered with laughter again.

Get out of here! Eah, tell her there is no way I'm switching hosts, she's crazier than you are! As well as a bossy old drag – you're right, she is, don't even worry—

I don't— Ea was appalled to hear it saying these things.

You can be honest, it said, *I mean you're full of it! Meanness, envy, neuroses: why else would I pick you? You're weak and vulnerable, you're fun! Or at least you could be, if you just let yourself go. Oh wait, you did. That's how we met!*

I'm so sorry. Ea clicked it to her mother, unable to bear what the Remora was saying out loud. She didn't hate or resent her mother; the only thing she felt was bitter shame for the trouble she was bringing to the pod.

Don't even worry, said the Remora, *they need a bit of a shakeup. Living out here in the middle of nowhere, no visitors, probably inbreeding and going mad with boredom by now. You're incredibly lucky I came along, right? Get celebrating, because—*

SHUT UP! GET LOST! Ea spun out of the water as best she could with the shallow draught of the nursery area and tried to slam the thing off her. She was not high or fast enough, so she just succeeded in stinging her own skin and the Remora was still there.

Oh dear, it drawled. *All those lessons you didn't want.* It had moved back to its first position behind her right ear. *Oh yah, we can do that*, it said in another accent. *We're terribly versatile.* Then to Ea's horror, it defecated.

She did not think but rushed from the nursery area to avoid its further pollution, out into the lagoon and toward the channel – but her mother blocked her.

So annoying, whispered the Remora, *when Mummy says it's not safe. Just wait . . .*

It was silent for a moment, then Ea felt its vile peristalsis as it concluded its excretion. She and her mother recoiled from the fouled place.

Copy her if you like, but Mummy's not the boss of us any more, is she? it whispered. *We are. And before you get any ideas, my life is also yours. Important you understand . . .*

Ea stared at her mother, pleading. Her mother did not answer for a moment. Then she clicked in Longi, loud, so that all the horrified pod that were gathered at a distance could hear. *It's true. If we tear off a remora, it makes a wound that will not heal.*

And guess what happens then? squeaked the Remora in excitement. *Hello Residents, hello Transients, hello White Goddess. Called by your own leaking blood . . . silly old Longi.*

BE SILENT! Ea's mother fired a pulse of sound precisely into the Remora, enough to stun it without hurting Ea, though she felt the force in her jaw. No Longi ever used their voice against another, but neither did they blaspheme by calling on the shark gods.

A remora must leave of its natural free will, Ea's mother went on, *or natural death.*

Downer, croaked the Remora, though with more respect after the sonic blow. *That was her last warning – if she tries that shit again, I'm going on your eye and believe me—*

Please— Ea had never felt her mother's rage before and it frightened her more than the Remora. Her mother immediately calmed herself for her daughter's sake.

Good job, Ea. You're in charge now, don't listen to what they say about me. What's a party without a few bad people? Anyway, takes one to know one, that's why we're a team now. Save me from those pious old mantas – all that praying and swaying, and the fasting? I couldn't tell if I was dying of boredom or starvation. No socialising either, until now. Just flapping on and on – I'm not even sure they know where they're going.

You were on the mantas? Ea was so shocked, she said it naturally.

How else did we meet? The Remora clicked in emulation of Longi speech and then hummed a self-satisfied little tune. Ea filled with rage.

Now now. The Remora instantly understood her change of mood. *We're going to be nice to each other, I'll start. Please go and eat something, so that you'll poop. I put it like that because you're all truth and light here, I know. Teeny bit squeamish. Or, take me to the calves. Not as tasty but I am starving.*

Ea remembered the circling mantas. They were supposed to be pure and holy, but they carried remora. If she hadn't been so bold and stupid—

Still by her side, her mother touched her in comfort.

Ea. They only call the strong. You had no choice. The mantas have them, even the—Her mother stopped.

Go on, urged the Remora, *say it! Let's call a shark, shall we? That would be fun! Ouch, what was that? What did you just do?*

Ea had done nothing, but felt her mother had retreated into the clickless communication of the womb, when Ea was not yet ready to be born, but fully aware inside. She heard her mother deep in her mind.

The mantas called you, Ea's mother said in the silence, *because they had a message. What was it?*

No they didn't! I went to them because I'm wicked and stupid! And Ea fled from her mother, the Remora cackling against her head.

Ea went to the moray wall and found them swinging from their holes, as if expecting her. Thirty or more of their snakey bodies made horizontal waves, all their hot little eyes trained on her as she arrived. Bearing this parasite, Ea felt uglier than the worst of them. She did not know if the morays ate remora, but it was worth offering it up. She would take her chances with the wound. But the morays only stared.

Hormone surge, shouted the Remora into her ear, unafraid. *Cortisol, adrenaline, woohoo, Ea, you are delish when you're upset.* She felt it slap its tail against her as it jumped to the other side of her face. *Ooh nasty things, don't eat me!* it squealed in mock horror, then changed its voice. *Eels won't touch me*, it said in a deep sinister tone. *That's my shark voice, do you like it? Not that I've heard one, I'm imagining it. Live in hope though. Apex predator, who doesn't want that? By the way, Ea, I know your plan and I'm sorry, your ugly friends won't touch me. There are many benefits to being unpopular. Plus I still need to feed. You will be going hunting tonight I hope? You can't sulk forever. Poop for me. Come on.*

You're disgusting, said Ea, disappointed and angry her plan had already failed. *I'm not hunting until you leave me.*

In retort, the Remora dug deeper into her face. *You cetaceans*, it said coldly. *Who do you think you are? You've got some nasty habits, don't think word doesn't travel. You tribes are all the same. And don't be so silly, of course you'll go out. You have to eat. Believe me, I can wait you out.* The Remora shivered against her, to show it was laughing. *By the way, what did the mantas say to you? I blacked out when they started swirling and making that weird sound. Come on, let's share a secret. What did they say? Oh, go away, you don't scare me.*

The Remora spoke to Ea's favourite, the big black killer moray who had now swum out of his hole in a dark wave, and who stared hard at her with his piercing yellow eyes. She had never seen his full body length before and, despite its mocking tone, she felt the Remora flinch a little at his presence. Then the great eel slowly opened his jaws to show his pharyngeal second set of teeth, pale spikes in the depth of his throat. Ea dared look in his eyes and the black eel silently hissed into her mind.

Keep your secret.

She turned away, hiding her gratification. The morays were indeed intelligent and sophisticated. They had just never chosen to speak to her until now.

I do need to go, she said to the Remora. *Right now.* And she left the moray wall and swam on the surface to the channel of waste, where many Longi were doing their business at the ebb tide. With clicks of sympathy and apology, everyone swam away as she drew near. Ea did not try to hide her humiliation, but held her head high out of the water while the Remora ate its foul fill.

Keep your secret. So the morays knew the mantas had visited. Ea wondered what else they knew, and why the Longi never bothered to socialise with the eels. Perhaps other creatures also knew things, perhaps the Longi did not know everything. She felt the Remora prying at her consciousness and shut down her thoughts by focusing on where she was. Swimming in the disgusting waste channel, with a parasite attached to her face. She was going to get rid of it, no matter what it cost her. Then a thought occurred to her.

You'd never do it, said the Remora thickly, still eating. *You can't even spin twice.*

Ea could, she wanted to retort, at least twice. She chose silence. The less the foul thing knew, the greater her advantage. Here at last was the best reason she'd ever had to practise Exodus. She would wait, and find the moment.

11

Remora Remora

Starving yourself is punishing you far more than me, Ea. Refusing to hunt a second night! What does the pod think of that, I wonder? Big strong girl like you can do it, though, for a bit longer. Don't worry, I'll bring you round. Meanwhile, this is a good moment to put a few ideas into your mind. As I mentioned, *parasite* is the wrong word. We, the Remora, famous and cosmopolitan traders, are in fact *commensals.* That means it goes both ways, but you're not going to get the benefit of our friendship until you accept me in your life. I'm here to stay, at least until someone better comes along. Thank you for your understanding. Also, please don't go thinking you can hide things from me, because I'm on to you and sooner or later you'll have to tell me everything. Trust me, it'll be a massive relief. But you're young and we're already doing very well, especially now you yourself want to get away from that overbearing mother of yours. I'll think it, you do it.

So, as you're my first mammal, let's get a few things straight.

What my people want yours to know, and I include all your relatives because you're into all that kinship stuff, is that when one of us takes up residence on your body, it is an honour. Yes, it is. Because we unconditionally accept you. All we ask for is a ride, and the reasonable expectation of snacking on leftovers, waste products and bodily fluids. In return, all your secret shaming thoughts and nasty habits are welcome! We accept you, we enjoy it all, the weirder the better, and there's very little we can't digest. And never worry about your place in the shoal, pod, whatever. To us, you're everything. We can also advise on health and nutrition, because we're closer to you than anyone and when you're latched on with our level of commitment, we're not going to let you get sick if we can help it.

We also advise on relationships, because we know how you really feel about people. Your body won't lie so we can taste the smallest changes, and soon I'll be able to know from bite to bite where you're at, who you fancy. There's going to be someone, trust me, even though I know you're a weirdo virgin right now. All this is going into your head while you sleep – and by the way, you're sleeping all shallow and flipping from one side of your brain to the other. I don't think that's healthy or everyone would be doing it and they're not. We, the Remora, can feel these things. We care about our hosts. But there's no gratitude in this world.

I hope in time you'll learn to appreciate me and my people, and stop thinking yours is the beginning and end of the ocean. Saying *commensal* will be a start. But don't worry, I'll pull you up on your language if you start slipping. Sadly, it's not just you mammals, it happens everywhere. It's a sign of how strong we are that we just stick on tighter. One day we'll get respect, because we're an ancient people as well as you. Just because we don't have an ancestral homewater, or go here and there in the season on pilgrimage or spawning, doesn't mean we don't have any culture. You'd be extremely surprised. You think we all look the same too – how many times have we heard that? Just like you probably think every squid or fish you eat is the same as every other. But you won't want to hear that. You're just as violent as everyone else too. But hey, no judgement.

Ooh, guess what else comes with trading? Language! We speak several – not that I'm boasting, it's just the truth. If you were only more open, you might learn from us. Plus, we spawn on the move, none of this risking everything to travel to a great big aggregate – I mean, stupid or what? Or staying in the same old, same old group, having tediously polite sex. I mean, take the sharks: all the scars on the females looks a bit rough, but it's got to be fun. You people are all about stroking and murmuring. Not that you even know yet.

Here's something else. People are jealous, because for us, life is the great moveable feast: one host, then another, we need variety. Some of us brag, I've heard it myself. Those who've once gone on an Apex Predator, or Resident or Transient, whatever you call them. I'd love to get a shark, sorry but it's true. That's why I went for manta when I got the chance, as they're related, but you'd never believe it. Learn from my mistake!

Anyway, good relationships are all about staying power. Once you're latched on, you've got to make the best of it. I'm making it sound like we're not romantic, but we are. Always hoping for the perfect host, someone who'll fulfil all our needs and give us the ride of our life. We also need a lot of food, so please no fasting. Also, no bitterness or moaning, like certain cetacean relatives of yours I could mention. I mean, the whales? Some people aren't happy unless they're miserable. You'd think they'd want our company, the way they go on about those long lonely trips, but they're absolutely not interested. Narrow-minded, I say.

I miss my friends! Commensals! Where are you? I want to be with people who take pride in being a hanger on. I want to be able to talk to someone who's also ambitious, who's not shy about wanting to upgrade to a shark one day. Can you imagine? Actually, I think you can – weird brainwaves – OK, I won't mention them again. To you.

You're quite something, Ea, I can make pictures in your mind so well! I could never do that with the manta, she always shut me out. Not a grain of humility, world of her own. Remind me to stay away from big wingspans, that was my ego doing that. I wanted the long voyage, and that's what I got. I was young, though. And here's a funny thing about us, we, the Remora. Although we stick on, we also get bored and we want change.

I was in a nice situation, a big juicy healthy host, group situation so good social security. People to talk and spawn with on the move, pretty high up the food chain, so good for the self-esteem – but then ... you get bored. Terrible but true. The good diet, varied scenery, luxury travel on the big wings and all that – but you find yourself looking around at other people's hosts. You start to wonder. Could I have done better? Did I jump too soon? Is this my fish for life, my diet until I die? Am I never to latch onto someone new and feel the thrill of swimming in someone else's excreta? Did I ... settle? So, don't go for someone who looks good now but lacks vitality and who's going to end up on the edge, or at the back. Don't hang with losers. We're a bit of a drag, so it's crucial to pick a strong host.

Which brings me neatly to this moment. When the manta had you in the middle and were going round like a school of barracuda with a victim, at first I thought you'd made a mistake, but my ride, the old misery who led them – by the way, I mistook her for an alpha male or I'd never have gone there – she was getting excited about you, then they all did. And we, the Remora, had heard about spinners, Longi, whatever you call yourself, and it was enticing. Highly promiscuous so lots of semen to snack on, show-offs on the move so a bit of a thrill, good hunters – what's not to love? I jumped right before the weird sound started, while you were just twirling around in the middle. You didn't even flinch when my sucker plate went in. Obvious we were going to have a great relationship. You're highly receptive. So last thing, then I'll let you sleep deeper. Your mother's right. Even if you have us bitten off, the wound keeps bleeding. Just a friendly warning. Sleep tight.

12

The Price

Ea took the Remora by surprise, racing straight out into the lagoon in the bright of day and flinging herself in great sideways slams. Let everyone think she was still trying to hear the music of the ocean, let them pity her – all she cared about was ridding herself of this hideous thing. Ea kept breaching and falling, but the Remora was still on her, dug into the protected space under her right pectoral fin. It was silent with rage but the moment she gave in to fatigue and stopped, it released its sharp sucker-plate grip and, with a cunning flex of its body, reattached itself to the top of her head. Ea screeched in pain as it slapped its sharp tail against her sensitive blowhole.

If you're not careful, it muttered when it recovered its own composure from all the wrenching and slamming it had endured, *I'll push something out, so it falls right down there. No, so it sticks to the side. How'd you like that?* Ea stopped moving in horror at the thought and felt it wiggle against her skin in what she knew was laughter.

Squid, it whispered into her mind. *I bet you're hungry. Big fat red shrimp, with the tasty blue tails. I know your favourite everything. When you finally do have sex, I'll shift to—*

Shut up! Ea leaped and made an ugly twisting breach so that she landed upside down and could not hear the end of that appalling thought. People carefully avoided looking over and, after a small pause, continued going about their post-hunt business as if nothing was different, when her whole world had changed. She was furious they were leaving her with her problem, even if she had brought it on herself. Having hunted well, enjoyed a caressing moil, now they were entering their afternoon drowse.

Ea tuned into the slowing chatter, the familiar friendly sounds as they lowered themselves into sleep. People were vulnerable when they slept; every calf was taught that when they learned how to alternate their brain hemispheres to let one side and eye rest, then the other. Part of the mind must always remain aware. But it occurred to Ea that when the Remora slept, it tightened the grip of its sucker plate and then seemed to completely shut down. Nor were there other remora to watch over it.

You're right. She sounded contrite. *I'm so hungry, you must be too. I've been selfish.*

Ea swam again to the waste channel, where the ebb tide was almost over. The Remora already knew the signs and wriggled in excitement. Loathing herself for it, Ea forced her body, and then felt the Remora gulping. Only when she felt it stop moving and the disgust of its swollen fullness against her did she move away.

She went back into the main area of the lagoon to where the last few people still awake were ardently discussing their best spins for Exodus. They were talking about the part called Flight, the climax of the whole ritual. Fast showy spinning with the loudest splash and the greatest net of bubbles trailing underwater. It was the one move for which the music of the ocean was not needed. Though Ea had not done it, she knew the technique.

She clicked quietly to her mother, to let her know she was there and not to wait up. Her mother's sleepy answer came back. She was already in drowsy synchrony with several other people, their brain hemispheres switching at the same time, sending a beautiful balanced wave through the pod. Ea listened until she was certain no one was talking any more. Then she let herself sink down almost into the same rhythm, carefully keeping her mind shallow and empty of everything – except the smallest motion of the Remora.

There, she felt it – the creature's pulse slowed. It pressed its well-fed body against her skin and now only its gills moved. She opened her jaws to test if it responded to her movement. Nothing. It was asleep.

There was the channel out from the lagoon, the sparkling blue light threading with gold as the sun lowered. Smoothly, calmly, just below the surface, Ea swam out over the reef terrace. She kept her mind full of the bright beauty of the corals below her so that she would not wake her passenger. The drowsing well-fed Remora only felt the gentle rhythmic stroke of the tide down its flanks as Ea approached the drop-off, where the reef sheared away in a cliff, and the deep lay beyond. As quietly as she had swum, Ea took breath and then dived.

The cooling temperature and change of pressure instantly woke the Remora and she felt it jabbering at her but she ignored it and prayed to the ocean. *Flight, please, let me just do it once, let me get rid of this hideous thing and then I will take part in Exodus, I promise.*

Down, down until she felt the colder layer even to the top of her fluke; Ea knew it was the place to turn. She powered round to arch her body tight, then began to beat her tailstock with strong steady rhythm. She kept her line straight as the surface got brighter and closer; she shut out the buzzing of the Remora, and the thought flashed like a fish that the leap began at the deepest point.

Ea increased her speed and burst from the watersky high

into her best ever spin. In the glittering coronet of water and light, for a moment she felt a new energy – she was flying like a bird, spiralling, the world was not split into above and below, it was one—

Down she slammed with a huge concave splash and she buzzed a loud pulse of joy and relief that, for the first time in her life, she had done it. Even without the music of the ocean, she had truly felt the spin.

Failure! Rubbish! screamed the Remora, biting its sucker plate hard into her skin. *I'm still here, and if you think that was anything to shout about—*

But Ea was already diving down again, feeling its frantic adjustments to tighten its grip. Now it knew what was coming and they were pitted against each other, but Ea was determined to win. As she went down, she felt the swell of the ocean and the knowledge went into her that just before the surge began, there was a slack, negative moment as when the tide changes. It held a tiny silence. Ea had always heard but never recognised it. She dived.

Stop struggling, trust the ocean—

At last Ea understood what her mother meant, at last she felt the arching of her body begin naturally. Here was the power surge coming through her driving tailstock, here was her spine lighting up with energy, here was the rising release as she broke the watersky again.

One, two, three, the spiral, the spiralling, and the whirling world slowed down, she saw the green of the palms on the shore, the luminous blue depth of the sky – *five, six* – but in her exultation at altitude, she forgot about re-entry. She fell in a huge clumsy splash.

EA! The long hard pulse was horribly familiar, coming from the lagoon behind her. Ea had not realised how far out into the vast she was, but the day was still bright and safe.

EA, COME BACK NOW!

Her mother sounded angry and Ea felt hurt and then angry too. Instead of being delighted that she had at last been practising, her mother was surely about to find some bit of protocol about the re-entry splash, which was not yet totally perfect but—

EA! EA!!

Her mother was charging for her, sending out furious pulse-bursts of her name in a rage Ea had never known. She whirled aside as her mother sped past almost hitting her, her fierce wake pushing her back. Ea was about to whistle in protest when she saw the enormous pale shape looming just where she had been. The grunt she heard was her mother ramming the shark with her rostrum. Ea heard her voice in her head: *GO, EA!!*

Her mother was a silver flash in front of her. Ea felt the heat of her mother's trail and the cold heavy curve of water as the great shark followed. Her mother came speeding in again, aiming herself directly between the shark's eye and its massive long gills.

GO, EA—

Ea reeled in the surging water as the White Goddess, *Carcharadon carcharias*, twisted round to seize her mother. The water bloomed red.

13

Surrender

Ea did not remember how she came back into the lagoon. The pod had gone out after Ea's mother had heard the clumsy splashing and raised the alarm, but there was nothing they could do except save Ea. She was alive and physically unharmed, but she would not speak. Despite their disgust at the Remora, they held her up like a newborn calf to breathe. The Remora was also silent, dazed by the shock to its host.

Ea woke the next day, ugly grunts in her head, or in the seabed, she could not tell. The familiar, menacing sounds that hurt her sonar. She did not notice the Remora, even when it bit down and shook itself. She was in the nursery area but through her headache could hear the pod, as if from a great distance. She felt a peculiar numbness inside her chest and it was hard to think. Something was missing, something was wrong, but she did not know what. Threaded through the pain in her head and the strange feeling inside her was the chirp and splash of calves playing. Lying at the surface she saw a bird streak across the sky's hard glare and she plunged down in panic. The world was horrific today in some new way, yet she had no sense of why.

Come on, the Remora snapped, getting her attention by slapping her eye. *None of this is my fault. If you're just going to be such a misery, at least let me switch to someone else. Go on, that's it, they're coming over.*

They were. A group of Longi elders approached, but their silence was alarming. The water carried their love toward Ea, but also a huge grief.

No closer! Ea remembered the Remora's intention. *It's not safe!* She felt danger all around, though she was in the lagoon.

What happened? she cried out, but the gathered Longi were silent.

You tried to spin me off, the Remora said sulkily, *but ha ha, you failed. Loser.*

Ea could not remember spinning. All she could think of were the circling black and white mantas, and the terrible thought they put in her head.

BREAK THE POD.

Ignoring Ea's warning, the Longi pod swam closer, very gently because they could feel her panicked state. She could feel their love reaching out to her, but could not understand the sorrow. In her inner ear the deep ugly grunt came again, louder and closer as if a great sea-serpent burrowed toward her through the seabed. She heard the calves starting to cry, picking up on the fractured dangerous feeling in the water. Ea's brain hemispheres flashed as if she struggled between sleep and waking.

The Remora slapped its tail against her again. *Stop doing that, idiot. Hurry up and go to them – hey, wrong way!*

Energy burned through Ea as she turned and swam away. She felt guilt and shame but dare not ask why. She had done something bad and she was unclean.

Break the pod.

Clearly she had not yet done that because there they all were, but that terrifying message now felt like a threat. To stay with her family must surely be to destroy them. Ea felt self-loathing like never before. Suddenly everything became clear. The mantas had not blessed, but cursed her.

I'm leaving. Ea clicked it over and over as she swam across the lagoon. She did not hear the grief and fear in her own voice, or the clicks and cries of shock as people realised what she meant. Her body swam of its own accord, carrying her frightened heart away from her family. They followed, calling to her not to go, that no dolphin survived alone – that no matter what had happened they still loved her.

At these last clicks, Ea swam faster. She could not bear to hear any more, she wanted the pain inside to finally come out and destroy her. It was a relief to stop trying to pretend – she was mad, unworthy and unclean. That was why she had the Remora and the mantas had cursed her. Someone had to be given up, to spare the rest of the pod. In some way she had always feared it would be her, and that was why Exodus was such a terror. This was her fate.

Ea swam harder as she went over the Edge, to get beyond the reach of the cries of her family calling her back. No one survived alone, but she would not weaken. She was obeying the mantas and breaking the pod by leaving it. Death must surely be close by. Gathering her courage, Ea went out into the vast to meet it.

14

The Wrasse of the Pinnacles

Out in the vast just beyond the edge of the Tursiops homewater was a deep-sea vent in the ocean floor. From this rose seven towering black mineral formations of different heights, the tallest one tipping twenty metres below the surface of the water. The vent still occasionally and unpredictably bubbled with hot sulphuric water, so the environment was inhospitable as a possible reef, though rudimentary life took hold regardless. On their successful colonisation of the Longi homewater, Tursiops scouts investigated and reported back that the water stung, fish stocks were poor and Transients passed too close for comfort. In addition, there was a bad atmosphere. The pinnacles, as they were known for navigational purposes, were assigned as an outpost of the ocean demons and thereafter left alone.

Geologically, the vent was an unhealed wound made by the

same occult event that vaporised one whole atoll of this archipelago. The pinnacles were unstable, fast growing and their stony structure around the vent caused the currents to distort. Here the water column was a hot hadal fountain. When the fading cyclonic turbulence deposited the body of a huge Napoleon wrasse within the black spikes, it appeared that he – for the prominent bump on his forehead proclaimed him a supermale – would rise and fall in these hostile waters until he decomposed.

The Wrasse himself wished to die. In his former existence he had been lordmale of a whole harem but he had failed them. When the storm caught him, he felt it was oceanic mercy, for he was too exhausted and broken-hearted to go on looking for his vanished people. As lordmale it was his duty to protect his females and control all males, yet in one shocking event, they were taken from the water, all together.

All my people, there, then gone.

The Wrasse had seen it with his own stunned eyes. His beautiful people gathered together, first by joy and lust and then by some incomprehensible outer force, pushed closer and closer until they were crushed and screaming, into a monstrous compressed mass – and then pulled up through the watersky, and gone.

Somewhere else, they must be somewhere else.

Surely he was only left alive to find them. The Wrasse searched unceasingly. Food was scarce and the ocean was eerily empty. When after two whole moons there was no trace of any of his people, though his will drove his thin body forward, his heart began to weaken.

Duty or death for the lordmale – protect the herd – the herd is gone – liarcowardfailure—

So circled the self-devouring thoughts of the Wrasse until the cyclone. No one could go against the ocean in her turbulence. With shameful relief, he abandoned himself to his end.

As the surge pushed him into a gap between the pinnacles,

the deep scrape down his side was the unwelcome reminder that he was still alive. Then came the excruciating sting of sulphuric water against the fresh wound, but far worse was his despair at remaining alive. The Wrasse barked his agony and rage from his great swimbladder and it echoed back sevenfold inside his black volcanic prison. He convulsed as if shaking his way through the tendrils of a poisonous jellyfish, then he saw large familiar scales caught on the twisted black stone. For a moment his heart jumped at the hope of another of his kind, before he realised they were his own – and marked the place where he had entered.

Cautiously the Wrasse went out and swam about in the peculiar deflected currents, all of which had bad tastes. Returning within the pinnacles he found the water still hurt, but tasted cleaner. Also, and this again enraged him because he still wished to die, it seemed to be clearing his head. The Wrasse shook himself at the seditious new thought, that this could be a residence. The pinnacles were a forbidding place in an empty ocean and he was honour-bound to leave them behind and go on into the wastewater ahead, searching until death. And yet . . . What if he stayed, and starved to death? Was he even capable of choosing that pathetic end? In his glory days, the Wrasse had a strong appetite. His broken-hearted wandering had killed it, but these strange waters seemed to be returning him to his senses. As his body clung to life, he became aware of his hunger.

The bubbling of the vent was growing stronger and a column of light fell down between the pinnacles. The Wrasse stared down into the twisting black water, where surely monsters lurked. This water was alive, it was malign. If he had courage, here was death. Racing his fear, the Wrasse plunged down to meet it.

Long before he even descended a quarter of the way, the Wrasse blacked out from the heat. The rising jets of the vent then carried him back up to the cooler water, and he came to from bumping against a ledge. The first thing in focus was vivid yellow algaeic growth, furry and healthy and right in front of him. He fell upon it like a greedy female of his lost tribe, scraping it off with his big white incisors and swallowing until there was no more left. The yellow algae were vital and tenacious enough to withstand the local conditions of the vent, and the Wrasse, who had not eaten in days, immediately felt the benefit.

His vision sharpened. He noticed tiny transparent shrimp, their bright blue intestinal tract the only thing that gave them away. They tasted foul but they instantly made him feel stronger. Next he saw starfish, great ugly black things with so many bumps and spines he had at first thought them part of the spires to which they clung. And clung, with that same tenacious force, releasing noxious black liquid as he tore them away. It was good to have something real and resistant to fight with, even a starfish. The Wrasse hurled himself on them until he was so full he was forced to stop his assault.

Algae, shrimp, starfish. He, lordmale of the whole herd, who would once have left these poor things to the females and the lesser males, and himself either hunted fish or chosen to demonstrate the power of his teeth on the thickest clamshell. No one to see now, no dignity to maintain.

No one at all. The Wrasse was no longer My Lord, or Sire. No court, subject, ranks of beautiful adoring females fluttering for his attention. He was uncertain how long he had been within this black fortress. He could not think; he seemed to remember diving down at least twice, seeing the midday beam of light shine down between the spires more than once. Perhaps many times. He now knew where to find the black starfish, and the crevices favoured by the clouds of tiny blue-veined shrimp. He could recognise the gleam on the black that was not sunlight, but the yellow algae.

Days passed in dark and drifting thoughts, bitter and vicious recriminations against himself, curses and insults that he was dying a coward. The colourful flash of his own fins, once the flaring honour of the supermale, now advertised him as a pretender. The Wrasse would have denied himself the relief of sleep, but his exhausted body overpowered his mind.

Like all supermales of his people, *Cheilinus undulatus,* the great Napoleon wrasse – now the Wrasse of the Pinnacles – had once been female. It was a miraculous natural phenomenon, a sacred mystery, that came to certain females if the dominant male of the herd was lost. Several would then undergo the Change, but as they emerged as resplendent claimants to the title of lordmale, they had to undergo highly ritualised combat with each other. The strongest, most gorgeously attired new supermale was chosen, and those other newly transitioned female-to-supermales would then decline to merely male. The Wrasse of the Pinnacles had experienced the most drastic hormonal transformation, and his new gender was a success.

As with all birth and rebirth, he had completely forgotten the traumatic experience. His first clear memory was emerging from some safe, nightfast crevice and hearing the sound of many troubled females. Coming soon upon the cause, the sight of three weakling supermale pretenders caused him to jut his immaculate new fins in outrage. He had grown a great thick tailstock with a high fanning caudal fin, and he could feel the heavy bounce of his body in the water as he balanced. His huge new head, with its massive hump, he only saw by his shadow and he felt his latent power of speed in his muscles.

The newly transitioned Wrasse glared at the imposters to the title of lordmale, all unrecognisable to each other as past grazing acquaintances, and most dominant females of the herd. Following the death of their aged lord, all of them had now metamorphosed into males. The Wrasse of the Pinnacles was the biggest, the brightest, the boldest of them and he, most recently the she with the most testosterone, made the hierarchy clear.

Submissive females whose biochemistry restrained them in stable gender, and who had not entered that turbulent hormonal sleep, clustered together to watch the defence of the claim. They delighted in how the Wrasse head-butted and barked from the depths of his newly enlarged swimbladder, and even the coral shivered at this new sexual force in the water. Here was the new Lord of the Reef.

Far behind him now. A period of a few glorious moons, when he ate his fill and watched his pretty females grow larger and more lascivious in their song and play under his great protective eyes, ringed with orange and banded with blue lace. He felt the arrogant thrill of display and heard the ladies enumerating his virtues. Their finbeats vibrated the water as he passed among them, everyone waiting for the Great Spawning, the oceanic festival of sex. This was the full moon when coral and anemone and bivalve and fish of many races would synchronise their annual orgasmic release, and the ocean would pulse and rejoice with the promise of new life for the strongest and luckiest, and plentiful food for all.

At the time of the Spawning Moon, the Wrasse would know each of his females as they released their eggs for him; he would pulse hard jets of his sperm into their midst and only then might the other males emulate him. Then the moonlit water glowed with lust and life, and he would swim guard of all. The lesser males were crucial as auxiliary defence and witness to his glory, because only with contrast could there be pomp.

What happened was surely his fault. Some false judgement of the tide, or the moon, or the signal from the corals that made him lead them to the ancestral spawning site too soon, or too late. Again and again had the tortured Wrasse gone over it in his mind, the females rushing ahead along bright coral-flowering currents, the milk of lust already seeping from lubricious coral citadels, whose million citizens pulsed to their own lunar laws. The

Wrasse could taste and feel it still, that night of excitement as the ocean herself began to flex and contract as the moon roused her.

Even here, alone amidst the pinnacles, the Wrasse shuddered with the sexual thrill of the memory. For a flashing moment he was there again in the moonlit water which seemed to get brighter and brighter with each arriving group, while he beheld his beautiful females and held them steady. They would not be the first nor the last to spawn, nor would he prematurely burst with pride. From all over the ocean they came, the different tribes of *Cheilinus undulatus*, to the ancestral spawning place. The people gathered for their orgiastic rite of joy, confident that on this one night of the year, not even a Transient would trespass.

The waters teemed with beautiful people, their gills flowing with the shared chemicals their bodies released. Energy spiralled and lit the water, the people were singing and chattering and then they fell silent. The moment was upon them. As the moon reached her apogee, the water trembled and the first coral burst out a jet of eggs. The ocean filled with sperm and eggs and the gathered people of the Wrasse were released to join in.

The females of all tribes shot up toward the moon gleaming down on them and then their lordmales followed. The Wrasse felt himself tight and full of sperm as his own beauteous females raced up toward the surface to release their eggs. The lesser males followed them into the great throng to make the cordon for their lordmale and the Wrasse was a synapse away from firing himself up into the concentrated mass of eggs, when three long black shadows slid in front of the moon.

Then the bizarre thing began. The sea clenched hard around the mass of females, and those supermales and males who had gone up after them. The water was full of eggs and sperm, but now the people were screaming in panic and pain as they were pushed, then crushed together. The Wrasse was paralysed in horror as the entire group of gathered tribes were forced together and dragged sideways by what force he did not know. There was screaming, the water still streaming with egg and sperm and now blood. He heard the hideous sound of bones breaking, spines snapping, intestines rupturing, and all the time, people crying out to be saved.

The Wrasse swam up to the horde of people but he could no more stop the great compacted mass of them being dragged up to the surface than he could stop the moon shining. A terrible rumbling started in the water and now he could see the fine black lines that criss-crossed and dug into the shining flanks of his people.

And then, they just disappeared. All of them. Crushed together by some evil power that pulled them up through the sky. The Wrasse swam about desperately, unable to believe that all those people, thousands of them, every single one but himself, had vanished. The water rumbled with growling sounds, growing fainter. The moon stared down in shock. The ocean went slack. The Wrasse was alone.

How many moons roving in search to bring him here, he did not know. He was certain death lay in the deep in the vent, but conditions were unpredictable. Some days heat did not rise at all, while on others, it surged up fierce and concentrated – but he was too far away. Or else he grew used to his new conditions. When he plunged down he no longer blacked out, but instead felt himself licked by the hot probing tongue of the vent. That pain was his shameful pleasure.

As he deserved to die, he needed to find another way. There was a broken black spike of rock that he might race at, to impale himself. If he did not kill himself outright, his injury would surely call a shark. Then he was glad, a coward once again, when the pinnacles conspired with the vent and he could not find the spike. The Wrasse gazed at the dark glittering spires around him, but seeing only the reef he had come from so long ago. He had travelled its many miles, from the colourful bustling civilisations at one end, to the bleak and desolate regions where all that was left of ancient coral cities was white ruin. He left the reef and wandered the vast, searching for his people. Heedless of danger he called out for his beauties, his knights and squires of his court, for anyone at all to hear him. In rage and grief he even called out for sharks to come and take him, but his suffering was to remain alive.

And then, as if the seal between some chambers of his hearing were opened, he heard an unfamiliar sound. A distant clamour, the rough buzzing and chirping of many hundreds. Instinctively the Wrasse shrank back. Predators – dolphins, he thought. Their uncouth sound travelled through the water, faint and fading, passing beyond his range. He did not know if he was sorry or glad.

15

Justice

The sound the Wrasse heard was the Tursiops pod in uproar. Despite Devi's prohibition on ever mentioning Yaru again, the detail of her physical injuries had passed in surreptitious click through the pod until every female knew she had been multiply raped. Many had already been harassed and insulted by those four young thugs. The noise of female distress and outrage grew, until the vira commanders literally could not hear themselves think. Devi was forced to speak to her lord Ku, on behalf of all the females of the pod. She was loath to do this but knew if she did not, she would lose her power base. Uneasily, she set this against the increased enmity she would rouse from the lord Split, whose son was one of the offenders.

The lord Ku heard her with a heavy heart. Peripheral females were often casually used for sex by those males who could not yet hold a harem, and their losses were mere collateral damage of maintaining the power structure. But these four youths had raped a co-wife of the First Alliance, defiling the sacrosanct male hierarchy they hoped to join. It was nothing less than a challenge to the political structure of society. An example must be made.

The four were rounded up. Protesting with contradictory accounts, they categorically denied any involvement in the accident. They had been doing their best at the back keeping all the stupid peripherals together, but it was impossible.

Why impossible? The lord Ku went close to them. So young and strong. He regretted what he must do. There lasted a rare and painful silence, in which the four felt the unpleasant focus of the whole pod's attention on them. *You wish to hold my harem? You plan to seize power?*

No! The four juveniles began to understand what was happening to them. They never meant it like that, it was never supposed to turn out like that – and so they damned themselves by their own abject excuses. Better had they kept to their unified rebuttal of the accusation, but it was too late now. Never had a wall of their own people looked so frightening, the suppressed fury of the females even more so than the males. Feeling the implacable group will that they should be punished, the four grew angry and broke out in bitter complaint that they were good enough to become vira, why were they never even allowed to compete in the games?

I am of noble birth! raged Split's son. *I am entitled to sexual privilege!*

The lord Ku heard the buzz of outrage from the females, immediately quelled by a sharp pulse from Devi. She knew justice was in the balance, but if the females angered him at this moment, he might choose pardon. A small minority of males held sexual rights, and only respect for that vira hierarchy prevented more rapes. To be in a harem was but fragile protection. She arched submissively low before her lord Ku. Observing this, her co-wives did likewise, and the movement spread through all the females of the gathered pod so that every male was witness to their plea for justice. Holding her position until she was short of breath, Devi at last felt her lord's jagged energy stabilise. He signalled to her to take breath. All the females followed her lead. They had affirmed his sexual domination, and in return, he must protect them.

The four young males buzzed in displeasure at this unexpected behaviour. Females fought and nipped and competed for the most powerful males. They did not act in concord. It was a sly trick, the lord Ku must see through it, they were innocent. But as they lost control of their breath and began blowing hard and vulgar at the surface, everyone saw their involuntary arching and downward jabbing of their pectoral fins. They could not hide it, they were posturing as if for imminent combat and their anger sealed their fate.

The lord Ku went by them one by one, swinging his head to tooth-rake each face in the same place. He gave them the harem stripe – security to a protected female, and shame for a male. It would forever show that the bearer had offended their lord.

A murmur of triumph went around the females. Now was avenged the insolent lechery and bragging, and the brutal way the thugs had beaten calves from their path. The murmur became a click travelling from the highest harem out to the lowest peripheral female, that Yaru's rapists and the killer of her female calf were marked for life. Once again Devi silenced her harem with the dangerous flex of her body they knew so well. Quickly, all the harems fell silent.

The lord Ku had not finished.

You four, he clicked to them when the whole pod was silent, *plead privilege and lust instead of discipline and loyalty. You insult those warriors who did not question orders but gave their lives for the safe Crossing of the pod. Good Lord Split your father, my second in command, survived, and all see the evidence of his valour. You shame him.*

No! cried Split's son, suicidally. *You are unfit, you are too old – we need new ways—*

Then make them. The lord Ku came forward, his body arched in anger, his lesions pulsing white around his eyes. *Make them out in the vast, your new homewater.* His crooked dorsal fin stood high and rigid. *For you are exiled.*

At first the four cackled in angry mockery. Just for rape, and the death of a female calf? Then when they still did not believe it, the vira made it plain for them, shoving and beating at them to drive them past the drop-off. A crowd of triumphantly buzzing females followed behind as the four went out, breaching and splashing in defiance. They cheered and whistled back at the pod as if they were off on some bold hunt; they pulsed insults back at them, that they would return and mete out retribution for this insult. They were stronger than any vira, that was why they were being thrown out! The females buzzed back at them, but Devi was silent. The lord Split flashed by her, hatred in his muscular wake. She saw him go toward the edge of the homewater and stop. She knew he listened to the last vaunting brags of his favourite son, fading out in the vast.

Charged with rage and adrenaline and disbelief at the shocking outcome of their little prank, the four maintained their high spirits for some distance, finding day-feeding shoals and devouring them without hunger. Of course hunting would be easy, for what were they but the best vira in the whole pod, had they only been given the chance to prove themselves? Then they teased each other about their harem scars, jostling as they aped becoming First Wife, and mounted each other in play-fighting and the constant struggle for dominance – when the thought of Devi's eyes came to them.

Devi, who had watched their fate in silence, and who was

ultimately responsible. The four knew it as well as she did, for if the harem had left one of their own behind – and the four were brutish but had still heard the whispers about how Devi kept control – then why mind if she were lost or damaged? Everyone knew the lord Ku did nothing without consulting her. In any case, they had thought that the one they had played with was a mere peripheral. Until now, who even cared? Hypocrites all of them – the females, the vira, and as for the lord Ku, he was getting old and why did no one say anything about that, or those diseased lesions growing bigger all the time? They had been exiled for speaking the truth!

But as they swam on, defiance became anxiety. The hard white reef was behind them and now they neared the edge of Tursiops homewater where the troughs and seamounts began. A disruption in the currents told them they were nearing those eerie black rock forms called the pinnacles. These were far below the surface and marked the start of the ocean demons' world. But before that thought spread as fear, they saw they were not alone.

A strange and delightful creature was travelling in the same direction, and the sight switched them into high good humour. It was a fugu, or blowfish, of whose defensive and psychoactive toxin the Tursiops were extremely fond. They were very keen on anything that got them high but did not kill them – sarpa overdose accidents were another reason for their rationing – so fugu fish were a rare treat. Demand for their irresistibly fun tetrodotoxin meant the Tursiops had greedily killed every last one in their range and too late did they consider saving any for the future.

Now, in a consoling gift from Mother Ocean, here was this fat frightened female, swimming away as fast as she could. They forgot all their woes as they swam alongside, teasing her with snapping jaws until she was forced to void herself of a good dose of poison. They shoved and jostled each other to swim through the narcotic cloud, opening their mouths for maximum membrane penetration. Then they began tossing her about on the surface.

The Wrasse was lurking in the shade of the biggest pinnacle, idly turning his huge body this way and that to catch the fading exhalations of the vent, when he heard the vulgar cackles – and the single terrified cry in their midst. He identified it as female, single, and in his territory. The cackles came louder and harsher, and with a flush of adrenaline and cortisol through his body, the Wrasse knew the yobbish voices came from his most hated foe, dolphins. Specifically, because he now recognised the accent, they were the worst kind, the dreaded Tursiops, who were known not just to predate his people but sometimes toyed with them first, pretending to let them escape.

The Wrasse growled deep in his body, feeling the base of his fins thickening to raise up his heavy dorsal war flag. He counted the cackles – four males. Bad odds. But he had rage to spare, and here was the chance to spend it. The Wrasse was two-thirds of the average length of a dolphin but his great beak was like bone or stone. His explosive bark could stun several small fish at once, and intrusion of these thugs removed all doubt: this was his home-water and they must be driven off. The Wrasse waited until the fugu's screaming had moved to where the hooks and spikes of the pinnacles could do most damage to sensitive dolphin skin. Then, fins flared and teeth bared, he burst from the shadows.

Tossing the inflated fugu between them and swimming through the last of her voided toxin, at first the four Tursiops bucks did not even notice him. It was the fugu who saw him first, alerting them with her wild swivelling eyes. They were so high on her poison that they first thought the vivid colours and great size of the emerged Wrasse were a hallucination. Then they noticed their penises had all come out, and cackled more manically.

Furious at their levity, the Wrasse shot forward and rammed

the nearest one with his beak. A great bubble of air burst from its blowhole and the other three took even greater amusement at his plight. The Wrasse stared. Clearly he had not landed a hard enough blow so put more force into the next one, backing it up with a vicious bite to the nearest fin. He felt his teeth touch in the middle and heard the gratifying squeal in response. Then he dashed underneath them, snapping savage bites in all directions. In their drugged confusion, the four Tursiops felt attacked by a raging shoal and rushed to surface.

The Wrasse looked up from below. For a moment, the long dark silhouettes of the dolphins on the surface reminded him of something else. For a moment he heard the screaming of his people. The Wrasse toppled, he struggled, he could not see properly—

Here, here, come in quickly!

It was the Fugu, shouting to the Wrasse in the crude Teleost speech of all fish. She was within the sanctuary of the pinnacles, but the Wrasse was uncertain what was real. Then he saw the tail flukes and the keel and yaw of the big Tursiops bodies above him, and the water clouded brown. With a jerk of outrage that brought him back to himself, the Wrasse realised they were defecating over his home. They clicked abuse in their guttural dialect and he recognised the word for revenge. He lunged into the falling muck, flared and ready to fight despite his disgust – but the four dolphins were moving on.

The Wrasse felt his eyeballs hard with anger and his heart thrum with stress. But the four fools were moving out into the vast, away from the direction of their homewater. His kinetic navigational sense had jolted into new awareness, and it restored some of his confidence. He wished the disappearing Tursiops all the ill in the ocean, of which there was much, then returned to his territory. His, because he had defended it. Now all he had to do was evict the Fugu.

That was an urgent matter, because as she deflated, the whole inside area of the pinnacles vibrated to her histrionic wails of distress. The Wrasse had no compassion for anyone, least of all this fugu. Thinking her a female of his own kin, he had risked all for a case of mistaken identity, and now those Tursiops louts would return with others. From earlier suicidal thoughts, the Wrasse now pivoted to outraged determination never to make a meal for those coarse mammals. He glared at the creature whose fault this was, and to emphasise his hostility to her presence, pushed hard finbeats at her. He was distracted by a peculiar sensation on his skin, almost as if he had been scratching his flanks on reef sand or had swum through tingling anemones.

There were no anemones here, and certainly no reef. Protective or defensive anger had always led to a pleasurable testosterone after-surge in his skin, but this was different. The Wrasse felt . . . sexually aroused. He wanted the Fugu to hurry up and go so that he too could shelter within the spires and dwell on it some more. He could not relax and enjoy it with her there. And now, pathetically, as if the Fugu did not know he was a supermale with extraordinary eyesight and other powers, she was trying to hide.

Get out. He spoke Teleost, instead of the elegant reef dialect that was his native speech. *Go away.* He felt a stirring around his genital patch. Surely it could not be time for the Spawning Moon again? Had he wandered for that long?

You seem dazed, she said in an arch voice, emerging at her normal size. *But then I am the most poisonous fish in the ocean, it's true. Did you try a little? Were you curious?*

The Wrasse did not answer. The feeling in his body was not from her toxin. He flexed from side to side, as if he could shake it into clarity. He did not feel ill, quite the reverse. His victorious combat against four great Tursiops males had energised him.

Don't get ideas, she said, checking her fins for damage. *I can see I excite you but it's so tiring being desired. It's the same everywhere I go.*

Do that, said the Wrasse. *Go. This is my home, not yours.*

Well aren't you lucky, she snapped, as if they were equals. *Mine—* She stopped herself, and ascended to where she pretended to look out. The Wrasse knew she couldn't see anything because the pinnacles were far out in the vast, and the water was thick.

Where is your reef? he demanded. *Did you see any of my people?*

Gone, she said, *and no.* She stared out, whirring to stay where she was. *Mine was a glorious reef, not like this dump.*

So was mine, retorted the Wrasse. *Where people knew their place.*

My place, she said, *was far above your ridiculous hierarchy. I ran the cleaning station, if you even know what that is.*

Of course I do. The Wrasse was annoyed she had engaged him in conversation.

Well then, when it closed down, she continued in an overly patient voice, *everyone who lived on the reef became homeless. Most died. Do you know, I think I'll stay here. I'm rather tired.*

You can't, said the Wrasse. *It's mine.*

Well then share, she said. *It's mine too now. Or kill me, I don't even care.* She fluttered out the better to see him. *We saw a few of your sort there, but nothing like your colours. What's going on with the tail fin?*

Now that she said it, the feeling became clear and localised for the Wrasse. His tail fin – yes. That was where the feeling concentrated, as if energy lines were prickling all down his body to culminate there. As if bright warm sunshine shone on that part of him. Despite his great size he curved round to see and caught a flash of pink.

This is new, he said.

Tell me about it, said the Fugu. *It's happening to a lot of people, a lot of weird changes. You see the world at a cleaning station, so nothing shocks me. Male to female, female to male, a bit of both . . . no one wants that though, do they? Although I suppose you're never lonely. Awkward for you, with the festival coming up. No way to take part . . .*

The Wrasse stared ahead, furious and distressed that she should so casually raise the Great Spawning Moon, diminishing it into 'the festival'. The anniversary of his catastrophe.

The Wrasse felt his body was roiling. He wanted to flex and undulate and release his mind to cloud with perverse sexual thoughts to block out the grief. Before she could further observe him, he sank down to where the vent pulsed hot and hostile and dark.

Pressing his skin against the glittery abrasion of a black volcanic pillar, the Wrasse let the fantasies come. He felt secret shudders then flashes of heat. First female, then lordmale – he was one then the other then both. He imagined himself watching, doing, dying, eating, being eaten. He went down further, where the heat stopped all thought.

16

Two Missions

The waves hurl and pull Google's battered body far from the dirty little harbour of his triage, into the angry open water of the vast. His skin is so burned and his muscles so bruised that it is a blessing he is barely conscious. He does not even try to dive and this saves him, because he is tossed to the surface where there is air to breathe. But the salt slap of the waves drags his mind closer to waking. Either way, there is pain.

Since he was nine years old and like all the Marine Mammal Assets in the training program, Google had been given a daily pharmaceutical cocktail. Tailored for each animal, his was titrated for enhanced endurance, resistance to pain and, as one of the larger males, the modification of behaviours incompatible with environmental conditions. In other words, while not physically castrated, his natural testosterone was suppressed to keep him docile in his pen. Amphetamines and steroids kept him active, and benzodiazepams and anti-depressants, stable.

All the bottlenose dolphins in the training program were intelligent but Google was also known for his wonderful temperament. He learned to lift himself up out of the water when he heard footsteps coming along the gantries, after discovering it made the anthrops happy, and they then gave him more fish. Though he always accepted it, food was never his major motivation. Google loved his drugs.

The daily dose, the tiny sting in an underside vein of his right pectoral fin, that was what he cared about. He knew if they visited him early, it would be a long day out in Work, and if they came late, after a day of high stimulation out in Work and often with pain in his head from all the noise, then the little sting sent him floating away in muffled peace. His young anthrops handler never gave the sting but Google liked him best because he could feel he too had a pain inside, but it went away when they were together. Google had a strong feeling of responsibility and did his best to keep him cheerful, by performing all his tasks as well as he could.

They went together to a new place of Work, transported by air to a new ocean for more serious games. Like all the other MMAs in his cohort who travelled in the great pressurised carrier, Google had emerged from the heavy tranquillisers shrieking in alarm. All the animals were immediately given more drugs to stabilise them. These doses were very high because the next operation would terminate their well-being.

None of the MMAs had the opportunity to reorient to their new Workplace. Waiting in his narrow travel tank, Google sensed tension around him. There were new sounds in the air and new anthrops' voices. By the time his own one reappeared, Google was seething with pent-up energy. He was winched out of his individual tank and into the transition tank, and he understood that though Base was different, he was still being prepared for games and exercises. As he secured the heavy fastenings on Google's neoprene harness, his young anthrops emitted a different energy. By the heavy attachment, Google recognised the familiar game. *Go Work. Go Snap. Find Base.* Feeling sadness from the young anthrops, he tried to connect with him, trying to make the sound that made the boy smile. But that day the boy would not meet Google's eyes.

His body swings high in a wave and slides down, high and down, so that his brain almost picks up a rhythm. The storm ebbs. Google's mind flutters, but some primal instinct to flee from pain sends it reeling back into memory.

They let him down into the water, in the regular sling he knew how to leap back into. He did not notice them pull it back up because he was already diving, swimming deep and fast to avoid all obstacles and complete his mission: press the attachment on his harness onto the target. He had practised many times but there was so much more noise in this Work, it was dirty and thick. Google reached the target, the side of a ship. He moved into position and felt the magnets clamp to the steel hull. Then as usual he pulled and twisted to break the seal and free himself, but these magnets were much stronger than those he practised with. He was stuck. From inside the attachment he could feel a small vibration and he knew something was wrong. With the strength of the steroids as well as his own, he wrenched himself free. Then he raced for Base.

Behind him the limpet mine detonated. The Workplace rose up all around him then crashed down in flaming chaos. The water pounding with the acoustic beating, metal shards and jagged pieces hurtled from all directions. Avoiding collisions, Google came up to the surface into a huge slick of burning fuel. His neoprene harness ignited, flames spread across his skin and when he went under again the molten plastic fused into his flesh.

Google kept swimming with all his strength and found Base pouring with black smoke. He could hear shouting and yelling, no one was there waiting for him but the sling was still in sight, though higher than it should have been. Google leaped for it and slammed down, screaming and blacking out as his burned skin scraped against the metal frame.

Later, when the ship had limped back to safer water, they found him and thought him dead from his wounds, until they began to excise his transponder chip. Then he moved.

Find Base. That recall was the first instruction Marine Mammal Assets learned to follow, and as Google regains ragged consciousness, it is the first thought in his mind. His shrieking nervous system shoves it aside because his body clock knows the drugs are late. Even here in the middle of a different ocean, thousands of miles from the people who know what he needs and can give it to him, Google feels himself raising his right fin as if they will come. It is time, he is frightened that they will not come, a terrible fear is swarming in his mind like never before and if he could beat his head against his tank he would, but his tank is not there. He wants his tank, he wants the sting – the last of the fentanyl is wearing off and he is in agony.

Google is already at the surface but he cannot control his breathing, his blowhole snaps open and shut convulsively, water goes in and he's drowning. He coughs and gasps as he sprays it out, the salt water blasting new pain through his burned trachea. It brings him round, and with intense effort he makes himself aware of his surroundings. There is nothing to see but Work, but he can feel this is not the same place. The water is different. He is different. His attention comes back to his body, all the sensations of pain colliding like the unfamiliar currents around him. His back remembers the burning harness and he goes under, but it is not there. All that remains are the livid lines he will bear to his death, and which will not have time to turn to white scar tissue.

The swinging weight of the ocean carries him on. Google has never known this mental torment of being lost, and it distracts him from the physical pain. No matter what direction he dives, he has no sense of the way back to Base. His world has gone.

Google dives frantically, he swims into a confluence of marine rivers and for a moment curiosity distracts agitation. One river feels better, so he aligns himself and it carries him. For a moment, he gets a flash of confidence. This river has a sense of purpose, it is almost as if it speaks to him, urging him this way. *Find Base.*

Joy explodes in Google's heart as he recognises the hammering engine sound of a ship. *Base!* He has found it, this river will carry him there and he throws himself forward. But the sounds are uneven, as if Base is listing – or even changing direction. That must be it – Base is moving and he must catch up before it is out of range. Google swims with all his strength and training, his attention locked onto the sound ahead of him. He knows as if from a distance that his body is struggling, but he focuses on his speed. The panic has gone and he is going to do this, he will finish his mission.

Base is still moving, so to secure its location Google braces himself and fires a beam of sonar out from his damaged melon. The pain almost blacks him out but he gets the reward: there in his mind is the blot of the ship, the real position up ahead. Google thinks of the face of his anthrops and he powers on, ready to burst his heart if he has to.

The Rorqual was exhausted. The great humpback whale had been travelling this particular ocean gyre and performing his song-cycle for three whole days, when the cyclone messed up the final movement. No one would be able to hear the details with any accuracy. Ever his own sternest critic, the Rorqual decided he must sing the whole thing in full again. If he left his warnings blurred and vague by his own laziness, some far-travelling whale kin family might meet fatal danger. Because of the shipping lanes the Rorqual warned of, this was one of the most dangerous parts of the ocean and also the location of two ancient whale songpaths. If he lingered too long, he too might perish.

The Rorqual was also starving because once he had started a song, he never broke off to feed. Singing the entire composition twice made him weak with hunger, and he was desperate to leave this grim region of death and memory. His annual navigations of the ocean gyres showed him more nets each time, heavier with more dead bodies of his own people and many others. Even great Transient sharks hung motionless. Over the years the Rorqual refused to grow used to the pain of it, but instead kept it raw, to strengthen his resolve. Each baffling death hurt him, each wasted life mattered, and he would sing with his last breath, to try to keep his people safe. Hunger reminded him he was still alive, and he denied himself the indulgence of loneliness, until one day it overpowered him.

The Rorqual could no longer hold back his own grief. There was so much pain in this world but he did not know what else he could do except bear witness and sing his song, despite no sign that anyone ever heard it. While he kept moving he could withstand the sense he was lost and alone in a dead world, and while he sang he could imagine his living kin, maybe safe beyond harm because of his warning song. Maybe that was why he was alone, because, despite the lack of response, his song had been successful and everyone had fled. Sometimes he held to that in hope, but other times when he was tired, he feared his loneliness would madden him. The Rorqual craved connection, to know and be known, to travel, to sing, to play and eat, and most of all, to sleep with one of his own. He craved family and closeness with a desperation that sometimes stopped him mid-song. He heard that break as the piercing tone of his own heart, and decided to use it in his song.

Coming as a shock in the middle of his calls and booms, this new element of silence resonated with all the love and power and pain of the whale's spirit. With a knowledge that was ocean-given, the Rorqual transformed his song. It was not enough to sing warning of external dangers, he must put himself as witness into his song. At first it felt vain, but then he felt the silence go out in waves, just as much as the sound. The silence of the nets, of the lost ones. And then his song again, his warnings, and his rage. His range increased and, though no one ever responded, neither distant male in approbation, nor lowing female beckoning the bliss of her presence, the Rorqual found new meaning in his work. He used the little archipelago in the middle of many songpaths as the locus of his great circuit, and while he did not choose to give up his mission to go and live there, the fact it hosted two dolphin populations gave him a remote link with family.

He was almost at the end of his second full rendition, when the hairs on one side of his face trembled. Something, or someone, was coming. Without interrupting his booming, the Rorqual turned. A single bottlenose dolphin sped directly at him. The Rorqual moved aside because otherwise this peculiar dolphin might crash into him – but the dolphin adjusted, then slowed. It twisted in the water going to and fro along the great length of the whale. It was clicking frantically and making other sounds the well-travelled Rorqual did not recognise.

Glad to stop singing, he rotated to examine the dolphin more closely. A male bottlenose, no sound of any accompanying pod. It was large and strong – and then the whale saw the injuries. Just as disturbing were the vibrations coming from the dolphin's melon. He was clearly communicating something, but all the Rorqual could understand was a feeling of anger. Then the dolphin hurled himself forward and rammed him. The Rorqual wanted to laugh, but it was serious. The dolphin had been in some physical horror and had lost his mind.

Google could not bear his mistake. The sound he raced toward was not Base, but this thing, this creature, he had never before encountered. This animal was pretending to be Base, it had tricked him and caused him to go so far from where real Base might be that now he might never get back there. Part of Google was stunned by the reality of this enormous living being he had rushed to join, and part of him was heartbroken at his mistake thinking he had found Base. He had never before intentionally attacked anyone or anything, everything had been a game or a mission or a test, but now Google was overwhelmed with rage and grief and all he wanted was that sting in the fin to take it all away.

Base! he kept shrieking as if the whale could help him. *Work!* he screamed as if this new ocean would transform back to the one he knew. Ramming the whale had taken the last of his strength, and his heart beat so fast he knew he was dying. His blowhole opened, water rushed in and Google began to drown.

He was being lifted. He was coughing and gasping at the surface, supported on the Rorqual's careful fin. He had no strength to move, it was like being in a sling at Base.

Base. The thought of it, the immobilisation, made him rest. *Base.*

The Rorqual considered what to do next. He kept Google at the surface, high enough to breathe but so that his raw body could be kept wet. The dolphin cried out the same sound over and over, and his distress reminded the Rorqual of when calves of his own family thought they were lost. Then the mother sang the low sweet lullaby to bring them back to her side, and the Rorqual did it now. The same song his own mother had sung to him, bringing such an ache of that lost love, it was hard to keep singing.

When he felt the little dolphin become still against his fin the whale thought the song was working, but then it began to convulse. The Rorqual felt the hollow vibration of exhaustion and hunger and pain. First it needed sleep, it would die without that rest, but something was stopping it. The Rorqual tuned himself more finely, to feel this small kin's brainwaves. He was astonished. No one could endure that clashing. The dolphin seemed to be fighting its own mind, and small as the dolphin was, it was painful for the whale to connect their consciousness. There was one other thing the Rorqual could try, but it was kill or cure.

The whale stopped the lullaby, made sure the dolphin was secure, and then, from the very depths of his being, brought up his howl. It was slow and long like waves from one far shore travelling out across the ocean to some distant reach. He let his silence follow, and then he wailed again.

This was the sound that Ea had heard, sweeping the ocean with pain and love and yearning. It went through every cell of Google's body, and the spaces between them. His breathing stopped.

The Rorqual felt the tension slip from the dolphin's body. So. He had killed him, the one person who had heard his song. But before the whale could begin his recriminations, he felt the inhalation, and Google's blowhole close softly. Very gently, the Rorqual sank below the surface, keeping the little dolphin secure on his fin. The whale waited, feeling for the breathing, feeling with his own mind, for that tiny characteristic moment when the brain hemispheres switched, which was the same in all whales, big as a blue, small as a bottlenose. He felt it. The dolphin was breathing again. He rose up, and felt the blowhole open again. But the whale did not trust he would be able to keep doing it alone, because he knew this was no ordinary sleep. He had put the little dolphin into the deep healing sleep in the way the whales cared for each other when there was sickness or grief. If they could be healed, the pod supported them at the surface until they recovered their strength. If not, they let their beloved fall into the ocean depth, and enter the unitive state. This was what he would do for this lost and wounded bottlenose, who had heard his song and found him.

As he listened to the staggering, slowing, stabilising heartbeat of his patient, the Rorqual understood something else. He had been mistaken. His song could not just be for his own people, he must sing for the whole ocean. And somehow, he also had to eat.

For all his booming and swearing in his punk arias, the Rorqual was a tender nurse. Normally after completing his song-cycle he would go straight to sleep in his upright, fluke-down position ten metres below the surface. On waking, he would go in search of food. Neither was possible without the risk of his patient drowning, because the whale had put Google into such a deep state of rest that his breathing had slowed far below a dolphin's natural resting state. Patience was a natural virtue of the larger cetaceans, and so, forced to wait at the surface, the Rorqual decided to use the time for reflection on his song.

His wide-ranging nomadic life had taught him much about other ocean peoples, but he had only focused on his own kind. And when he had found that group of humpback bachelors, their relentless good cheer felt vacuous. They in turn had rejected his truth. Checking the wounded bottlenose was still safely positioned between his fin and his body, the Rorqual reconsidered. He sang of unbearable things not through choice, but a compulsion to tell the truth and warn other people. Those bachelors kept to their tiny patch of ocean, singing the same fragments of happy travelling songs for journeys they showed no sign of making. He left because he thought it pointless and their falsetto style, stupid. Now he wondered: why were there no seniors, no calves, no females? The young males of his own extended family were sometimes sent off together, to play their rambunctious games a little distance from the pod. What if something had happened to the larger group, what if they had already experienced something of what the Rorqual sang? He had found them near a songpath. Maybe they had been so young when they were lost that their voices had never developed. Childish songs in childish voices, clinging to that time.

The Rorqual's deep groan of understanding woke Google. He lay still, allowing himself to absorb his extraordinary position, supported at the surface on the fin of a whale. Despite the rumbling groan in the great cavern of his protector's body, he felt safe. It was almost like being at Base.

Google let himself think this without struggling or panicking. He could feel his sore body but it was bearable because the mental anguish was gone. He was able to tolerate the knowledge that somehow he was separated from Base because now he felt stronger. Without moving, continuing to breathe quietly, he located the place on his right fin where he got his sting. He thought of it, but the frantic compulsive hunger for it was not there. Instead, he felt the long rolling wave of the whale's energy holding him as securely as the colossal fin kept him just at the surface. Google did not know he was being treated as a calf because he had no memory of that. Born in captivity to a wild captured mother who went mad in her tank, he had been given to a captive-born surrogate who miscarried her own calf but was kept in suckle for others. Google did not remember anything of this, but his calf-hunger for love and closeness woke in him. Google did not understand why he was trembling, neither did the Rorqual, but as was always his response to strong feeling, the whale began to sing.

This time it was soft and so low that Google did not know

but only felt that it was for him alone. He felt surrounded by protection and the sound joined him to the whale's loving heart. To his delight, Google understood him better than even his own anthrops, or any of his MMA colleagues. This giant barnacle-encrusted dolphin was reassuring him that he was there, the family was there, the pod was there, all was well, little one—

Google heard the sounds and strove for meaning. The Rorqual felt the break between their minds and stopped singing. Google slid off and into the water, able once again to dive. The Rorqual gently lowered himself and watched as the little dolphin explored his wondrous size. He was greatly recovered and the whale felt a deep satisfaction.

Kin . . . Google clicked it naturally in Old Pelagic, then looked surprised at himself. The Rorqual was also surprised, but the healing sleep he had administered was from those times.

KIN, he clicked back. Then, *Where is your pod?*

Pod? That particular sound again. Google did not know what it meant but he was excited to be able to communicate with this great being the size of a ship.

Pod, kin, your people. Those you love. The Rorqual was grateful he had saved Google's life, but now wanted to go off and feed. He needed the deep.

Google let the whale's carefully enunciated clicks go into his mind. Meaning stirred through the sounds – and then he understood. He spun in excitement like a calf.

Anthrops! he clicked. *Kin, people, anthrops!* As he formed those sounds for the very first time, he heard himself speaking. Wonder thrilled him like a sting in the fin, but better, because he was still conscious. He moved his body and, though there was still pain, he could bear it. Now more than ever he wanted to get back to his anthrops, his kin and people.

Pod, Google clicked urgently to the whale, *Pod is Base, Find Base, Find Pod! They are waiting for me.*

Base. The Rorqual did not understand. *Ah. If you can cross these currents in time, before the ships come, you will find your pod. You will hear them!*

And Ships? Google felt the whale's tension rising in the water around them.

Ships, yes! This dolphin must surely have heard ships, he could not be out here without encountering their pulverising sounds. *Ships! Very dangerous, we have to move* – and to make his point the whale sang a fragment of his song, the ugly repetitive grunting of an engine, radiating for miles.

Google became ecstatic. *Yes! Where can I find it?*

The Rorqual could not believe him. The bottlenose was alive but had lost his mind.

No, ships kill us—

Ship is Pod! Ship is Base!

You don't know what you're saying. We need to leave this place, we will die if we stay here, they will be coming, you can hear them surely—

All the receptor hairs in the Rorqual's face were tingling. As the ships came closer from both directions the feeling would get stronger until his whole jaw would vibrate in warning.

Anthrops, clicked Google, high and desperate. *My kin! My Pod!*

The Rorqual sent a pulse of sound zooming through the water so that Google could follow the trajectory. There was no more he could do for him. *Your pod's homewater lies there.* He threw a sound beam toward the end of the archipelago, where even a half-deaf dolphin would be able to hear the great Tursiops rabble. *Base, pod, kin*, the whale told him.

Whatever had happened to this poor fellow was a mystery, but the dolphin's only hope was to find the Tursiops tribe. The Rorqual only knew them by the sound of their click, with its obscenities and harsh contractions. It was hard to understand how they tolerated the acoustic conditions and the amount of filth in their waters, yet they seemed to thrive. As the whale's jaw began to ache, he knew the ships were closer and there was not much time.

Go, he told Google, pulling in a great draught of air. *Quickly, or you will die here.*

Google felt the distant thump in the water. He recognised the sound of ships, but something in him hesitated. The sound was different to Base. With a profound shock, he remembered the explosion in the water after he had attached his toy to the target. He had trained in this game many times, with MMA colleagues, but there was never an explosion or burning water. Something had gone wrong in that game.

I want to come with you. Google did not mean to say this; he had never used these words or had this feeling.

I go too deep. The Rorqual sent his love and urgency into the little dolphin's mind. *Quickly, while you still can. In that direction . . .*

The Rorqual sang another great beam of sound out from the depths of his chest, out through the featureless ocean, so that Google felt it in his own body. He turned toward that path. Behind him, around him, he felt the deep pull and flex of the ocean as the whale left him. It was like a sting to his heart instead of his fin, the pain of being left.

He felt the ocean tripping and stuttering. Sounds were coming, *Ships. Base.* They were louder all the time, and he could hear they were stretched out in a line. They were travelling fast in this direction. The sound was hypnotic and deadening. The tremor was building. Before Google could think, the first one was there, a colossal monster ploughing forward.

17

First Impressions

Ea was slowing. The initial adrenaline of her great self-sacrifice was wearing off, and now she was horribly aware of how far out she was, how empty the vast, and how lost she was. She had thought she had gone in a straight line and was not scared of travelling past the hills of the furthest Longi hunting grounds, but she did not know about the deep pelagic river systems that carried her far beyond them. She was now in the western ocean, feeling the last swells of the cyclone. She circled, trying to feel for home – not that she intended to go back. But just in case.

Idiot-idiot! the Remora yelled into her brain with all its strength. *Find the way and go back while we still can. Hurry up, imbecile! You can't do anything right, can you?*

Ea had made the grand impulsive bargain with the ocean, her life for the life of her whole pod – but the ocean was not honouring it. Instead of giving her the quick and painless end she assumed was her right for her selfless act, this ocean was making her suffer by having to wait in fear. Ea felt a rising anger, her usual reaction to being upset or scared. This ocean was not beautiful and kind and wise; it felt thick and foreign and even as if it was deliberately ignoring her. She came up to breathe, then, in sudden temper, slammed the water with her fluke.

Losing it! screamed the Remora, panicking. *Come on, let's go home, you've made your point, I won't go with anyone else, I'll stay with you forever – come ON, are you deaf?* It thrashed from side to side as if it could whip her back to the homewater.

It only succeeded in channelling Ea's vague impotent rage at the ocean. This remora was the reason she was here, this vile thing—

Come on, hate me, your blood's getting warmer, I love it, now let's get you home—

Ea remembered why she had left. The Remora was the living proof of her wickedness. And someone had said that to tear if off was to bleed to death. So be it. She could not bear the waiting and the loneliness any more. And she hated the Remora with all her strength.

Ea took a great hunting breath and plunged down. She beat her tailstock as if the thing she chased were fathoms below. The higher salinity made the water denser and she forced deeper, as if the ocean held her back in spite. Flashes of light pulsed in her head and Ea knew she was deeper than safety, but she did not care. She was just a witness to what her body was doing. She went down until her body rebelled against the pressure and her rostrum jerked and turned her in a sharp curve. She felt the arch of her spine and the fast, powerful beats of her tail.

Ea twisted through the surface and was airborne, spinning off toward her left side so fast she could neither count nor feel her axis but she knew it was high and with many revolutions – and then down she slammed on her side and the water rose up in a huge translucent bowl where she had fallen. A great sparkling cloud of bubbles slowed and held her as she went down – then she felt the re-entry complete, and aimed herself deep again. She did not dare think, just let her body go deeper, until the pressure turned her.

Ea came speeding to the surface and cleared it in a high twisting arc. She saw the dark ocean spreading to the edge of consciousness, the flashing white of the sky – black sea white sky – and she slammed back into the water, faster and more painfully than the last time. The bubble cloud slowed her but the impact had stunned her and she was dizzy from the spins. She rested at the surface, feeling how fast her blowhole snapped open and shut.

black sea white sky

The sound of the waves became detailed and overlapped in echoes. Her muscles burned with fatigue and adrenaline. She felt the slow uncanny breath of the wind on her back and the panting circle of her blowhole. It was as if the attention of the ocean was coming to bear on her small body. Ea felt herself observed—

Four great dark dorsal fins rose up around her, bodies gleaming huge and colourless, light streaming from their shiny skins. Twice her size – and they had blowholes. Dolphins, but not Longi. She could feel their power as they pushed the water at her, and instinctively she went down. They came with her, effortless and muscular. Young males, she could see that – and all with the same strange new wound on the side of their faces, only just healing.

Ea whirled away from a bubble stream blown directly at her spiral – a touch so intimate and unbidden it could only have been a mistake. Whoever these dolphins were, they were very young for their size – but another hard bubblejet shoved at her spiral, and Ea realised it was not a mistake.

She dived at once but they came with her, clicking uproariously to each other in their coarse dialect. She made out the click for spiral, a word which to the Longi meant the holy structure of life as well as the female genitals – but she knew barbaric dolphin tribes used it as a term of abuse. Surely these boisterous young foreigners did not intend such an insult. But they did. They kept her in the middle, and circled her to view her from all angles.

Ea, not impressed by juvenile males of any description, forgot she was in the middle of the vast and made it quite plain by her tail that she wished them to go. She ignored the tiny part of her brain that was telling her there was danger.

It's not part of your brain, you idiot, it's me. The Remora had slid out from behind her pectoral fin and was now lying flat and still against her head. *You don't want to annoy them.*

But Ea was already too indignant. *Who are you?* she clicked at them. *How dare you treat me like this.* She revolved in the corral they made, refusing to be intimidated. She saw one of them going deeper beneath her, readying himself to strike – but she was faster, speeding through a gap between them and turning to face the assault, her pectoral fins stiff with anger. She sent it out to them, hard and emphatic as she would if any young Longi male had been so insolent – *Do Not Do That!*

The four absorbed her message then burst out cackling together, as if she had made the funniest joke. In their guttural pulse-stream to each other she caught the word 'spiral' again, and 'female', and other repeated ugly-sounding clicks that she did not understand. No other delphinid people had ever visited the remote Longi atolls, but suddenly Ea knew who they were. All the young Longi were schooled to avoid their dire example.

You're Tursiops! From being terrified then indignant, Ea was now excited. Her whole life she had been warned about these people, and though they were big, crude and uneducated, they were dolphins and therefore kin. The Longi had never dwelled on how powerful and impressive the Tursiops were. Ea knew how exhaustingly courteous her people were. Manners could be taught, and perhaps she was the one to do it. As if they were visiting her own homewater, Ea made the ceremonial whistle to introduce herself.

I am EA.

The four Tursiops listened, then again cackled with laughter. They whistled back at her, one after the other with no pauses for the basics of courtesy.

One, Two, Three, Four. Ea understood they shared the same particular whistle coda, meaning they were part of a family. But no family could have four calves of this age and size, so it must mean something else. Before she could ask they surrounded her again. When she saw mischief in their eyes, her heart began to thump.

With click and buzz and posture, Ea made it clear they were not to touch her. They might be big uncouth young males but she was a female and her wishes were still paramount. She had only to politely turn aside to dissuade the most ardent Longi suitor – but these Tursiops ignored all her signs.

She took breath and dived – and they came with her, blocking her at every whirl and circle. Ea kept her head and tried to escape but they followed her every move and one of them was directly in front of her when she finally had to surface. She backed away and felt another behind her. She kept clicking *NO*, the same in every cetacean dialect, but they ignored it. The four pushed closer so that escape was impossible. They were turning her – Ea could not quite believe she was being held against her will – and then she felt it.

The appalling violation. When she struggled against it she felt a new pain – their teeth in her pectoral fins either side, and one biting onto her fluke to keep her in place for his friend. She knew she would tear herself apart unless she kept still. They kept bringing her to the surface to breathe, but each time she was deeper in shock, so that her mind was no longer in the body they still used, nor watching, but somewhere out in the ocean, unconscious.

When she came to, they were travelling. They were still taking turns holding her up so she could breathe, but by the nips to her tail fin, they were now tired of this and wanted her to swim by herself. The sky was light, she did not know what had happened, only that her body was sore and raw. The four Tursiops males synchronised their tailbeats to propel their captive forward, and as soon as she could, Ea shook herself violently to make them move away. But every time she attempted to break out of their diamond formation, one of them would nip her, and once, the one in front paused to tail-slap her across the rostrum, which caused her agonising pain in her sensitive sonar melon.

Ea waited until they had travelled on then tried to leap out ahead, but she had neither speed nor strength, and the attempt just seemed to amuse them. They struck her again then shoved her on.

The only reason I'm still on you, came the tiny sibilant whisper of the Remora into her head, *is because they taste so disgusting I cannot believe it. Their skin is covered in something revolting, and as for the rest – you do not want to know. Bad, very, very bad. And you didn't help. I got hit when you were being stupid and resisting, but luckily my sucker plate is amazing. Or you really would be on your own.*

Ea would never have believed she would be glad of the Remora. She could feel it now, the familiar serrated dig of its sucker plate discreetly under her chin.

Less likely to get slammed if you do something stupid – which of course you will. Or you can listen to me, and learn. Feel like doing that now? Because you didn't turn back when we could, did you? And while you've been out of it, I have been busy, because I'm a highly intelligent individual. I have some news for you.

Ea relaxed her muscles around the Remora's grip to show she was listening.

Well, Ea! Our life is about to become a lot more interesting, and maybe you weren't such a bad choice after all. You, my dear wilful imbecile, are going to become the centre of attention. They're just thrilled to have captured a fancy foreign spiral, that's what they keep saying. And other things I'm too well mannered to repeat.

Spiral is not a term of abuse, Ea thought angrily to the Remora. She was about to go on but nearly choked as one of her captors voided himself as they swam. It was foul and she felt the Remora press its plate harder against her and open its mouth.

Ugh, it gasped, when they had moved through it. *Needs must, but what do they eat? We'll find out, because we're heading home. Not to yours, that's all over, forget about it. To the Tursiops homewater, if you don't mind, to the megapod! And guess what's going to happen to you when we get there?*

I can't. Ea's mind was fogged with exhaustion and pain, but this was still news. The Tursiops homewater? But that meant the original Longi homewater.

If I were you, the Remora said, *I wouldn't dwell on old stories. They won't go down too well. Just think of our new life, and all the great opportunities you're giving me! Variety, new people – surely they can't all taste this bad?*

For the first time in a very long time, Ea burst out laughing, and her four captors curved round at the strange sound. The Remora immediately detached from her and ostentatiously swam in front of her so they would notice it, darting to and fro. They recoiled.

I'm her personal assistant, it said in surprisingly fluent Tursiops. *She engaged my services at an exclusive cleaning station. I travel with her to keep her in good condition but if you hit her any more, she'll be damaged – and a damaged gift is an insult.*

One of the four opened his jaws in menace and the Remora quickly reattached itself to Ea's underside. *My people are great admirers of yours, so I just thought to pass that on.*

The Tursiops buzzed an obscenity at the Remora, and Ea felt the sonic slap in her own body. They swam on. When it had recovered, the Remora wiggled for attention.

Not that I expect thanks.

Thank you, Ea thought to it. *But a person can't be a gift – I don't understand!*

Ha, said the Remora. *You will.*

I will not, Ea clicked out loud, *I am a Longi!*

The first Tursiops rapist turned around. Sensing his love of violence, Ea was silent. She hid her fear and her anger as on they went, toward the Tursiops homewater.

18

Leverage

Before investigating the bizarre breach-and-splash of some small creature in the near reach of the ocean, and making their exciting discovery, the four Tursiops exiles were severely downcast. Absence had definitely made the heart grow fonder and they now knew what an easy life they had lost, with protection on all sides and plenty of food, even if it wasn't always the tastiest. However, their fear that the vast was crowded with malevolent sharks searching for them had not materialised. This must surely be because they were fierce and intimidating, and their diamond formation as good as that of any vira. In fact, who was to say they were not now their own vira? They adapted their juvenile names to the more martial and impressive vira numeric, tagging themselves with the same code at the end to show they were a unit. Split's son was One, and the other three vied with quick decisive violence to establish their dominance.

When they were forced to stop and rest, they kept their

diamond formation and slept in shallow relays. Being renegade vira restored their self-esteem, but now they needed to develop that impressive ability of the top alliances, to communicate privately while in the midst of the pod. This was harder than they thought because One was biggest but Three had a faster mind. Supposedly all females could do it at will, but they were probably lying, as they so often did. Scheming complaining females had caused their punishment and were now their sworn foe, and on this they all agreed. From reckless youths they now felt grim-minded adults, ready to do whatever was necessary to establish themselves in a new homewater. And when they did, they would make sure every female was under complete male control.

The breaching sound was too small for a whale, too narrow for a manta, too frequent for a hunting shark slamming down on prey. It could only be a dolphin, but alone? Out here? It must be sick, or it would not be drawing attention to itself. When the four came near to Ea and observed that she was a female Longi, they felt that Mother Ocean herself had rewarded their fortitude and virility. They made the plan quickly and with minimal clicks – they went around her and then drew in, so that they could come up and surround her.

What great good fortune to find her, one of the famed and lost Longi people, presumed extinct! Surely a peripheral, cast out there alone. She fought of course, that was the feminine way to demonstrate sexual readiness – and they could all see that she was of age. They each instantly lusted for her slender body with its dramatic dark cape, the silver stripe, the pearly underbelly and the famed Longi spiral so provocatively small and neat.

Her face fascinated them as did the strange language she spoke, and her extraordinary imperious way of addressing them. She spoke like Devi, as if she thought herself equal. The four absorbed her long delicate rostrum, so different to their short blunt beaks. They noticed the black and white lines that circled her eyes and gave her a most engaging expression, even as she became more excitable. Eagerly they struck their sonar out and around for her pod, confident they could batter any males of this delicate species – but she was indeed alone. They could have her.

Ea was a stunning prize to have come across, and the nascent hierarchy of their vira strained as they struggled for mating rights. By the time they had achieved fair distribution and reasserted it at least twice each, their prize was quiet and passive. This made her easier to transport. The plan came to them all at once, further proof they were doing the right thing: what vira commander would not want her in his harem? Instead of sharing her between themselves and using her up – for she was much more delicate than the few Tursiops females they had managed to catch – why not use her to buy their pardon? Why not return and present her to replace the female they had damaged?

The four imagined the thrilling chatter and clicking of the pod as the notorious exiled bucks returned, not in craven shame but as a new vira, tested by the ocean and found valiant. What a fine tribute to bring their sovereign lord Ku who, with his insatiable greed for sexual novelty, would never be able to resist. Pardon was assured. They slapped their tails in triumph, but they would be very careful of her. No female could be trusted, even a mad lost peripheral from another tribe. Especially a mad lost one, so careless of herself she had even picked up a remora, which marred her beauty. To their disgust, it had now attached itself to her belly, and its body waved unpleasantly close to her torn spiral. Even Split's son, who did not scruple to take an old female when lust was upon him, found it off-putting.

The Remora listened to all this with resentment. These Tursiops people ate so badly that even a remora shuddered at the taste of their waste, and here they were planning to dispose of it. All cetaceans were unbelievably conceited. The Remora only knew self-love, but a healthy host was part of that. Ea showed signs of starting to heed its counsel, and it needed to keep her alive until it had a new host. *No mammals ever again*, it vowed. The Remora moved its tail carefully into the slipstream of travel, and listened again. Ea was a valuable commodity and they were discussing the fastest way home.

Also, it noted rising tension in the alliance. They were arguing and no one wanted to be the first to acknowledge what the Remora realised: they were lost. In their anger of exile, they had used the fast drift current to get out quickly into the vast. It had taken them beyond what their mere bodies could swim in two days and their sense of geography was minimal. They had not found any new homewaters to conquer but they did now have this Longi female. She must have come from somewhere, and once they got her home – and the Remora heard their click change in relief at the thought – they would mount an expedition to find out where that was. From exiles to explorers!

Home now. Quick-quick. The Remora felt extremely pleased with itself; that tiny little squeak could have been a Tursiops click.

None of them knew who said it and each took credit for the idea – of course they must hurry home quick-quick. A dying gift would not work and so speed was of the essence. The megapod was easy to find because it was where the sun set. And now they had focused their minds, they could tell where they were.

The Remora had been so busy trying to keep Ea alive that it had barely noticed the signs, but the Tursiops four were looking around them. Pieces of curious white and multicoloured moult, from some creature the Remora had never yet identified, drifted in the water. The Remora was unafraid; moult had never hurt it and had no gastronomic appeal, so it had not given its source another thought. Some strange shoal or foreign coral or crustacean no doubt. But now, sensing the shared apprehension of the four, the Remora recalled snippets of conversation from the mantas.

They feared moult and made great detours to avoid a place it came from. The Remora focused its memory on the name.

The Sea of Tamas! it clicked in a crude Tursiops accent, from its hold near Ea's spiral. Ea's four captors stared in amazement. At once, exhausted and battered as she was, Ea arched her little body in threat and pointed her fins down. She clapped her jaws and stared cold anger at them like a moray.

The four stared back, then burst out whistling with laughter. She was their good fortune, she was proof that not everything the vira said was true. It seemed likely this moult came from the Sea of Tamas, a place no one was supposed to go. Well, the Longi were supposed to have perished, yet here was this young female, very much alive. The Sea of Tamas was probably maybe even a source of more fugu. The First Alliance had too much control and a little moult was nothing to be scared of. They put Ea in the middle and nipped her to keep her moving. All four liked it when she whirled on them – a little fight showed she was healthy. They wanted to take turns to hit her to calm her down, but One insisted on his right to do that, until he got bored.

What do your lot say about the Sea of Tamas? the Remora whispered to Ea, once she had recovered from the last blow. They were moving along inside the diamond formation. *Is it a big Longi thing?*

Ea did not wish to answer, but it was an advantage to have a translator. The Sea of Tamas . . . yes, she had heard of it. It was the one part of Exodus with no spinning or splashing and it did not need to be practised. All that mattered was to get through it and rejoin the dance. For a moment Ea forgot her captors and her injuries and remembered something else. It was the part where sometimes people lost their minds with fear.

19

The Sea of Tamas

The four had form in trapping females, and though Ea was quick, they were bigger and faster. After each foiled escape they enjoyed nipping and bashing her back into place – before reminding each other they must not present a damaged gift. One swung his huge head against hers to make things clear. He pointed out to the others how he did not knock her unconscious, just enough to keep her dazed but still moving forward.

The four of them communicated constantly and loudly, rudely buzzing and clicking over and around her body. Ea felt the timbre of their pulses and squawks, and though their dialect was guttural and unappealing, she started picking it up enough to know that they too feared this new area. The Remora was also silent, or else Ea had lost sensation in her body because she could not feel anything except the sting around her eyes. The water went bright and dark as the big grey forms of the Tursiops loomed around her. They had stopped their clamour and were travelling at the surface, where the weak sickly waves made no sound.

As her captors slowed, Ea tried to rouse herself to vigilance in case she might still get away, but there was something here that sapped her energy. A dull feeling of dread built up inside her. She no longer wanted to break away; whatever was here was worse than being in this brutal little pod. The water itself was alien and hostile, in a way that was not current, tide or weather. Shaking herself to check if the Remora was still there, she felt the answering buzz on her skin as when it was speaking to her, but that too felt slow and fogged.

They moved on, the four males slower but intent on forcing forward, travelling at a shallow depth below the surface. The sun was a dull grey glow whose light did not penetrate the water, which felt dense and itchy. Ugly white moult of some unknown creature floated by and Ea avoided it, but there was more. All she could hear was the heavy labour of their passage and the uncouth blows for air when they surfaced. And then her inner ear gave a sharp new signal: a dolphin calf crying for her mother. Instinctively and forgetting any other danger, Ea responded. She dived and pulsed her sonar to locate the calf, which sounded close by, but no sonic picture came back. There were not even any fish nearby. The water was uncannily empty, except for all the moult.

The cry came again, closer. It was a little female, her call for her mother so piteous that Ea immediately whistled back in Longi, once to soothe the calf that help was near, and then in the Tursiops she had learned, to call out to the mother. She heard a distant cry in response, a word she did not understand. Despite the pain in her head from the beatings, Ea used her sonar again to try to find the dislocated pair. She looked up and saw the four Tursiops at the surface, doing nothing.

What's the matter with you? Ea buzzed up at them. *They're your people!*

It was stunning to her that they did nothing, so Ea went deeper to search. The water was hard and resistant and when she used her sonar again, again she saw nothing but drifting moult.

Ea looked up to see the four of them still hovering in their defensive formation, doing nothing. Cowards, she thought. For a moment she was dizzy and then the water seemed to change. It was no longer thick and hostile but crystalline turquoise, swaying her to and fro in that friendly way of the Longi lagoon.

Ea . . . ! Hearing her name and the Longi voice, Ea felt a rush of happiness, but when she turned, it was to see an approaching shark, huge and pale with dorsal fin towering and, far behind, hypnotically graceful, the immense tail fin sweeping the water. It swept by close enough for her to see scars on its fins, the serrated rows of teeth, the dark blue eye – and then it disappeared in front of her eyes.

Ea thrashed screaming to the surface, trying to tell the four males about it—

There is no shark. There. Is. No. Shark!

They were highly agitated themselves, but they had been down and there was no shark, no crying calf. She had imagined it, they would have known, they were not frightened of any shark nor had they seen one when they scanned, looking for the calf. They wanted to know if she had seen a female with it, why had she said the name she said, what did she know?!

Yaru? All at once Ea understood that she had felt something from their minds. She listened with her inner ear, and there it was, the faint sound of the calf crying. *Yaru lost her calf,* she said, unaware she had clicked it in Tursiops.

Not our fault! Not our fault! They chanted it to calm themselves.

Ea felt the slap on her face from the Remora's tail. She had not noticed it move.

Pathetic, all of you. Frightened of ghosts and visions. If anyone would listen to me, I could have told you about this place. Just ignore them! But well done for drawing on my experience, you can now click Tursiops. Not that you'll thank me—

Who was that calf? Ea turned to the four. *Who is Yaru?*

They turned on her with screeches and clicks, but did not hit her. Two denied they had seen or heard anything, Three and Four protested their innocence. One said nothing, and Ea knew then that they were liars as well as cowards and rapists. She saw too that fear had broken their alliance – and she believed what the Remora said. There were ghosts and visions in this place, and her captors were frightened. So then she would be strong.

Ea had never been violent in her life except on the hunt, and there the Longi observed strict rules and protocols of respect. This was different. As if she were fully charged with pod hunting power and stunning a baitball, Ea sent a violently hard pulse of sound into the melons of each of them. She fired her sound so fast, and so mercilessly close and precisely, that they cried out at the shock attack.

NEVER TOUCH ME AGAIN.

She braced for their retaliation, but instead they ignored her. Ea waited. Violence could not be such an easy answer. It would be sickening if so. But there in front of her, they moved into their diamond formation and began swimming away.

If you want to get out of here alive, you filthy spiral, called back One, *come now.*

Ea hesitated. The water was closing about her, tight and dense. She felt the negative charge of it, and strange calls of pain reached up out of the murk to pull her down.

Go! hissed the Remora. *Quickly, you've made your point.*

It took some effort to catch up with them. They travelled with very long submerged breaths, but despite their greater size, Ea could retain her own breath for at least as long. She could feel the

Remora smirking: it had a way of swaying against her skin when it was pleased.

They were shitting themselves! Not that anything could make the water worse. But least I got a meal.

You're disgusting.

Thank you. You're just boring, except for when you hallucinate sharks. I wish it had been real, then I'd have the exciting glamorous life I deserve. The Remora wriggled the way it knew she hated, but Ea was distracted. The moult was proliferating, it swirled and bobbed on the surface scraping against them, it drifted below as deep as she could see. The colours were unpleasant and the pieces of shell or skin collided and broke apart, thickening the water. Ea had never encountered anything like it. She wanted to ask her captors, but since she had pulsed their heads, they had ignored her – knowing she would stay with them for survival. They went deeper, and Ea wondered if this was the worst part of Exodus. If so, it was very unpleasant but she could bear it.

As the casts and skins in the water grew more numerous and variegated, Ea began to experience a growing inertia. Though it was disgusting here she was so tired she thought of resting for a while. She was hungry and maybe she could eat some of this moult, it had to be from some kind of creature that shed its skin and would be better than nothing. Yet she held back, because none of the Tursiops ate it, and they were also hungry and tired. By the tone of their clicks they were uncertain of the way, but they pressed on.

The four were now totally focused on their own survival and appeared to have forgotten about their captive. Ea could not go as fast and when she saw their grey flukes disappearing into the bedraggled dirty water ahead, fear of being lost drove her on so quickly that she felt scratches down her sides from the drag of the moult. Some of the pieces were so huge that she could not imagine what creature had discarded them. She hoped not to meet it, but there was no sound in the water except the peculiar whine of detritus rubbing together, stretching in all directions and slowing their progress. None of it made sense: these animals discarded skins like some ugly jellyfish, thin and billowing, some white like ghosts or alien colours like headaches. The density slowed them so much that now they had to push their way through and feel the repulsive touch of the moult all over their skins. They abandoned the diamond formation but kept together as much as possible, and again Ea felt their fear at this place. Sometimes one of them would dislodge one of the floating dead things and it would spill some stinging or oily residue into the water, and before long all five of them were smeared and smarting from their passage.

To think that this piece of water was commemorated in Exodus – when she got back she would have something to say about the lack of detail. Faithfully, Ea's anger replaced her fear. Why wait for Exodus to tell people what the world was like? Just tell the truth and warn them, so they knew! She beat her fluke in frustration and felt her strength increase. The memory of the Rorqual's song came to her. *He* warned people, *he* sang, maybe even of this. Ea felt a burst of love toward him, whoever and wherever he was in this ocean. Even if she never met him, the whale was still her friend, and the thought made her stronger.

When they next came up to take breath, all five dolphins were silent at the sight. The surface was solid with moult as far as they could see. The waves were suffocated, the air was still, the only sound was the dull tapping of all the shed scales, or skin or carapaces.

Giant plankton, said the Remora. *Fast breeding, seen it before. Shallow and deep.*

Ea did not trust the creature. No plankton could be this size because then the fish that ate them would be colossal. It was not possible. Also, if it were plankton, it would have some residual life force, and this had the feel of dead stuff.

Ea could just about swim through it, but her spirit was sinking. The four Tursiops also seemed stalled, their fight and their brag were gone. Then far out in the dismal morass, Ea heard a splash and a struggle. Something thrashed on the surface, then sank back down. All five of them saw it, and understanding they were stronger as one, they went to investigate.

Deep within a sprawling strangle of moults was an old female turtle. Her neck was almost severed by a transparent loop that twisted tighter as she struggled, so that Ea saw the pale raw flesh where the moult cut in. The turtle was near her end but feebly continued trying to free herself. Lower down were more creatures – a drowned flock of birds, and rotting fish and a huge shapeless piece of flesh that might once have been a whale calf of some kind.

The evil stuff bumped her on all sides. As if the sound was suddenly turned back on in the ocean, despairing cries and wails of agony flooded her brain – and then shut off. Ea forced herself to look. The moult formed a hideous spreading mass, solid enough to hold together, loose enough to trap the countless creatures Ea now saw as corpses. Many different dolphins, turtles, sharks – and mantas. She came up gasping.

Shit, said the Remora. *You've lost them.*

Ea looked around. They had left her there.

Idiot, it snapped at her. *You've killed us.*

Shut up, she thought furiously to the whining Remora, *or you'll be right!* It stopped buzzing and she controlled her fear to locate her erstwhile captors, now her only chance of survival. Her sonar only brought scrambled pictures of the moult, but her inner ear flared open. Distorted cries bounced amidst the trashed water, but Ea pushed toward the sound and feeling of Tursiops panic. By accident she caught something white and curved over her rostrum. It was coated in something slimy and the feeling was so disgusting, she was about to shake it off – when it reminded her of sponging. Overcoming her revulsion, she kept it there. The edges were sharp against her skin, but the covering let her push ahead faster.

Some distance below the surface, Two, Three and Four swam frantically around another mass of moult in which One was caught. This moult was different: it was a transparent membrane of lines, finer than jellyfish tendrils and almost invisible except where it bunched together. One was twisting in it with all his strength, screaming out uncontrolled bubbles of precious air the more he struggled. The more he struggled, the tighter the trap became.

Ea truly hated One, the leader of the gang and also the most cruel and vicious to her, but that did not stop her joining the others to try to free him. Nothing worked. He was too fear-crazed to hear them and his clickstream of terror was using the last of his air. In his struggle he had turned himself upside down so that now he was looking into the black of the deep and the drifting dead below, caught in this same net.

While the others shrieked and buzzed at One to try harder to free himself, as they could not do it for him, Ea went close to him. She looked in his eyes and knew he was dying. He had hurt her and raped her and part of her triumphed at this justice. The message of the mantas was suddenly in her mind. Losing the leader, even of a group as small as this, was surely breaking the pod.

Yes, and Ea tasted revenge in her heart. *Break the pod, lift my curse with your death* – then she was ashamed. No dolphin left another to die. She could not do it, even to her Tursiops rapist. They could not save him, but they could be with him as he died.

All Ea's hate was gone. One tried to click and his last air bubbled up to the surface. She saw his blowhole open and the filthy water rush in. One gazed at them as he drowned, and Ea felt he was begging them to wait for the end. They did, then rushed up for air.

Two, Three and Four lay at the surface, stunned by what they had witnessed. Their breathing was ragged and they shuddered uncontrollably. Furious at their weakness, because if they perished so would she, Ea swam across them to turn them away from the place of One's death and the trailing membrane she knew was still there. Then she used her fluke hard across their faces, to break the horror trance. Violence was part of the Tursiops language, and she was both disgusted at herself for using it, and startled by how well it worked.

Which way? Quickly! Ea pulsed it strong and rude into the head of Two, who was now the default leader. All three males came to their senses. They conferred too fast for her to understand, then forged past her. Ea accelerated to take the missing part of the diamond formation, for her own safety. They swam on in silence, but for the weird atonal bumping of moult in the waves.

Ea's body swam, her mind in torment. She was polluted, body and soul. The feeling in her heart when she saw her tormentor dying was the worst of all. She truly would have saved him if she could, but she had tasted the satisfaction of revenge. She could be cruel too, and now she understood the Shriving Moil of her own people. They tried to live in perfect love, but there was a secret savage place in everyone's heart, not just hers. After how long she did not know, the light began to fade and her muscles slowed. The numb shock of One's death was changing to mere pain in her body, but the water was clearing. The three males slowed and rotated positions so that Ea was now on the right flank of the formation. They rested at the surface for a while. No one had eaten, no one had slept because they needed to put the horror behind them. Night was coming but Ea knew they could not hunt in this state. No one could be vigilant; she would rather go hungry. She could not remember her last meal. Perhaps she would starve to death, perhaps that was the ocean's fate for her.

Suddenly the three Tursiops cheered, a hoarse exhausted sound. *Tursiops!* they cried.

Ea heard a dull heavy rhythmic sound in the water, coming from far away, looming louder then fading. It was so familiar. The ugly grinding in the water, the sonar-thudding pain was massively loud but each time it came, the three males whistled and cheered.

She listened in astonishment. These were the sounds that no other Longi but she could hear, and insisting they were real had made her a freak and an outsider. Yet these Tursiops could not only hear the very same sounds, but they were also rejoicing at them. How could it be that every cell of her body wanted to get away from the noise, but the three of them turned directly toward it, their grief at the loss of one of their cohort forgotten as they began chanting, their spirits rallying:

Tursiops, Tursiops!

Ea felt a rush of loathing. The Tursiops loved filth and noise and brutality – now was the time to leave, but as if she had clicked her plan aloud, Two, Three and Four were immediately around her, guarding her again. They cackled with laughter, and shoved her forward. Ea lunged down and put on a burst of speed – which only took her into stronger noise vibration so painful that she had to stop. The sound came through the water so hard it was like being struck directly on her melon. Ea's captors did not even need to touch her now, just keep her moving forward on the path they chose, because any deviation from that acoustic corridor made her pain far worse.

She felt a tail-slap as she dawdled. Their confidence restored as they neared home, Two, Three and Four had resumed their physical bullying, as if Ea's presence of mind in the Sea of Tamas had not saved them.

Relax, said the Remora. *It's just the demons, I heard them say so.*

Demons? Ea immediately thought of all the dead hanging in the nets.

Who make the noise, said the Remora. *I'd shut up and learn if I were you.*

Ea didn't know who she hated more, the parasite or the Tursiops, but one thing was clear. She was going to escape and find her way home. The Remora could eavesdrop on her impassioned thoughts, but not her prayers. It could not hear her heart.

Mother Ocean, Ea prayed, *forgive me. Mother Ocean, let me escape.*

But as they swam on into thicker water and grinding noise, Ea could not hold back the thought that she had brought this on herself, and Mother Ocean had abandoned her.

20

Neighbourhood Watch

Directly en route between the Sea of Tamas and the Tursiops megapod, the Fugu was now a squatter at the pinnacles. Impervious to threat, trickery or coaxing, she ignored everything the Wrasse said or did, because if he fatally attacked her, she would poison the water. And as an exhausted refugee who had survived a terrible journey, all she cared about was sanctuary.

Here at the pinnacles she had found a strange and bad-tempered guardian who had already protected her. The Fugu had no heart to go on, but as she recovered her deflated state, she looked about her and saw potential in these dour spires. She had been carried here by strong currents, and the presence of those brutish dolphins meant there must also be fish. She had not passed a single cleaning station since leaving her own collapsed, and she began to wonder.

The Fugu had lived on an ancient glory of a reef, full of interesting characters and many languages and cultures. The best holes and crevices were always hotly contested but there were enough ledges and plants and accommodating anemone communities for everyone to get along. Most people anyway. The Fugu observed the small predations of daily life, but she enjoyed her special immunity and imagined herself a celebrity. Her favourite pastime was mingling with the cosmopolitan crowd of deep pelagic types that visited the cleaning station, for the personal attentions of the tiny wrasses and other worker fish. She liked to hurry them along so that large glamorous ocean travellers did not have to wait too long to have their parasites removed. Beauty and grooming required a peaceful atmosphere, and too long a queue could cause dangerous frustration. Sometimes the Fugu even wished for some skin condition of her own so that she too could be the subject of soft and flattering nibbling, but it was not possible to be so impressively toxic and also get groomed.

She revelled in her status as self-appointed hostess of the famous cleaning station, but when the coral turned nauseous colours, when the workers began to sicken and die, when everyone began asking her what was happening, she did not know. No one knew. The customers stopped coming because their exfoliation now stung too much since the water had changed. The coral paled to white, and died.

There was nothing to eat on the reef and no more work. Fights began as people struggled for what was left, whole communities sickened and died, and the survivors went away. The Fugu was the very last, pleading with people not to leave, hoping somehow the reef would get better and the customers would return. Then the moult began arriving, and the Fugu finally abandoned her beloved home. She assumed there would be other, lesser reefs nearby. She was right, but as she travelled on, she saw that they too were dying.

The pinnacles were the best place she had found, which was not saying much. The water was painful at first and then invigorating, and she began to notice several familiar-looking tiny fish darting about nervously. Little local variations on groomers and cleaners, the kind she had ordered about in her old life. If she had found her way here, so must others. Despite the forbidding aspect, the pinnacles might indeed make a good cleaning station. The Wrasse could remain the big boss, and she would be the lady. A purely business relationship.

You're an emotional eater, she told him in her native reef dialect. *But you can't eat all my workers, and I've seen you, you go killing when you're not even hungry and then you just leave them. Not even sharks do that.*

The Wrasse knew she was right. When he was overcome with rage and grief and memory and when his skin was too sore from self-harming plunges into the scalding vent, he would kill small fish for the temporary relief of the ambush strike. These unnecessary takes were then followed by self-loathing if he left them to sink, or nausea if he forced himself to eat them regardless of his hunger.

In the few days since the Fugu's arrival and her incessant chatter, the Wrasse became self-conscious about his kills. The Fugu proclaimed herself a benign moral influence and set about rounding up the little shrimp in the hope they would begin to clean the great Wrasse. She begged him to let them practise, but he could not help himself and ate some when they tried to go into his mouth. The Fugu simply recruited more, and the Wrasse noticed that she was making the pinnacles a busier place. He had been so engrossed in his misery, he had not seen all the tiny fish that were now appearing.

To get away from the Fugu's chatter, the Wrasse began making long surveillance trips around the pinnacles. Each time he went out further and noticed new details. Here, the algaeic growth was faster, there the budding of some new kind of polyp. More life than he thought, though not all of it welcome. Between two particular spires he felt a clogging in the spirit of the current, travelling toward the megapod of Tursiops barbarians.

On the other side, facing out into the vast, were ominous wavelengths of a sea he did not wish to travel. In it were predators which even he, a lordmale of his nation, would not impress. *My nation.* In his wanderings before the pinnacles and since his arrival, he had never detected the smallest sign, chemical, auditory or visual, that any of his people remained in this world. Sometimes he relived the moment in his imagination. The joyful gathering of the Spawning Moon, the crowds arriving at the fertility grounds. The spiralling rise to meet the moon, the luminous pull of light, the thrill swelling his body—

And then the screams as they were crushed together. The massing horror, the smell of blood and egg and sperm in the water, swimming up to the outside of all those screaming people crushed together – and pulled out through the watersky. Every single one of them, gone. Then the Wrasse wanted to kill anything he saw, and had to remind himself where he now was. The pinnacles. The tall jagged black spikes that day by day were less inert mineral forms, and more strangely sentient spires. He felt they were responding to his presence, that within and around their hooks, spores and current-washed planes, was some unspoken mystery. With its scalding chemical tongue the vent was trying to speak to him. *Die here*, it seemed to say. The thought gave him peace.

The Fugu disapproved of his masochistic deep diving, or anything that took attention away from her. The Wrasse was audience for her stories, and gradually he allowed himself to be nibbled at by cleaner shrimp, just because it was easier than constantly driving them away, or risking her ire by eating them. The Fugu was grateful, and the Wrasse found himself pitying her more than resenting her intrusion. She worked so hard to find common water with him in their shared past of colour and glamour at home on their different reefs, and talked so much about her past popularity and status, that the Wrasse understood she too was bitterly lonely.

You may stay, he said. *But no one will come.*

I will and they will, she said.

Thank you, said the Wrasse pointedly, to remind her of her manners.

You're welcome. The Fugu was oblivious to sarcasm or despair, but fixated on her grandiose plans to recreate the cleaning station, and all her future glamour and power. The Wrasse let her talk flow over him – it blocked out darker thoughts. Then she got his attention.

You're still changing, she said. *Physically. Did you not notice? In the beauty business you see it all, but as a very feminine female with no desire to change, I always find it unsettling. At my cleaning station, a most sophisticated and tolerant place, we saw many high value individuals – mantas, sharks, turtles – transitioning. A lot of them confided they hadn't chosen. I think it's the times we live in. There's something in the water.*

The Wrasse absorbed this in silence. The Change happened in his people, but only in response to the loss of a lordmale. He had never heard of a lordmale changing again.

The way you're moving, and sometimes your voice, I think you're going female again, she said. *And don't take this the wrong way but aren't your females a bit dowdy, compared to the males? Whereas you're as male as male could be, you're getting flashier by the day, but there's something feminine all the same. I'm sorry, but it's true.*

The Wrasse felt indignant at the double affront. The ladies of his court were not dowdy, they were demure delightful beauties. True, as a lordmale he eclipsed them all but that was his risk and privilege. The Wrasse scanned his body again.

Flashy . . . in what way?

Such triumph for the Fugu in that invitation, such affirmation of her authority

Flaunting it, mused the Fugu. *Bright green lateral spots like*

a moray, then those new yellow tail bands – no one's going to miss you, are they?

The Wrasse managed to twist around to see. He thrilled at the glimpse of the new gold-trimmed flash of his own tail. He flared his pectoral fins wide and swivelled his big eyes to each side. How magnificent: two shining gold frills that brightened the water. He felt deeply gratified at such personal glory, even if only the Fugu was there to see.

I don't know who you think you'll spawn with like that, she said. *Just who are you trying to attract anyway? Wait – where are you going?*

The Wrasse had heard an unusual sound, like a heavy gnawing. Made by someone large. Stealthily he swam the outer waters of his stony keep toward the sound. The sight was pure outrage. A great orange-striped triggerfish was busy attacking a giant clamshell, attached to the outside of a spire. By the bump on his head, the marauder was also a lordmale. And the clam! The biggest the Wrasse had ever seen, yet he had missed it on his patrols. It must be newly arrived or he would surely have noticed it, because clams were his favourite food. Indignation charged his blood. Not only had he missed this delicacy, but the insolent trespasser was ignoring him.

Not quite. The triggerfish casually swivelled one black and white eye before returning to work, making loud grunts of satisfaction as his heavy beak made progress. Little fragments of clamshell drifted toward the Wrasse, along with a swirl of tiny multicoloured round things that detached from it. The Wrasse stared in angry wonder as the triggerfish continued. This clam was embedded with these little things. Perhaps they were eggs, but on its shell? It was too soon for the ocean to spawn, yet what else could they be? His appetite thrilled to the delicious chemical distress signal from the clam. Soon this bastardly fish would get the prize.

The Wrasse's pectoral fins flared with such new force that the triggerfish felt the current. The two dominant males stared at each other. The Wrasse took in the orange stripes and the high eye position of the triggerfish, who in turn assessed the smooth cliff of the Wrasse's face. The patterns around the big hard eyes. Then the triggerfish merely raised its dorsal fin – a great orange spike that hoisted a serrated descending row of smaller ones going all the way down its flaring tail – and pulled off another multi-coloured plaque of clamshell.

The Wrasse filled his swimbladder and barked. Both fish tasted stress hormones in the water – their own, and those of the clam under attack. Somewhere in the Wrasse's brain, he registered a strong drift of other clam hormones coming from behind him in the pinnacles. The triggerfish smelled them too, and in its moment of distraction the Wrasse launched his signature move, a speedy head-butt hard behind the beak and under the eye. It would have been a knockout blow but the triggerfish sprang back in time and the strike only glanced him. He whirled round faster and more vicious than the Wrasse expected.

As the two titans fought above, the moult-encrusted clam flushed more stress into the water and further excited them. The triggerfish had seized a gold-trimmed pectoral fin of the Wrasse in his jagged beak and was trying to tear it off, when the Wrasse changed direction, using the force of the triggerfish to throw them backwards. They spun in a tight circle toward a spiky black spire.

The triggerfish would not let go. Understanding what the Wrasse was trying to do he dragged him back around, so that now the spikes faced the Wrasse's bright flank. He grunted through his beak, as he gripped the Wrasse's fin, that he was younger and stronger and was going to take this place and eat that clam.

Younger but not wilier. Ignoring the pain in his fin joint, the Wrasse twisted upside down and rammed his body close against his foe to lock their scales together. Then with the shadows of the pinnacles to orient himself, he barked directly into the head of the triggerfish.

The shock of the sound made the triggerfish release his bite and spring back – impaling his own tail on a spike of a pinnacle. As the first trickle of blood leaked out, he began a stuttering electro-pulse of pain. Furious his foe would now call even bigger ones to the pinnacles, the Wrasse went below him and used his great solid humphead to shove him off the spike. The triggerfish fled.

As the Wrasse beat his tail and whirred his fins to dispel the loser's blood, the triggerfish's pulse faded into the distance. He felt a powerful flush of pleasure. He was a winner, a lordmale, and if something was his, he ate it, mated with it, or defended it. Now his reward would be the peculiarly adorned giant clam – but it had vanished.

The Wrasse looked again. Giant clams were sessile things, they did not move like starfish or anemones. But this one had flushed a huge amount of stress hormone into the water, and the Wrasse had not only tasted the hormone, but could now detect more coming from deep within the pinnacles. There were more of them. The Wrasse stopped flashing to and fro, and hovered on his pectorals. There, below him, inching down the steep black spire on a large and yellow-striped muscular foot, was the daring clam. The Wrasse had never before seen such behaviour and decided to watch before enjoying his reward. Feeling his scrutiny, the clam drew itself down tight against its foot and stopped moving. The Wrasse went down and gave it a tentative gentle gnaw. Tiny pieces of multicoloured moult detached and rose toward the surface. The Wrasse had another try, this time exploring what manner of stuff this was. His big teeth pressed some together. Too hard for eggs, or else too long travelled, long dead before they could hatch. He wondered how they had attached to the clamshell.

As he studied the peculiar encrustation, the Wrasse had the strong sense the clam was urging him to go. Further evidence of his growing madness, because clams were just a food source – they did not have wishes. And yet, this one had . . . made a dash for it, was the expression that came to mind. He tried to remember his reef: there were definitely clams there, though none of this size. Did they ever move? Not that he could think of. Yet sometimes they did change position, so they must do that when no one was looking. He was just in time to see the yellow foot disappearing as this one secured itself to the rock.

The Wrasse was amazed. This wily clam was indeed aware of him and had used his moment of inattention. He swam down and nudged it. The clam, a good half-length of the great big Wrasse himself, remained motionless. He studied it more attentively. By the deep undulations of its shell, it was old, and striped with colourful detritus in its crevices. He shoved it harder to try to get a taste of that yellow muscular foot, and it sent out another chemical distress signal. Almost at once, the Wrasse tasted the same in answer, drifting out of the pinnacles.

The source was a group of giant clams on an inner ledge of a spire, about ten metres down. Many also had the little egg decoration, and all were of an age and size as the fugitive. Prisms of sunlight rippled down into the dark of the pinnacles, whose inner edges glittered black. It warmed the body of the Wrasse as he descended to the clams, just in time to see their fleshy frilly mantles wave from their parted mouths, as if they too enjoyed the sunlight. Their secret soft bodies were translucent at the edges and miraculously coloured, all different, blues and purples and pinks and gold-ringed black spots, with bright green lines.

As his shadow fell on them, in muscular synchrony all the clams closed their shells so fast that the water lifted the Wrasse. He hovered above his new treasure. The biggest clams he had ever seen, and the deepest. They had managed to escape his vigilance, but now he would come here exactly when the sun fell down the centre of the pinnacles, ancient signal to ancient life form. Now he understood. The decorated clam had arrived on a current, and was moving to join the others down on the ledge. It too had travelled the vast.

The Wrasse searched and saw it clinging to the stone in a new place. He drew back to show it he was not going to attack. He agreed with himself he was mad, why else would he imagine he was communicating with a clam society? He was lonely, but they were not. He stared down, a banquet at his fin tips. The water was traced with their thin delicious mucus secretion as they hurriedly closed their shells. The Wrasse lingered on the very brink of alimentary arousal, so that his muscles quivered with pleasurable anticipation – but for the first time in his life, the thought of ripping one of those beautifully coloured mantles out from inside upset him.

He turned his body to enjoy the overhead warmth and feel how it refracted off the pinnacles. This was why the clams had chosen that platform. Bathed in these intense prisms of sunlight for a certain time, the rest of the time they were secure in the depth and shadows, and yet they had the warmth from the vent. The Wrasse postponed the difficult question of eating them. For the moment, he decided he would guard them. Motion caught his attention. As if the decorated and molested clam had understood and was testing him, it rose up on its muscular yellow-striped foot and, there in front of him, it began to move.

Only mortal threat could have distracted the Wrasse from this extraordinary event, and it came in the screech and squawk of his nemeses, Tursiops dolphins. They were coming in from the vast, heading no doubt for their cacophonous megapod on the far side of the pinnacles. They would pass right by. Exhausted from vanquishing the triggerfish, the Wrasse took cover in the shadowy fortress of his black keep and peered out.

The buzzes and clicks resolved into the moronic group signal he had learned to loathe: *Turs-iops! Tursi-ops!* And here they came, shouting their presence to the ocean and, by the general disturbance of his waters, using their sonar to find his pinnacles. Those young thugs had vowed revenge after he had mistakenly defended the Fugu – was this it? Their click-chant grew louder; he counted three voices. The water told him they were almost upon him and the combat-weary Wrasse prepared to flare his fins. Yes, the same thugs with the raked faces. Would he hide like a coward, or go out and defend his honour to the death? Death it was—

But the Tursiops were passing by, paying no attention to the pinnacles. The Wrasse counted three big males and one small female, she of a dolphin race he had not encountered, though on principle he disliked all cetaceans. Highly sensitive to beauty, the Wrasse noticed the female's long pointed rostrum, black cape and pearly belly, and the distinctive black ring around her eyes. He also noticed that she was not chanting, and that the males appeared to be guarding her. Then they were gone. Relieved, he slid out when they were safely beyond. He truly was mad, talking to clams, and imagining the water was now traced with grief from the female. He was ill. He wanted his old self back, clear and emphatic. *Eat, mate, defend. And then, search. Keep searching. Do not stop.*

It was too late. The Wrasse had stopped, taken a new territory, even accepted a small garrulous fish under his protection, who was now trying to take over his territory and make a cleaning station. He swam back to the clams. If they were together, then he was not mad and he would protect them. If they were still apart, he would eat every single one of them whenever he felt like it. He did not know which option he preferred, until he reached them. They were tightly gathered. The Wrasse noted fine gold threads around their feet, as if they had laid security lines around their position. He blew down on them, and felt a shimmer in the water. They felt him. He felt them.

His pinnacles, his clams. Perhaps he would even try letting himself be cleaned.

21

Pressure

By the sickening vibrations in their guts and the pressure in their heads, the Tursiops megapod knew the ocean demons were active again. They were not yet shrieking and roaring, but deep unnatural soundwaves rolled in from different directions of the vast and the seabed groaned at her wounds. The pod almost craved for the battle to start so the anxiety would be over – provided they first had sarpa.

The First Harem kept quiet as Devi listened out for news from the vira command, currently travelling the homewater to decide which bay offered the best protection. Only then would they give the order to go for sarpa, so that even with dulled minds and slower reflexes, everyone would know where to go. Devi heard her lord's distinctive click coming closer, and then all the co-wives of the First Harem backed away in arching respect as the lord Ku entered, with his second in command the lord Split, and then the top alliance commanders with their own first wives. Devi made deep obeisance to all, followed by her harem, but her lord did not make his usual acknowledgment. She noticed how the lord Split surveyed the First Harem.

Sarpa stocks are short, the lord Ku told her. *The people clamour in this time of need.*

A shared resource! the lord Split clicked. *But stocks are too low for all to partake.*

Devi felt their tension. Something dangerous had transpired, concerning this harem. The lord Ku came to her. *Do you know why this would be?*

No, my lord. She clicked it softly, keenly aware of scrutiny by the lord Split and all those behind him. She maintained her submissive posture.

You have not let that pampered son eat at will? The lord Split could not restrain himself, and Devi heard the involuntary buzz of displeasure from the lord Ku. She gently rose to the surface for breath, and to control her anger. Her co-wives rose with her, and pressed themselves to her sides in silent support.

My son is unable to eat sarpa, Devi clicked. *Along with his many other deficiencies.* It enraged her that Split would attempt to blame Chit for failing sarpa stocks, and force her to acknowledge his weakness in his defence. Split was using him to publicly humiliate his parents. Devi could not help herself – she looked directly at Split, and found him already watching her. She looked away.

The lady Devi is strong as a male, the lord Split clicked to the lord Ku. *Perhaps we should have a female vira.* The gathered company clicked and buzzed at the joke of it, the lord Ku as well.

I am as loyal to my lord as any vira commander, Devi retorted. *If that is what my lord Split intends.* The lord Ku swam between them and turned on his First Wife.

You will respect my brother vira, lady Devi, if you wish to hold your position. The whole pod thanks him for his valour on the Crossing, do you forget?

The lord Split held out his torn pectoral fin for all to see.

Perhaps the lady Devi could take on a shark, with her wayward ladies and her son. The lord Ku laughed at this and the pod followed. But the look he gave Devi was clear.

I dread to offend my lord Split in any way. Forgive me. Devi abased herself until she burned for breath, and the lord Ku signalled for her to rise. The water was shaking with the rumbling from the vast, but Devi felt it as her own anger and humiliation. Her son Chit pressed beside her to give or receive comfort, and she could feel he was about to burst into his strange chanting. She willed him to contain it.

The demons move away. The lord Ku swam to the front of the bay and the pod followed, positioning themselves around him to feel the truth of it. The screeches were receding into the vast. The ocean seabed was quiet. He turned back. *We conserve our sarpa. Do you understand, my lady?*

Yes, my lord. Devi was heartbroken. Her lord Ku had borne her shame, and taken Split's cause against her. It was the price of keeping Chit safe. She remained in her submissive posture as the water surged with the group departure.

Lose no more wives, the lord Split clicked to her as he left, *and give your lord better sons.*

Yes, my lord. Devi clicked back softly, but her heart was full of sharks.

The First Harem knew not to come close until she had recovered her dignity, but Chit never understood this. He swam around his mother expressing her distress, until she slugged him away with her tail. The co-wives were ready to let him try to suckle – something he always wanted after his mother's frequent rejections, despite her love for him – but instead, he pointed himself out into the vast and began waving his body from side to side as if in threat. The co-wives were exhausted and longing to sleep, but losing Chit was unthinkable.

Devi watched them cluster officiously around him, knowing they were performing loving care for her benefit. Their unswerving loyalty safeguarded their place in the First Harem, and also kept her son safe. No one slept until Chit was settled, and there was an unofficial rota of sleep-mothers, whose challenging duty was to link his chaotic brainwaves to theirs and then manage him down into rest. Devi looked on, knowing it would have to be her. Chit was peaceable and loving except for those unpredictable times he fought sleep. Only then did Devi recognise anything of his father's mental toughness, which she matched with her own. She prepared herself for this new battle, and crossed the bay to where the co-wives were increasingly desperately cajoling and caressing him to come with them.

Chit even ignored his mother. His attention was trained out on the vast, in the direction of the eerie black rock formations, from which sometimes drifted a faint taste of sulphur. He had long wished to go there, but Devi and her co-wives dissuaded him with stories of pain and monsters. But Chit was older now and, though still simple-minded, was big and strong enough to ignore them. If he took it into his head to leave, Devi would have to take some co-wives and go with him, or call vira guards to stop him. In desperation, she rolled beside him, offering to suckle him, but Chit refused to break his focus. Instead he began to chant in the way that sometimes presaged a seizure, or was sometimes mere high spirits. Devi called to him softly, in the loving whistle of his private calf-name. He flicked his big tail in her direction to show he heard, and to urge her attention.

They're coming, they're coming, he sang, high and tuneless. He rolled and splashed in the bright water to show his happiness. *They're coming!*

Seeing nothing but the glittering vast but aware Chit sometimes heard things that others did not, Devi shot out her sonar to check. The rumbling of the demons was still moving away – but then she let out a pulse of amazement, because Chit was right. A small group was coming in from the vast, she could hear them. They were chanting as they approached the homewater.

Tursi-ops! Tursi-ops!

By now all the co-wives were behind lady Devi, whose well-being was their own.

THEY'RE COMING! Chit buzzed over and over in joy, not caring who heard. He swam out and the First Harem went with him. Many other people had heard the commotion and were also going out, shooting their sonar to discover the identity of the visitors.

Three Tursiops and a foreigner. By her size, a female.

22

The Gift

The acoustic pain of the demons was receding, and Ea's excitement grew. Even as a captive, she was about to enter her stolen birthright: the fabled Longi homewater. Then they would be out of this rumbling dirty water with its sinister rock formations and pulses of heat. These thugs had beaten and raped her but she had survived. She was strong, she was a Longi female – she would bide her time and then . . . She pushed the thought down so that the Remora did not hear her. It had been quiet for some time and that was a relief.

But there was some grave mistake about their destination; these stupid brutes must have navigated wrongly. The homewater of the Longi was pristine and pure. It was bejewelled with ancient coral reefs of astounding variety and beauty, and Ea had heard all her life how to grow up in its lagoons was to be educated not just by one's Longi family, but by all the creatures who lived there. She knew there were species that went back countless generations living in this one place, building on the wealth of their different civilisations to make this one homewater. Life there was full of wisdom, harmony and beauty.

This could not possibly be the same place. This water was filthy with particles of moult, streaks of filth she did not recognise and, above all, constant noise. This was now overlaid with the males chanting louder and louder, *Tursi-ops! Tur-si-ops!* sending it out ahead of them. There was a distant call back of countless voices, *Tursiops!* and the three males whistled and cheered. They drove Ea toward the sound of the mob.

The megapod was deafening. Clicking, whistling, buzzing people, and then the constant grinding in the water. Ea's eyes were sore and she was too exhausted to be frightened, but she had never seen a crowd like this before. Enormous Tursiops people surrounded her, dark and gleaming grey and all twice the size of the Longi. Their blowholes snapped and sprayed in vulgar excitement, their energy was fierce and probing.

Excitement flashed through the pod: the young delinquent males had been exiled on pain of death, but they had survived and returned. Ea understood the dialect now.

Three out of four, but who's that?

A female!

Who's with them? Who is it? How many of them—

A foreigner – a female! A Longi female!

LONGI SPIRAL!

The clicks rushed through the crowd, the anxiety about ocean demons now diverted into rabid excitement to see this freak. Jealously guarded sleeping places were abandoned in the thrill of the news. People plunged and shoved to see the returning valiant boys with their prize – surely all the Longi had perished when they fled the good judgement and natural order of Tursiops dominance? Was she as beautiful and witchlike as they said? What heroic young males . . .

Their exile was already forgiven. No male could clearly remember why they had been cast out but every female did, and felt the silent pulse of resentment in her heart. None dared click it. In any case they were too busy rushing to see a real live Longi.

Foreign female! Longi female!

Tursi-ops! Tursi-ops!

The vira acted swiftly to instil order, driving the crowd back to open a wide channel between bodies, allowing the three males and their captive to advance into the main lagoon. Ea felt their attention dragging her sides like dirty seaweed. No moray ever stared harder than these barbarians, in whose guttural click she made out many crude expressions, familiar from her abuse. In a new form of outrage, some even shot their sonar at her, taking intimate impressions of her body.

Eager as he was to see this living gift, the lord Ku waited in dignity for the proper presentation, his biggest most fearsome vira commanders ranked either side. Exiles had never returned, there was no existing protocol and so what happened now would set it for the future. He had never even discussed that possibility with Devi, his most reliably discreet and pragmatic advisor, no doubt waiting with her harem in an excellent viewing position.

Wishing she could be with him, the lord Ku lay on the surface and felt the air drying the swollen lesions – now on both his eyes. They had also spread to his genital patch, and he could feel hard swellings under his pectoral fins. Other vira commanders had them, the elders who had made the journey across the vast also showed signs, but his were the worst. Or, he decided, the best. The new sign of power and authority. That would be how he carried himself, and he rose up out of the water and breached.

The huge male surged up out of the water in front of Ea and fell so heavily that his splash drove everyone back. Ea reacted instantly to the terrifying attack, standing up on her tail and instinctively clapping her little jaws in defence. Silence fell on the pod. Threatening the lord Ku meant the death penalty. And then: his harsh clacking laughter. Everyone followed.

Ea fell back down, her body aching from the stress of the pose she had never taken before, one that her body instinctively made as she thought she was about to die. All around her the sound of derision and anger pummelled her brain. As she turned around for a way to escape, she saw a group of females nearby – one of them so much bigger than the others at first Ea thought she was a male. This one was not laughing, but stared with hard intent. Wisely, Ea did not clap her jaws at that danger, though she felt it as distinctly as a tail slap.

The great male moved his head, and the pod understood this signal and fell quiet. The three males went forward. Ea watched, trying to understand what was happening. One by one, they submissively presented themselves to, arching their backs like females, completely silent. He opened his jaws, and the pod held its breath. Then, slowly, he closed them. The three passed on before the other large older males, then pressed together side by side like young calves. Ea had never seen her captors behave like this, their demeanour the opposite of their brutal arrogance with her. To her shameful relief, she felt the Remora's wakeful attention.

Shh, it said in a tiny voice. *Let me concentrate.*

Ea took its advice. Observing that the teeth pattern of the great diseased male matched the scars on the faces of her captors, she now understood the click they had made so many times on the journey, *the Ku this, lord Ku that. KU* must mean the leader, to whom they prostrated themselves. He now made a loud click-train, repeated by the males of his alliance.

Then came raucous cheering led by the males of the pod – this too she recognised. *Tur-si-ops, Tur-si-ops!* She guessed he had given his mercy to the three males, and that it was to him that she was being gifted. Then the chant came again from the females of the pod, and to Ea's ear, loud but without conviction. So the males and the females were not in vocal harmony . . . Whatever had just happened, Ea felt female anxiety like tendrils in the water.

She was also highly anxious because her captors had disappeared into the crowd and she was alone in the middle of the mob, facing the lord Ku. She felt the sickening rumble in the water again, and her vision was blurring with the pain in her head. The water was sickly warm and she felt him coming closer as if he were a predator and not another dolphin. The heavy white scarring at the base of his dorsal fin was the horrific sign of how it must have been almost torn off, before it had healed at a crooked angle.

Am I very ugly? the lord Ku asked Ea. *I heard the Longi never lie.*

Start now, hissed the Remora, *if you want to live.*

Ea pushed down her revulsion and forced herself to meet his leprous eyes.

No, she said. *But I think you are sick.*

SICK? He reared in front of her and she thought he was going to strike her. Then he made that tearing sound that she understood was laughter. After a moment, the pod broke out cackling in abuse and relief.

Sick! Sick! Stupid foreign spiral, show her—

Without a sound or splash, the lord Ku dived beneath Ea, inspecting her from all angles. He stopped and looked at the Remora, and Ea willed it to leave her. Instead, it secured its grip tighter on her belly. *Get ready*, it whispered, *this is—*

The Remora grunted as it was squeezed hard, as Ea felt herself lifted on the lord Ku's back like a newborn calf by its mother. He knew how to balance her, he held her aloft in public display, and she felt the great baritone of his click going through her own body, intimate and awful – and completely intelligible.

Behold the gift I now accept. Behold the lord Ku's newest wife!

He flung Ea off his back and she tumbled into the water, flailing for balance. She reared back up, ignoring the frantic flapping of the Remora.

I am not your gift! she clicked hard into lord Ku's face as he came upon her, his long white penis snaking out. *I am a free Longi female and I demand—*

The strike was so fast and sharp that at first she did not know what had happened, only that one side of her face felt a thud, then burst out in stripes of pain. While she was in shock, he forced himself into her. Males of his alliance stood guard against her escape.

Ea shrieked out at the stinging feeling moving inside her, she wanted to vomit in pain and disgust, but he brought her to the surface, still belly to belly, so that the whole cheering pod could witness it. She stared into the sun to take away the pain, to take away everything, while her body jerked and tore.

23

The Harem

If Ea could have extinguished herself by will alone she would have done so, but her body clung to life. She knew she was no longer surrounded by the mob and the water was cooler, but not that she had been retching, or that even Devi's loudest clicks straight into her head had left her unresponsive. Her mind was bright and blank but now she became aware she was swimming with females. The large one she had instinctively feared nipped her hard to keep her speed up. Ea was still dissociated from her body so she felt the bite but not the pain. Nor could she feel the Remora or hear anything but the nauseating throb in the water.

When the lord Ku had finished with her, he passed Ea over to Devi. His First Wife hid her resentment. The last thing she wanted was a new addition to the harem, and everyone had now seen that the legendary beauty of the Longi female was a fact. The upside was that the lord Ku had given permission for Devi to use sarpa as required. The pod was in a volatile state, the lord

Split was hostile, and once again she had serious sexual competition. Devi hid her own craving for sarpa, and knew she must be careful about dosage for the Longi female. There must be no more accidents in the First Harem. With three of her most loyal and discreet co-wives, she took Ea to the kelp grove.

The guards officially ignored them as they passed into the deep narrow inlet. Heavy green vines hung down the wet black walls. The air was still and cool, with no birdsong. The only sound was water slapping against rock, and the huff of their blowholes. When Devi came in front of Ea, Ea thought of the sun and waited for the blow. *I am a free Longi.* The unbidden thought gave her courage. She clicked it out again, directly into Devi's head. *I AM A FREE LONGI.* Let the worst be done, let it be over. But no blow came.

Devi did not seem offended by this extraordinary rudeness, in Longi terms. Instead, she clicked, soft and careful, back into Ea's melon, *Follow.*

Very obviously, as if Ea was a young calf they were teaching, the females took a strange double breath and sank down. Immediately there was a hissing in the air of the cove. In fright, Ea copied them and went down to where they waited for her. The hissing blocked out the rumbling in the water and came from the giant kelp forest that grew from the depths. There was no current in the cove, but each flat frond moved sinuously, so that the whole grove flexed like a vegetal gathering of sea-snakes rising out of their holes. The hissing was the sound of the fronds touching and recoiling from each other.

Ea saw how the plants opened to ease Devi's passage as she led the group deeper. The watersky was a pallid glow and the hissing of the kelp almost soothing, though she felt the Remora press tight against her, as if anxious. She began to notice details. The fronds were different shades of darkness, green, brown, running with thick black veins that changed colour at leaf junctions, where they joined in long blisters that showed red in the dim light.

Ea, whose breath control was excellent even on the deepest, most exciting hunts, found it getting short. The surface was close above but she felt unable to rise up to it. Devi came alongside and her look told Ea to wait. It was not a threat, just an instruction. All the females were angled in the same direction, their attention trained on little flashes in the darkness of the kelp. Then the fronds drew apart and five silver fish swam forward, one for each dolphin.

Ea stared. They were small and gleaming with a single lateral line of lurid yellow that she knew meant foulfish. Though tiny, their faces showed a grim mouth and hard cheek plates, predators but for their scale. Ea had never seen any fish with those odd reflective cataracts on their eyes that hid all emotion then suddenly flashed, as if they stared back. One in particular seemed to have chosen her. It swam up to her face then stumbled in the water, sending out panicky electrical pulses as if wounded. Surely a foulfish – but Ea felt a perverse compulsion to eat it. She looked to the other females, each apparently hypnotised by the same bizarre behaviour, even Devi. Devi looked back at Ea, then opened her mouth and the sarpa fish swam in. Still holding Ea's gaze, Devi closed her mouth on it.

Revolted but fascinated, Ea also opened her mouth and the sarpa fish entered. As she closed her jaws the fish swam down her oesophagus. She gagged and as she felt its body burst, the disgusting taste went up into her brain. She wanted to vomit but she could not move. She felt herself rising. Devi was carrying her up.

Energy waves bounced to and fro between the walls of the cove, the water hummed and hissed, the sky pulsed hard and white – and then it all stopped. Ea's head no longer hurt, her body felt no pain. A great calm suffused her. She looked at Devi, who had lost her frightening aspect and was now merely imposing. The other co-wives looked at Ea, and they too were no longer harsh captors, but grand females.

Sarpa, said Devi, and her click echoed in Ea's mind. *Dreamfish.*

Strong for you the first time. Stay with us. Ea understood but could not reply. The other co-wives went behind and around her and Ea was glad of them, because as they left the kelp grove and passed through public waters, she felt the penetrating male stares and heard the crude clicks. The water was still clouded, and the noise vibration was still there, but far less painful. Ea's anxiety was muffled as if her soul was stuffed into a sponge, and that thought made her laugh, a peculiar sound that was more of a cackle. She did not feel happy at all, yet her outer self was laughing. The co-wives cackled back at her, always glad to join in anything to raise the spirits. Ea's slow brain searched and felt the heavy spot on her skin where the Remora was still latched on, slack and silent. Perhaps it was dead. Then she felt it twist.

Disgusting, it slurred. *Sarpa. Hurts. Don't . . .*

It tailed away and Ea felt pleased. She would eat some more to get rid of it. Her mind began to surface. She became fascinated looking around at this very large atoll they were travelling along, with its many bays. This was the famed Longi homewater? So crowded and dirty? The sarpa opened up some more of her brain with a painful twinge, and then the clicking, buzzing, whistling din of the huge pod began to separate into words and phrases.

Banal chatter, mothers chiding squabbling calves, raucous youths swearing, all the crude expressions. Non-stop clicking, squealing and buzzing, covering up the grinding sound in the water. Around Ea, the co-wives chattered about nothing; pieces of seaweed, who said what to whom, the last hunt, the next hunt, the lord Ku's greatness, Devi's greatness – anything to wall their minds off and distract them. And from people all around, chants of *Tursiops! Tursiops!* as if to reassure themselves.

Devi came alongside and Ea swam more strongly in the same direction so that the First Wife had no cause to nip her again. She still felt threat from Devi, but now mixed with something else, though she could not have identified what it was. Devi knew exactly. It was an intensified version of the resentful admiration she had felt about Yaru. Ea was not only beautiful but also intelligent and resilient. Devi led the way into the bay of the First Harem, and all the drowsing females woke and hailed her with the whistle praising First Wife.

We live here, we belong to the lord Ku alone, Devi clicked, *and he gives us and takes us as he pleases.*

The co-wives repeated the whistle. Ea understood and copied it. She felt the Remora twitch on her chest, but not what it said. She felt pain on her face, three strong lines that throbbed hard, and a faint fourth – and her torn spiral. Immediately she split her mind away from that and recalled the taste of the sarpa fish bursting in her throat.

You think you're clever, clicked Devi, *but all your Longi ideas are wrong here. He will not want you to have ideas at all. That is not your function. Do you understand?*

Ea knew who he was. The big white encrusted eyes, his belly slamming hard against her body, the twisting lashing pain inside her.

Answer.

I understand, she clicked back in Tursiops. *More sarpa. Please.*

The co-wives cackled incredulously but stopped on a look from Devi.

For that, Devi said, *you must be under the protection of this harem. He will ask for you only because you are new and foreign, and he likes that. We do not. There are no 'free females' here, Longi or otherwise.* She turned to her co-wives. *Who here wants freedom? Who wants to be a peripheral?*

A clamour of clicks of refusal, horror, ridicule for that thought. This foreign spiral was surely going to be a problem for the great Devi, so not only would they have the illicit pleasure of witnessing Ea challenging her, but also the satisfaction of seeing the First Wife deal with her. Every harem needed a Yaru, or an Ea. Not too many, though, nor too often. They made everyone feel inferior.

But I am a free Longi female. The sarpa made Ea fearless.

The co-wives willed Devi to knock her across her pointy little beak. Why did she hesitate?

He will tire of you, Devi clicked in the soft tone far more frightening than her rage. *Then I will be your only hope. Your choice is to be a slave here, or a free female for use by all the males. Our lord Ku chose not to see the state in which you arrived, or he would not have accepted those thugs back into our pod, for first defiling his gift. But we did. So you have already had a taste of being a free female. Answer me, Slave. Before I strike you.*

Yaru, clicked Ea. She instantly felt the fear it released in the co-wives. Then she knew, through the decomposing sarpa in her brain, that the sound was hanging there in the water, like a shadow. The water whispered it. *Yaru.*

No, Ea . . . slurred the Remora, pushing through its own drug haze. *Shut up—*

Devi came up to Ea and pushed her backwards. *Where did you hear that name?*

The water told me. In the Sea of Tamas. She searches for her daughter.

The co-wives jerked in shock, but Devi did not flinch.

Yes, she clicked, *Yaru. Who defied all sense and so was lost in the vast.*

Ea stayed very still, sensitive to the lie. Devi stared at her, willing down her own fear.

Long-gi! Long-gi! Chit's high chanting broke the tension. *Tursiops! Long-gi!* The great adult-calf, his tiny penis out, swam toward them and tried to suckle at Devi. She slapped him away with her tail and he whistled out in sadness. A couple of co-wives rushed to console him and take him away, but he was too big to force, and fixated on Ea.

Pretty! he cried out in his strange young voice. *Pretty!*

Ea held herself rigid for the assault, but he only bobbed around her like a young calf, whistling his admiration.

Your toy, Devi said to him, *when your father has finished with her. It won't be long.*

Long-gi, chanted Chit, as he was led away, *Tursi-ops!*

Devi waited until her son had been removed, then turned back to her.

So what is your choice? Freedom as a peripheral on the Edge, for the quarter moon you might survive, or security as a slave?

Ea felt the Remora flapping weakly on her abdomen in desperate plea. It was thinking only of its own life, and frightened of the Edge. Ea pushed her truth down and arched submissively before Devi.

Slave, she clicked in Tursiops.

What was that? Devi wanted everyone to hear. *Who is a slave?*

Ea imagined the blinding sun as her anger. She answered quietly, *I AM A SLAVE.*

Whose slave?

Of the Tursiops.

And?

This harem.

And who is the head of the First Harem and all females of the Tursiops tribe?

YOU ARE, DEVI! You are! The co-wives could not restrain themselves any longer. Devi had triumphed, the newcomer was theirs. Ea was spared more humiliation by a new sound that made everyone twist around in its direction.

It was not a distant rumble or a grinding in every drop of water, but a small, localised and harsh mechanical noise, coming closer. The First Harem began whistling in excitement, and now Ea heard it coming from all over the pod.

Godaboves! Godaboves!

She had no idea what this meant but she felt the thrill sweeping through the water, as everyone rushed toward the sound. It was coming toward the bay. Caught in the crush of the First Harem, Ea was going to discover the source.

24

The Boats

The First Harem surrounded Ea as if she had always been one of them. She felt the friendly – if very muscular – jostle and push as they all went out into the vast together, gathering with the pod as the vibrations in the water got louder. Following her first dose of sarpa and compared to the huge general rumbling she had heard on arrival, these sounds were bearable. She kept her nerve as whatever was making them approached.

As she waited, she once again tried to get a sense of this place as the homewater of her people. This ocean was neither pure nor joyful with all kinds of life, as she had been taught it was. Despite the currents and waves, this water had a thick and sullen quality and Ea compulsively checked her skin for stains or smears. When she looked around no one else seemed worried, but instead the pod was chattering. The Tursiops talked all the time, and being loud was the only way to be heard. Their vulgar clicks and buzzes and squeals filled the water with a group vibration, and Ea felt a surprising desire to join in. She started copying sounds, and discovered that sending out her own noise eased the pressure on her head. If there were even the smallest lull, someone would start the tribal chant, and soon it would be a chorus. Then it would ebb back into separate voices.

The Longi had no group chants nor fear of being quiet. It hurt her to think of them.

No need! shouted the Remora, apparently also recovered. *Boring old Longi!*

Ea remembered how much she hated the filthy thing, but wanted to concentrate on keeping her place with the females. The thought was very clear in her mind. Stay with the females.

That's me saying it! yelled the Remora again. *Stay with the females! And in case you're wondering, I'm only still on you because so far everyone else tastes worse. Don't start thinking I like you, because I don't. I jumped off to check but I came back.*

Ea had not noticed, and the missed opportunity made her angry. The hideous thing continued speaking but she did not hear any more, because the clicks of the pod rose to a frenzy of excitement as the vibrations – now two clear sources – emerged from around the headland in the form of two boats. Now the Tursiops screeched in joy, people swimming as fast as they could to get there. They pushed and dived over and under each other to get close – the First Harem with Ea securely in the middle were extremely vigorous and successful, because Ea could now see the wood of the boats. Their black and white markings looked like mantas.

The pod was loudly clicking and chanting the familiar *Tursi-ops!* but mixed in with this was another click Ea did not understand, until she realised it was in greeting to the strange upright animals with the hard-jointed limbs, two in each boat. They each held a big identical piece of white moult that looked heavy. Then the vibrations stopped.

God aboves! clicked the pod. *God aboves! Tursi-ops!*

At first Ea thought these ugly animals on the boats might be the anthrops of Longi folktale, dangerous creatures best avoided, but the bold Tursiops showed no fear. Instead they crowded as close as they could. Something in the water trailed a bad taste, but Ea forgot that as, with an increase in excited clicking from everyone, up on the boats the two godaboves hoisted the heavy white moults, from which poured out a great shower of silver fish, right onto the heads of the Tursiops.

The water churned as people struggled to grab as many as they could, and Ea recoiled at their terrible behaviour – at the same time that she felt her own massive hunger rear up. Shoved this way and that in the lunging squealing First Harem, Ea forgot her manners and grabbed a big mouthful. But even as she was swallowing, she felt the taboo. These fish were already dead, but it was too late, she was gulping more of the icy rigid bodies. As they went scraping down her throat her body knew it was still food, and Ea lunged for more, before the First Harem were barged aside by the others. The first wave of people to eat were pushed back by progressively lower orders of vira and their harems, until finally the last few fish were fought over by the uncomeliest, oldest, weakest dolphins. Then the two small engines whined back to life and the boats circled and headed back the way they came. The weakest of the weak who had not been able to get any fish raised their open jaws out of the water, helplessly hungry.

Those are the peripherals. Devi was beside Ea again. *Some are younger than me, but their hard lives age them. They are our gift to the Residents.*

You give them to the Residents? Ea felt sick at the idea.

Of course. Because sometimes the ocean demons even attack the sharks, they maim them and leave them alive as warnings to us. She stared at Ea. *You judge before you understand, because that is the Longi way. Your people judged us when we came. We don't need your approval. We have our own laws and we are glad of the godaboves.*

Godaboves, Ea repeated, to show she knew the word.

They are on our side. Sometimes when the demons scream in war, they know it is hard to hunt, so they bring us food. Godaboves!

Godaboves! clicked back her loyal First Harem, who then had to stop Chit from endlessly repeating it. As they turned to go back into the bay, Ea could still feel the fish cold inside her. The Longi taboo was stupid. Food was food and her escape would need all her energy. This was the time, right now, while the pod was still excited by the godaboves and the treat of free food without hunting. Some were even basking in the sun. Ea watched Devi go to check on Chit, then made her way to the edge of the slow travelling, endlessly chattering First Harem. A shadow fell on her, made by a huge crooked dorsal fin.

My gift is leaving the harem? The lord Ku blocked her. Ea could not speak for fear, and once again Devi was there, the glint in her eye letting Ea know she understood exactly what was happening.

She longs for you, my lord. She wished to find you. Who can blame her?

The lord Ku made a sudden harsh sound that made his whole body shudder, and after a moment Devi and the now-clustering First Harem echoed with their own laughter.

What a wise prize. Come, little Longi gift.

Ea dived before he could press against her, glimpsing his large curved penis, now coral red and projecting from the white lesion. But he was in front of her again, faster than she was and making that pulsing sound she knew was his laughter. He came close alongside and she felt the feverish heat of his body when he nudged her.

You pretend to escape, to excite me. I want you to spin for me.

Ea looked him full in his disfigured face. She refused to be afraid.

No. I can't.

Every Longi can spin – what is wrong with you?

For a moment there was no sound. Ea saw the black and white wings of the mantas.

I am deaf to the music of the ocean.

The lord Ku burst out with violent shudders, a sign of his amusement.

No one can hear it any more! That is from the ancient times, you would have to be a thousand moons old to know it. But you can still spin for me. Little gift, do not refuse.

Please, the Remora said into her brain. *Give him anything, I mean it.*

Ea looked out into the vast. The day was new, she had a whole tide before the predators rose for the night hunt. It was possible.

No it's not! the Remora cried, understanding. *Don't even think of it—*

I need more space, Ea clicked. *My lord.*

The vast is yours.

The surrounding Tursiops whooped in approval to see the foreign spiral perform. Ea saw how suspiciously Devi watched her.

My lord Ku— the First Wife started to say, but he silenced her with a look. To Ea, he clicked, *You will show us Longi tricks. Then I will show you others.*

Ea pushed her anger down, arched submissively and slowly swam back out where the boats had fed them.

Long-gi tricks! the crowd chanted. *Long-gi tricks!*

These people must be stupid to be so easily roused to a rabble, Ea thought, but it was useful. She judged that in a crowd of this size and noise and in bright daylight, it was unlikely the Residents would be around. She did not want to follow in the wake of the stinking boats with their dead fish, and then she remembered a seamount with tall black spikes. Go there first, avoid the Sea of Tamas but strike out and find a current.

Ea took off at speed, the pod behind her. She went down and they went with her, and when she threw herself up out of the water in a few very poorly executed travelling spins, they were delighted. Some Tursiops tried to copy her and achieved height, but none could spin. Ea felt her lack of power. Whether it was the beating, the different water or the sarpa, she could not get higher. She could not combine velocity with the technique, it all fell apart before her body had even cleared the surface. The Tursiops did not seem to mind. Soon so many people were flinging themselves out of the water in emulation that they were landing on each other. Scuffles broke out and Ea seized the moment.

She dived and sped away for as long and hard as she could, but she knew she was being followed. The water carried their buzzes of excitement at the chase, and she dreaded what they would do to her if they caught her. They were faster and gaining on her. Ea was ready to fight to her death here in the vast rather than go back – but they came alongside. No one hurt her or tried to turn her back. Instead, they all went with her, letting her choose the direction, simply keeping pace. The lord Ku was there, and Devi, and she felt the muscular frightening energy of the big males around them all. She felt the tendrils of warmth and knew she was near that strange black rock form they had passed on the way to the megapod. Ea's muscles were burning with the speed she kept and her violent changes of direction, but the truth was plain. This was a new game and they were letting her tire herself, before taking her back. Ea raced and swerved until her muscles burned and her strength flagged. She was coming into the clearer water near the pinnacles, with its hot streams and sulphurous trails.

Now the Tursiops came in front, and on all sides. They were turning her with their wall of muscle, they made the water do it for them. Ea knew what would happen next, and it did. The lord Ku appeared underneath her, his great curved penis flaring out of his belly. Devi herself took one of Ea's pectoral fins in her teeth to ensure she did not struggle too much, and the lord Ku took his gift. In punishment for her escape attempt, he then allowed two of his vira to do the same.

Torn and exhausted by her failed attempt, Ea heard the

conversation as they travelled back to the thicker homewater. Her Tursiops was improving; she understood the abuse, the jokes, the high spirits at this new entertainment, the rebellious runaway Longi spiral. She was good value, they would play this game again and different vira would get a turn at her, while she lasted. By the time she was a peripheral, only a shark would want her.

My lord. Ea recognised Devi's voice close by. The First Wife was beside her, pushing her along. By the sound of it, they were back in the large gathering bay. *My lord*, Devi clicked again, louder. *Forgive my presumption, but I promised the Longi to our son, when you were finished. If she is to become a peripheral, perhaps he could have her first?*

That thing is not my son, Ku replied, *but he can try.* Though there had been no blow, Ea felt the pain radiate from Devi's body, and heard her soft appeasing tone, though not her words. She took Ea back into the First Harem bay before she too beat Ea, and the co-wives called abuse on her for how she had shamed them. Ea was ungrateful, had endangered all their safety with her Longi pride and vanity and pathetic attempt to escape. There was nothing good past the pinnacles, and if that was spinning, no one thought much of it.

They left her behind as they all went to the sarpa grove. The water was trembling as the ocean demons began to fight once more, and Ea's muscles clenched at the pain that was coming. She wanted sarpa desperately but they had left her to suffer without it. A large shape drifted alongside her. It was Chit, who was never allowed to eat sarpa, or talk to her. But no one else was there.

Pretty, he whistled softly. Ea waited for the shove of violation, but it did not come. *Long-gi*, he whistled, *Tursi-ops*, over and over, and Ea felt the Remora unlatching itself from her. She heard Chit's giggles. It was too good to be true but it was – the Remora was fixing itself onto Chit's underside, discreetly back from his left pectoral fin. She saw the serrated plate on top of its head that had caused her so much discomfort. It caught Ea's eye with its own bright black one.

No hard feelings, it called out, and it was such a relief to hear its voice so far away. *But you know, the heir apparent. Doesn't do sarpa, very protected, thinks I'm funny, which I am, though you never appreciated it. I did what I could, but now you're on your own. I won't be speaking to you ever again and I hope you know what you lost.*

Chit giggled again as the Remora secured itself.

Go back and sleep, Ea clicked softly to him. *Be good and someone will come and suckle you when they get back. Go on.* She wanted the Remora as far away as possible. Chit obediently swam back to where his co-mothers would come to dream off their sarpa.

Ea still felt pain, but the foul thing was off her. And it was good she had not fought when they caught her, because just as she ate foul food and wanted it again, she would do anything she had to, to get another chance to escape. Without the Remora spying on her thoughts, she already felt stronger. She would make a new plan, they would not stop her. She was even glad of the thundering pain of the water, the great booms and rumbles travelling through the seabed itself and feeling like they exploded in her head, because it meant she was conscious. If she had gone to the sarpa grove to dull herself, the Remora would still be on her. But the demons were shrieking and made her want to do the same. Her sonar melon felt about to burst with their sonic blows.

Devi and the co-wives returned, and Devi came up to her at once. *Open your mouth*, she clicked at her. *Quickly, if you ever want to hear again.*

Ea opened her mouth. Devi did the same, and a live sarpa fish swam out, and into Ea's. Ea closed her jaws and the fish burst in a narcotic bloom that went straight into her brain. The pain receded from her melon and her torn spiral.

All the co-wives were high on the sarpa, but Devi was still fully functioning. Though she did not apologise to Ea, she checked her all over for damage. Ea wanted to ask Devi why, if she hated her so much, she had spared her from being sent to the Edge, but the sarpa was taking hold. The water shook and screamed the war between the demons; the Tursiops pod felt their bodies churn and their heads reverberate. The drugged co-wives clung together, Ea too. But under the sarpa, deep in her mind she held to her truth: the Remora was gone, and somehow, she would find her way home.

25

A Family Visit

Far away in their tiny homewater, the Longi tribe felt Ea's soul strain toward them. Not a night's hunt nor a day's rest passed without them grieving her loss. Many people still believed she would return and the pod did not give up hope. But Ea's mother was gone, and some had seen her terrifying end. It was not just the loss of a beloved family member; she was the pod's chief dancer, who inspired them to overcome their fear and let go so that they could spin body and soul together and unite with the ocean. Without her, that was harder to do. And Little Ea, as they still thought of her despite her newly adult status, was their cherished, difficult, awkward one, who carried their failings for them. Without her, other people struggled to contain anger, or selfishness, or doubt at the traditional teachings.

Some of the Longi blamed themselves for not making more effort to bring Ea into the group, and for making spinning such a central part of pod life. Debates on how they could have prevented this double tragedy became increasingly fraught and the feeling spread that they no longer wished to spin. Some people stopped, and then claimed they heard the noises Ea had been plagued by. Others admonished them to spin more, then they would ignore them, but doubt spread. Had Ea heard real sounds, after all? No one had believed her, and everyone had pressurised her to spin and be normal. Her many faults were so plain that everyone felt more gracious by comparison. How could they not have seen that cruel pride in themselves?

The Longi soul-searching became more painful. What if it were not the remora fish or her mother's death that had driven her into exile? What if . . . it was them? The thought was so disturbing they put it from them, everyone reassuring everyone else of their kindness, ever more courteous to prove it. And yet they spun less, and more people thought they heard ugly sounds in the water, coming from far away.

But nothing happened, even though the spectral dorsal fin of the White Goddess of death swam through their minds when they went out to hunt. This they did discuss, in the moils they still held, but these too had changed. Instead of being uninhibitedly erotic and polyamorous, now the moils were about comfort and reassurance. They shared more of their fears, hoping they could still trust their ocean mother. They decided they could, and did, because the White Goddess would have passed on. She had no homewater but the wide world, and the Longi had paid their overdue tithe to her.

There was still the matter of Exodus. Each night the moon and the water told them that the Great Spawning of the ocean was nearing, and with it, the festival of sex. There was no question of not performing their rite of gratitude – it felt even more important now. Ea's mother had always led the company, but there were many people as technically proficient as she, if not as charismatic a teacher. The Longi felt the obligation of tradition – but now like Ea, they also felt a strange dread, which manifested itself in the growing reluctance and heaviness of their bodies. This in turn caused unspoken fear, resistance to practise, and the cycle intensified until one day when they gathered in the lagoon after hunting and rest, and at the normal pitch of the sun, everyone waited for someone else to begin.

The pod procrastinated. They counted their blessings, they admired the gold shimmer of the water and how beautiful people were. They checked on the calves, on the young ones. They inspected the boundaries of the home lagoon, and decided it would be a good idea to make group sorties around the atoll trinity of their homewater. They were returning from one such circumnavigation, with nothing now to do but actually practise for Exodus.

They began to spin, heavy and flat. Each leap stumbled and they fell back in crude splashes, instead of the flamboyant confident falls that Exodus called for. It was as if the water itself was pulling them down and holding them back. They persisted – the practice no longer joyful but a grim duty. All their sadness and doubt was in their movement and, one by one, they felt Ea in their hearts. And that erratic vibration in the water – how had they never felt it until now? They all listened. Now they no longer spun with the same intensity and time; their hearing was changing. They could no longer deny it. There were sounds.

People turned to each other, grief-stricken. The lagoon was safe and yet they felt a sudden apprehension. By instinct, everyone turned to face the vast. Something unfamiliar was approaching, but no one had that involuntary spasm of fear, once felt never forgotten, that signalled an oncoming Transient. Nor was it the regular adrenaline surge in the blood at sundown, when deep below the Residents began to stir.

Trusting their shared instinct, the Longi gathered on the defence. If it was more mantas, then after the disaster of the last visit, let them pass by unfêted. But the horizon was clear of their bright leaping arcs and as the Longi trained out their sonar to try to discover the source of their anxiety, they touched each other for reassurance. The picture was forming.

The water surged with a great motion and the image reached them – but it made no sense. All of the Longi saw some kind of irregularly shaped and moving black wall. Repeated sonar pulses showed more detail, as the wall came closer. It was not a wall. It was a pod of pilot whales, gathered so tightly that at a distance it looked like one giant creature. It was moving directly to the Longi lagoon.

Our calves. The pilot whales. This memory was supposed to be contained in Exodus, not swimming toward them, fear building with every wave. Paralysed, the Longi did not move. The pilots would chase them down if they fled, which they would not, because they would never abandon their young. They also knew they could not fight.

The elder Longi gathered together, trying not to spread distress. The Tursiops were the cruel barbarians who had driven the Longi from their original homewater but never hid their brutal nature. Whereas their pilot cousins ... The refugee Longi pod had been so relieved to encounter them in the vast, and totally trusted them for protection.

The two pods had travelled together, the Longi grateful that the pilots knew the ocean areas to avoid, where there was black slickwater and little food. The marauding Tursiops had spoken of this as the reason they had left their own homewater, but the Longi did not believe a click of it until the pilots confirmed it as the reason they too wandered the vast.

Food was scarce, then there was none. Everyone was starving, and the Longi, who used spinning to compensate for all manner of discomforts including hunger, no longer had the strength to do it. Each time the pilots went deeper in search of food, the exhausted Longi hoped for surface prey so that they too could eat, but there was nothing. And then there was horror. A starving male pilot attacked an ailing Longi calf.

Everyone knew the little fellow was dying from weakness and hunger, but he was still alive. His mother launched herself to protect him, but she could not break through the ferocious mass of pilots now struggling for a mouthful of his flesh. It was over so quickly that there was not even much blood. The Longi did not wait to find out if more calves would be taken – they fled their cousins and, from that day on, disowned them.

That was in Exodus too, the movement of Betrayal. The role of the cannibal pilot was taken by one of the strongest young males of the pod, who then had to choose the weakest Longi. There would be a chase, and a symbolic attack. There were no spins or falls, unless the chosen victim truly panicked and began leaping in earnest. It was one of the most frightening parts of the dance, triggering the final terror, flight and, ultimately, sanctuary.

It was not a dance, the Longi were not performing a ritual. The pilots were here, in reality. They outnumbered the little dolphin pod by at least three times and each one was more than twice the size of the largest Longi. When the pilot pod entered the channel into the lagoon, the Longi knew it was a raid. With no time to say goodbye or explain, the oldest females led those who understood out to meet their dread cousins. They were giving themselves to spare the calves.

The huge dark matriarch of the pilot whales dipped her head in universal greeting and did not attack. She pressed forward, followed by the massed ranks of the pilots, all entering the lagoon and pushing back the Longi. Now they were close among them, the Longi people could hear all the pilots gasping and moaning. The lagoon water swelled tight with their exhaustion and pain, and the sensitive Longi felt the pounding, bursting feeling in their cousins' brains. Every single pilot was in agony.

The old scarred matriarch swam aside and her people staggered past her until the lagoon was crowded with dark and foreign bodies. She turned a dazed stare to the silent Longi.

We – cannot hear. Demons took – our power – forgive me shouting—

She spoke loud in Old Pelagic so that no matter the dialect, they understood.

We have travelled far – to die—

The Longi people cried out for their cousins and went to them, and swam among the huge bodies, now almost inert. The pilot whales felt them and pressed back in gratitude.

We were hunting, the demons screamed all around us and our melons began to burst. At this, the Longi cried out in horror. It was not possible – nothing could destroy the sonar, the brain, the hearing, of a whole pod. Yet now they were close, they saw the congealed black blood around the pilots' earholes, and the blank terror in their eyes. Some were making sounds of pain; others were rocking in silent agony.

We wish to die – with your forgiveness. We know what we did. The matriarch used all her last strength. *If you will forgive us – we can join ocean mother. If you spin – we will feel it. You can free us.*

Her great body trembled in the water. Behind her, many of her people were trying to speak. Calves came out and swam in fearless wonder in front of these great cousins, and saw their eyes flicker at the precious gift of trust. Longi elders went to the matriarch, caressing her with love and forgiveness, urging her to take her family back into the vast, to try to live. A whole people could not be killed by the sound of these demons—

No more pain! the matriarch called out, and all the pilot whales who understood echoed the raw sound. *No more pain. Our sonar is destroyed, we cannot hunt, we did not even know if we would still find you before the demons. We live as family, let us die that way.*

Then all the Longi heard the water whisper what the pilots could not say:

Bless us – bless us—

*

Filled with their dying pilot cousins, the lagoon gave no room for the Longi to spin, so some went out beyond the drop-off and risked themselves in great twisting leaps and falls. The vibrations travelled through the water, into the souls of those leaving their bodies. Other Longi moved between the dying, bearing witness, giving forgiveness for the wound between their families and willing them safe passage from their bodies back into the ocean. The air turned silver with their last breaths, then the drumming in the water died down.

Beyond the drop-off, those spinning Longi gathered up the dying souls of the pilot whales into their dance, releasing the energy into the ocean and the air. They kept dancing until the last pilot, the matriarch, died. She waited until all her people had passed before she too let go of her pain.

The Longi all went back into the lagoon, now still with the dead. There should have been horror, but a strange feeling of peace was upon them. The water was grateful, the agony was over. On the beach they saw that some pilots had stranded themselves and they feared they were still alive, but there was not a sound or a movement. Dead pilots outnumbered the Longi living. And there was no way to move them.

A high little call broke the trance, coming from a pilot whale calf, still alive. It nuzzled its head at its dead mother, trying to suckle. A Longi mother whose calf was growing well went to the young pilot, and small as she was, turned her belly to him. Starving, he understood and latched on.

Now the shock set in. This was beyond belief yet it had happened. A whole pod of pilot whales, their ears blown out by the sound of demons, had come here to beg forgiveness, and for help to die.

The lagoon swayed black. Soon the predators would come.

The homewater was gone.

26

The Hunt

While Google made a lonely living in a foreign ocean, learning to hunt his food or else die of starvation, he continued along the current the Rorqual had shown him. He now thought in Old Pelagic, his native cetacean language that emerged after the whale put him into the deep healing sleep. This true expression changed all Google's perceptions. It revealed life-saving instincts but it also shattered his faith. He still heard ships, but now something in him hesitated. *Find Base*, that was never far from his consciousness, and yet . . . when he heard the engines rumbling in the water, he told himself *Not this one, not that one.* None of the sounds were right, the natural compulsion to race home was gone.

He was too busy staying alive to consider that he had not had his drugs for a long time. Never before had Google noticed the phases of the moon, but now he felt the connection between sky and ocean. Some new power was speaking to him, and sometimes when he had enough to eat, he raced for the feeling alone. Then he began to leap. There were no toys, no targets, no pontoons, and no safe tank at night. That no longer mattered, because Google decided for himself to dispense with regular habits. He slept when he needed, which was not much, ate when he could, which was less than he wanted but enough, and kept travelling the route the Rorqual indicated.

Though mainly a whale route, because of the strong magnetic signal from the seabed, it was used by many other creatures, and there were several shark crossings. The sharks left kinetic trails that Google, with his military training, enjoyed detecting. When he saw sharks they did not frighten him because he had no knowledge of any peril. When the sharks saw him, with his wounds and his peculiar energy like no other dolphin they had ever encountered, they left him alone. He was not prey, and when one sub-adult tiger shark became too curious, Google remembered the game of tag, and butted back harder than the juvenile had touched him. That was all it took, one contact and another part of Google's instinctive mind opened up. *Shark.* Now he knew, but he was still not frightened of them. He was not frightened of any outer situation, only the feeling inside himself, when he thought of his anthrops. How the boy would not meet his eyes. There was something terrible in that feeling – and then Google felt the pain of the burned stripes in his flesh, where his harness had been. Where the boy had secured it with the new and heavy magnets. Then Google swam fast, blinded with confusion, so that he had to stop and find his way again. The magnets they had put on his back were crude. The lines in the seabed were delicate and told many routes. For the first time in his life, Google was wild.

And while, far away in the vast, Google began to free himself, in the Tursiops megapod, captive Ea succumbed to the addiction of sarpa. Everyone did. It was the only way to numb the acoustic pain of the water. By her second fish, her nausea was gone; by her third, she welcomed the bursting sensation in her throat because it was immediately followed by the calming hit of the toxin. It did not just tone down the ugly sounds and desensitise her to the erratic vibrations in the water. Sarpa also transformed the mindless buzzing chatter of the megapod into a sense of security. So many people gossiping, talking about nothing, surely meant nothing was wrong. Ea found herself watching petty fights and flirtations and joining in with rumours, but she felt remote and sarpa-numbed. She was no longer revolted by the daily violence around her, the way people hit and swore at each other, including mothers to their calves. Bullying was the way of life, from calfhood onward. Ea witnessed and was dulled to everything, including her fear of being summoned to visit the lord Ku.

He was very pleased with her new docility. While he lunged and shoved against her, Ea's mind went to the moray wall and the wicked hook-jawed face of her favourite killer. Through the distant haze of bodily pain, she saw the hot little yellow eyes staring. The thought came to her that she had been going to visit a very old and dangerous creature, but she had been naturally fearless. Fear was no use when the danger was upon you. The lord Ku was big and brutal but he had done his worst. She was surprised when he asked her if she wished to remain by his side.

Give me enough sarpa and I will not care.

He made his disturbing cackle of a laugh.

Too much is not good for you, little gift.

The Longi spiral amused him, he told Devi later that same day. *Keep her in good health for me.* Devi made deferential sounds to cover her resentment, but when she returned to the First Harem, she saw that Ea was sickening. Perhaps the sarpa was too much—

I need squid! Ea had not meant to screech it, but she felt a sudden savage hunger that sarpa did not reach. She needed proper food; her body was craving her first diet, the squid and live deep-water shoals of the Longi homewaters.

And here it is! Devi buzzed her angrily, because a great swathe of moult had washed closer to the megapod, in which was tangled countless tiny dead squid. Many Tursiops were already gulping them down, heedless of the pieces of moult they swallowed with it. But even in her hungover state Ea would not touch it. Her sarpa numbness frayed into a rage of physical hunger. She had eaten the cold dead fish from the boats, she had gone with the co-wives to hunt the shallow edges of the homewater, but the fish were poor and tasted bad.

I don't care what you say. I'm hunting tonight.

The co-wives stared at this small thing, her eyes trembling, her spiral torn by their lord. Surely Devi would not permit this delicious insubordination. But Devi merely cackled loud free laughter. Ea was welcome to risk her life hunting, but the vast beyond this homewater was very dangerous. Only the strongest most able females went out with the males—

I am as able as you. My lady. Let Devi hit her, she would hunt anyway.

Devi scanned her co-wives for reaction. None met her eye.

Plenty of harem females are glad to stay close to the homewater, she told Ea, *and eat from the forage-stock around the reef, but of course as a Longi, you are too good for that. So please, risk your life. But we do not guard each other. That is not our way. Is it?*

Ea twisted around, aware she was missing some unspoken communication in the harem. Feeling the danger of reticence, the co-wives chattered their agreement with Devi.

You are right. We Longi do not eat corpses. Her click was high and angry and beyond her control as she felt the pain coming back to her body – the stinging corruption of the water, the rumbling in her melon and the visual distortions. *We hunt deep, we hunt live food and we give thanks to the ocean not to – godaboves.*

The co-wives felt the water shimmer their shared anxiety. They had all eaten, without thinking, what Ea called sick dead food. Devi had not stopped them, so surely it was acceptable. But now they became aware of their uneasy guts.

Of course you may hunt. Devi's click was dangerously smooth. *You will surely cope.*

The co-wives knew what was happening. Everyone could see how weak Ea was.

I will, Ea shot back to her, *and I will show you how we Longi hunt. If you can learn.*

Devi stared at her, her pectoral fins stiffening for a moment. Then she relaxed, and forced another laugh. The co-wives laughed too, but the thought passed between them: if this small weak Longi female was willing to go out for the rare treat of squid, why should they stay behind? They were stronger and more able than she. Devi could not permit Ea and stop her co-wives – and the click spread through the harems, that tonight the females would also hunt deep. Devi heard Ea's name many times, but once again hid her anger.

Evening came. Ea had to admit the rowdy muscular gathering of the megapod was exciting. She expected to be able to go out at the front in her usual position, but the co-wives held her back – Devi had been granted permission by her lord Ku to lead the females, on the understanding they would follow the bigger, faster, cleverer male alliances. Devi reminded her cohort of all the complicated piped signals she used to direct them, and Ea listened but did not bother repeating them to show she had understood. Hunting was hunting and she thrilled to the energy of the pod heading out.

At last the First Harem began to move. Fused into the greater motion and feeling the ocean again, Ea pushed forward alongside Devi. Up ahead was the massive kinetic power of the male alliances and she let it run through her whole body.

She had never experienced this in the Longi pod, but here the male energy was so much stronger. Devi glanced across at her and speeded up. Keeping pace, Ea did not even notice. She was focused on the unfamiliar choreography of the Tursiops on the hunt. Her own people had never mentioned it and Ea could not help admiring how they constantly shifted into different patterns, a well-practised team. She recognised two of her captors by their raked faces, now in the back of the last vira alliance. Far at the front were the lord Ku and his First Alliance, and any orders were repeated back and back through the male ranks, until by the time they got to the female cohort, it was reduced to the two compressed clicks that meant *Keep up!* and *Pay attention!*

Ea felt the water change in a promising way. She wanted to circle – that was what the Longi would instinctively do. She ignored the pieces of drifting moult because here the water was colder high at the surface, and then she caught the trace of the deep scattering layer of the tiny creatures that rose up at night to feed, and were the preferred food of the squid. A waxing moon shone down; the conditions were ideal. But travelling just below the surface, the oblivious pod was speeding on, making so much noise that the wily squid would escape.

When Devi ignored her quick sharp buzz for attention, Ea barged her intentionally. Devi whirled with open jaws at this outrage and all the co-wives drew aside, slowing their whole rank. The time had come at last and none would interfere with this conflict. Ea had been warned, they had all heard it. But instead of seeming frightened, Ea clicked in rough Tursiops. *Squid here now. Follow or lose.* Then she took the long sounding breath that every dolphin knew and went down.

Colder, deeper, not a bubble to betray her presence, Ea went deeper still. By the ripples of excitement in her body she knew the squid were there, but she needed a hunting partner. She felt the unnatural poise in the water that was another sign of the squid, a wily enough prey to stay still to hide. The Longi taught calves to stay motionless and feel for the animals, which would be close by. Clever, hypersensitive, difficult Ea, despite never hearing the music of the ocean, could always sense them.

And here they were, she was sure. She tipped her head down and sent a very small silent sonar pulse. The image returned clear. A big group of them, hanging without movement in the thick rising cloud of the deep scattering layer, the larval fish, the copepods, the small crustacea coming up the water column in the evening rise. They were even using pieces of moult to shield themselves. Ea's skin tingled at how close they were, but to attack now would be to lose them all. She needed a partner – and the water flexed at Devi's stealthy arrival.

QUIET, Ea thought to her. One click and the prey would vanish. She felt Devi's rush of indignation, but the First Wife restrained herself. *Go across*, Ea continued, *they're somewhere below*. The water barely stirred as Devi curved away.

They were communicating in Longi. Devi understood – it was amazing, but Ea could not dwell on it because now was the riskiest part of the manoeuvre: where the hunting pair slid apart, each vulnerable from behind, while they homed in on the location of the squid.

Ea slid down further until she felt the exact and subtle level the squid favoured, where the temperature dropped and the pressure tightened.

STAY HERE. She felt Devi was at the same level, far across in the dark. They must be fast and certain because they only had one chance. Too close now to check with sonar and with her oxygen level much lower than she was used to, Ea hung in the water and felt out with her Longi sense. *There they are . . . there they are . . .* the subdued pulses of the shoal of large squid, spread out and camouflaged amidst the cloud of tiny creatures and the deep drifting moult. Almost invisible.

Come down, come down – and Ea held in her excitement that Devi was receiving and understanding her – *and then we spiral.* She could not say more, only hoped it would be clear.

At first, the feeding squid felt only the current gently moving them. Engrossed in eating from the deep scattering layer, they missed the subtle pair below them, one large, one small, winding them tighter together. When the squid were corralled so close that they touched each other and realised, it was too late. Ea and Devi struck from below.

Above them the co-wives were in position to contain the first attack, circling the shoal to prevent escapes. Now Ea and Devi accelerated the upward drive and Ea let out the fast-ratcheting pulse of sound beneath them, panicking the squid together. A split-second later, Devi added her harsh buzz. The squid leaped toward the waiting jaws of the co-wives.

Ea felt how the sarpa in her blood slowed her and could not risk losing her meal. Flouting Longi etiquette, she seized what she could and ate it at once, instead of waiting for everyone to have their turn. This was normal Tursiops behaviour, they had no manners. On the hunt, there was success or failure, food or hunger. In the pod there was power and obedience, or disobedience and death. The sweet taste of squid blood streamed in the water and drew back the male alliances. Torn tentacles drifted, ink and blood mixed, and even those weaker members at the back became frantic at the taste in the water and found new strength and aggression to get into the mêlée and grab what they could.

Appalled at her own behaviour but starving and unwilling to let her rightful meal be taken from her, Ea lunged after the particular squid she was chasing and snatched it before a large male turned his head to grab it. Ea had her prize but as she bit down and killed its struggle, she recognised the opportunist: the lord Split. He clapped his jaws at her as if she had stolen it from him. She understood he was telling her to relinquish it to him. Ea swallowed it and flashed back into the scrum for more. Live squid after so long was an instant strength transfusion, and she and Devi had been the key to the success of this hunt. She was not giving up her rightful reward to Split or anyone else.

The Tursiops were a blur of hunger and bloodlust, and only when there was not a squid left alive did they go on from the clouded water. They sated themselves on a small shoal of forage fish Ea knew from home but did not care for, then at last the hunt was over.

The megapod went to the surface under the sinking moon, and Ea was amazed at their numbers and bold confidence out in the vast at night.

Tursi-ops! Tursi-ops! they jubilantly proclaimed, singing their own praises for their skill in this historically successful hunt: was there nothing the vira could not do?

Tursi-ops! Tursi-ops!

The First Harem listened eagerly to hear their own alliance called out in praise, for the great Devi had told Ea to go down first, then led the hunt to the feast. They heard the vira leaders claim credit, one by one. The cheers went on. The co-wives listened, silent for once.

The sky was purpling with dawn as the pod came back. Ea wondered at how they dawdled until she felt it for herself – the great swell of the waves building up into rollers. The vira alliances whistled and whooped to each other as they got into formation and Ea felt Devi's tension beside her.

How did you learn my language?

Devi swam on without answering for a while.

Know your enemy. And you talk in your sleep.

What about? Even as she asked, Ea dreaded knowing.

Devi came alongside, letting Ea feel her greater size.

Your fears. Your secrets. Why you left your pod.

Ea leaped ahead as if something had bitten her. She wanted to get into the thick of the crowd in front, noisy and shoving, and distracting from the dark stirring thing inside her that Devi had awoken. She saw they were all male, but she was property of the lord Ku, he had told her she was safe. As she went closer, they started to breach and dive down, and she felt the swell. They were going to surf.

Devi was there again, cutting her off.

Harems do not surf.

Ea pushed her aside.

And harems do not win the hunt, but we did—

The co-wives came forward in a line and made a chevron with Devi front and centre.

We did, Devi, you led us, and we hunted and they didn't even recognise us—

We won the feast!

YES WE DID – and Devi threw herself out of the water in a mighty travelling breach, as strong as any male, and dived. The First Harem followed, Ea too. They sped underwater to catch up with the vira alliances and keep Devi at their centre. As they came up behind them, Devi veered aside, still at her full speed but so that they would not break the line of the males.

The First Harem started clicking in uncontrollable excitement: they were going to do the long-forbidden thing – Devi was searching and found it for them, the strongest-travelling swell. The First Harem stayed close together, and Ea tucked in behind Devi like any vira second in command, and then they felt it.

Not yet a wave but pure ocean energy. The First Harem let themselves be downswept deep below the surface, then as they felt the rise they accelerated, and it was the easiest thing Ea had ever done. Smooth and fast with the gathering wave behind them, the First Harem held their line as the wave rose up into the dawn light and carried them shoreward in a translucent wall of water. It was as if Ea had been doing this all her life; she dived back down with the harem, keeping her place beside Devi, and felt the rhythm of all the females going in as the waveline fell, back down to catch another surge.

We do not do this! they whistled as they took another.

It is not allowed! they cheered to each other as their silver line sped forward in joy.

Two more rollers and then Devi buzzed them and turned them away from the breakers, for in their surfing euphoria they were speeding away from the Tursiops homewater. Lines of energy rippled between them, until they saw the phalanx of males waiting for them at the white reef edge. The harem's joy turned to fear at the way Devi faltered. She led them forward and the lord Ku came out to her. He swung his head against hers in a blow. Devi grunted in pain.

You shame me, he buzzed into her head. *You are an unfit wife.*

There was a high squeal from behind the line of males. Chit burst through the vira and rushed to his dazed mother's side, crying out in his strange voice and nuzzling at her to give her comfort. The harem closed around Devi and they swam back to their bay under a hard white sun, their exultation crushed.

27

Shame

Though the First Harem logged on the surface as if it were a normal day after the hunt, everyone knew better than to speak to Devi. Her lord Ku had never treated her so before, and they were frightened. Chit alone stayed by his mother and, to Ea's relief, she saw the Remora was still on his belly. Once bearing its shame had been the centre of her world, but now that was Chit's problem. Devi whirled away from her son's clumsy caresses, went down – and also saw the thing stuck to him. She turned on Ea.

Look what you've done to my son! Your filthy parasite has gone to the only pure person in this whole pod. Why did you come here? We thought we were rid of the Longi, we don't want you! Longi witch! Trying to take over our minds, turning my lord against me—

Devi lunged to strike Ea with her tail, but Chit twisted around to protect her, so that his mother's heavy blow landed on his head instead. He clattered with laughter.

I didn't want to come here! Ea danced back out of range, but her heart was pounding. They had hunted together, they had surfed – were they not friends?

You're destroying us but I'll destroy you first. Devi clapped her jaws at Ea and advanced on her. *Don't lie about being brought here against your will – they found you in the middle of the vast, why was that? Were you abandoned? Did you get left behind?*

Like Yaru? Ea buzzed it back at Devi, remembering the name that caused her fear. The co-wives became very still. Devi swam closer.

Longi witch I say! We've heard about your tribe, how depraved you are, how weak—

And we heard about you, Ea buzzed back, furious. *And it's all true! You're brutal and cruel and—* She got no further because Devi launched herself in rage, and Ea had to dive and twist to get away from her. The sleeping cove of the First Harem churned with Ea's struggle to escape Devi's sharp slashing tail, which lashed many co-wives as she tried to reach Ea. Then Devi realised they were blocking Ea with their own bodies. She surfaced, blasting furious sprays into the air.

Which one here told you? Devi buzzed low. *Who told you those lies about Yaru?*

No one! Her name is in the water! Ea felt the truth of this as she clicked it. Her vision was clouded with black patches that began to shape themselves into a dolphin. She heard the crying calf. *She's still here*, Ea said softly, and all the co-wives cried out in horror.

Silence! Devi struck the nearest one to her. *This harem will obey the rules. The Longi witch is trying to take over your minds, do not let her! She has already lured us into surfing, against the wishes of the vira. She brings discord and danger to us, she must be sent to the Edge.*

Chit began to wail and Devi struck him too, despite his size. Then he put his big body between his mother and Ea and started to croon, *Leave her alone, leave her alone—*

Nothing could have enraged Devi more than her own son

protecting her nemesis in front of all the co-wives. She would not stoop to the indignity of a physical struggle, but her intuition found the weapon.

Why were you alone, Ea? Devi pressed. *What did you do? What wakes you in terror?* Devi turned on her co-wives. *Because everyone here has a secret, don't they? Each of you has come to me about how you tried to help her but the others stopped you. Cowards! Liars!*

The co-wives looked away but they began to click nervously, stammering their own whistles as if they were being summoned.

Devi turned back to Ea. *So tell us, Ea, put those dreams together. What did YOU do?*

She killed her mother! Chit let out a screech and twisted in the water. *The thing is telling me! It's in my head!*

Vile thing, let me kill it now. Devi went to tear the Remora off but Ea blocked her.

Do that and his wound will never heal. The sharks will come.

SHARKS! squealed Chit. *That's what it wants! A shark! It's talking to me!*

You lie, Ea, you want to hurt him, you have no love for him—

Again Devi tried to get the Remora in her teeth but Ea stopped her.

Chit has never hurt me, I know what he suffers—

Ea killed her mother, Ea killed— Chit sang it in the Remora's horrible intonation, and then came back to his own voice. *Sorry, Ea, sorry, Ea—*

Ea could not hear any more, because her mind was flashing black and white with the manta's wings. All the sound in the world cut out except the beating of her blood. No longer in the filthy buzz and grind of the Tursiops pod, she was out in the vast, spinning to rid herself of the filthy thing, in water that was cool and clean, and the afternoon sun was sinking fast.

STOP, EA!! her mother buzzed with all her force, and the water lifted Ea as her mother sped past. She was shoved aside, lifted by more than her mother's wake as a great pale force whirled beneath her and passed so close she saw the huge blue eye.

Then as she twisted in the water she saw her mother's silver shape curving below her, aiming herself at the shark again. Ea watched it powerless from above, her mother hurtling at the oncoming shark, the impact blow, and then the turbulence of the struggle. Her mother lost in clouds of red.

The screaming was from Chit, because Ea was thrashing to and fro in a seizure. The co-wives were around her, trying to keep her still, and on the surface, the vira were coming to see what the disturbance was during sleeping hours – any altercation was disobedience.

There is no altercation, my lords. Devi came forward and clicked most respectfully to the vira officers, each of whom bore a split fin to show their allegiance. *My lord Ku, leader of the Pod, forbids me to permit entry to other males without him.* And she blocked their way with her own body, of equal size and power. Her posture was submissive but her energy was not. She waited until they left, then whirled around. The co-wives were holding Ea up to breathe, soothing her, stopping her struggling. Devi went to her, and saw that Ea was still in the grip of whatever tormented her mind. Her blowhole snapped frantically, even though she was at the surface. The co-wives looked to her, clicking in agitation.

Calm yourselves! Devi commanded. *Sarpa is the privilege of the First Harem. If we are challenged, we are playing a game, of carrying each other one by one.*

The narrow inlet was more menacing in the bright of the day than at any other time. The shadow was denser, the glare more hostile, and the vira guards resentful of unscheduled visits that disturbed their illicit sleep. Ea still had the black patches floating over her vision and kept having tremors of fear, but she knew where she was. The co-wives went alongside her but this time they touched her gently in reassurance. Inside between the high black rock walls, it seemed to Ea that the air was hissing more than usual but her terrifying vision had taken her ability to speak. They all logged on the surface taking shallow sips of this strange air through their blowholes, until they had enough, and Devi signalled they dive.

The kelp was different. Instead of relaxing to let them pass, the black-green fronds pushed against them as if to resist. The hissing was louder and some fronds snapped against each other. There was not a sarpa to be seen and they pushed in deeper, their need acute. Normally the sarpa fish came out to greet them and this delay unnerved them.

The First Harem turned in all directions looking for the sarpa, and just as Ea thought the sound of the fronds would madden her, Devi lunged into a tight clump and broke them apart. The plants hissed in pain and then they all felt it, the trembling in the water that came from the seabed and travelled up into the kelp leaves. The overhead sun illuminated a spot on the seabed far below, where they all saw the roots of the kelp pulsing red. They were distracted from this odd phenomenon by a silver flash of sarpa fish emerging from the fronds. Immediately they all knew something was wrong.

Instead of the usual one fish per dolphin, they now swam out in great numbers, listing and weakly flapping as if already dying. They clustered around the co-wives' faces, jabbing at them. Ea felt her heartbeat stutter and looked to Devi. All the co-wives were doing the same, watching Devi hesitating. The water seemed to pulse tight then slacken, and the kelp twitched. Ea saw the red now rising up from the roots, glowing in streaks and gathering in the nodes of the towering fronds. She wanted to speak but found she could not. She was short of breath as if she had been diving for a much longer time. The sarpa were all around her face, their mirrored eyes clouding and their movement frantic.

Just then Devi broke from her trance, lunged forward and took a sarpa. The other wives did the same but Ea's breath was gone and she had to go up for more air. As she moved, she heard a huge hiss and felt the kelp snapping at itself. Then there was a high scream that she knew was from the plants themselves, and the swollen nodes burst into the water. Ea closed her blowhole quickly as the stinging red liquid poured out of the plants. She felt the spasm of many hundred fish – and then it stopped. She took some clean breath at the surface and recoiled from the snaky struggle of the dying plants now sinking down. The others came up after her, shocked and disgusted. All around them, dead silver sarpa fish floated up. Devi was the first to start convulsing, trying to retch hers up. *Back*, she said. Then all of them started vomiting, all except Ea.

The First Harem managed to get back to their private bay, but they were seen in their sickly state. Even the great Devi was sick, spread the vicious click of gossip, the sarpa was all dead, the First Harem had eaten it all, it was the Longi witch's fault – *witch, witch!* the click spread, every female in the pod terrified and furious if the sarpa was all gone.

Panic roused the pod from their sleep, their bellies still full and their minds staggering under the hard sun. The First Harem tried to keep the vira out but they were too weak, some still retching empty guts – and Devi's shocking state confirmed the rumour. As the new gossip spread, Ea saw the terror in the First Wife's eyes.

I'm here, Ea spoke without click to her, as she had done while hunting and how the Longi mothers spoke to their calves when they did not want to wake anyone. *I'm here. And Chit is safe.* When she felt Devi's big fin jerking in a spasm of pain, she put her body against it. Devi was shaking with what the sarpa was doing to her and Ea signalled to the other co-wives. Themselves recovering also, they kept Devi at the surface and made a cradle with their bodies. Her safety was still theirs too.

The vira blocked the kelp grove. Poisonous bloodworms coiled up out of the silt and fed on the last living roots of the towering plants. Even if the death of the sarpa grove was not the fault of the over-privileged First Harem, it was the chance to overthrow them. The initial excitement at Ea's novelty had curdled to old fears of the vain and talented Longi, with their supernatural powers. This was what came of letting in foreigners: she had even tried to kill the great Devi.

In the First Harem, Ea heard her name being whistled and buzzed out in the pod. The co-wives heard it too, and knew the most vicious pulses came from other females. They were no longer obeying the rules of decorum and there were cries of protest as the vira males began to beat them back into submission. Then the lord Split himself came to their bay.

My lord Ku is beside himself with the shame of this harem. He requires you will present yourselves at once and in total. He turned to Chit. *And you.* Then he left.

Not good! cried Chit, in the high small voice of the Remora. Then he arched himself to see the fish stuck to his belly. *I won't hurt people*, Chit buzzed at it. Anyone who did not know would see him acting crazier than ever. Ea understood. Chit strained and twisted to see his parasite. *You won't make me—* Then he screamed and shook himself. Devi looked across, frantic with worry.

It's biting him, Ea told her. *He's fighting it.*

Devi hustled her son into the co-wives, trying to hide him. *Keep him quiet. Please.*

*

The chattering pod was mustered in the home bay but fell ominously silent at the arrival of the First Harem. A prominent space had been left for them, but as Devi led them in, vira males intercepted Chit and took him away. His chanting turned to cries of protest, then stopped. Ea felt Devi shaking in anger and fear for her son, but she maintained her composure. The First Harem looked out at the sea of shining backs.

Hard threatening puffs of air came from many blowholes and some people took rigid postures to raise their dorsal fins higher. Ea could feel the grinding in the water but something worse was emanating from the pod. Hate. It was so frightening, Ea shut it out and separated herself from Devi. She wished she could think herself away, stare at the sun, imagine herself at the moray wall, but that power was gone. She could still feel Devi's fear.

The lord Ku appeared, one eye now almost closed with the white swelling.

We are the Tursiops, strongest tribe of the ocean, First People. We do not need sarpa. We need the strength of our vira warriors, and the obedience of our females. That is what has saved us and brought us across the dangers of the vast, that is what will save us now. We will have order in this pod.

He came before Devi. *First you shame me by leading my harem in that unseemly display after the hunt. And then to go to the grove in secret, to take so much sarpa that you killed the grove? This calamity is on your back, Devi.*

On her back! The clicks came very quietly, but from different parts of the pod.

The water trembled. The lord Ku beckoned to Devi. She left the co-wives and swam out to him. Ea watched, trying to keep the numb deaf feeling. At once she knew the trembling in the water was the fear of the co-wives and all the sensation rushed upon her. They were terrified of what was about to happen, the pod was pent up in anger, somewhere Chit was in pain – Ea felt it all.

Then the lord Ku was clicking again.

You have abused your privilege, Devi. He paused. Many females murmured assent. *You have shamed your lord.* This time the vira males clacked their jaws at the insult. *By your greed and wilfulness, you have destroyed the sarpa grove, sickened all my wives and cast the whole pod into fear. For these crimes you must be punished and, as my lord Split requests, your weakling son will no longer endure the humiliation of the harem, but will enter vira training.*

Our son, my lord! And he will never survive it, you know that! Please, my lord, I will go to the Edge—

The lord Ku dealt her a mighty blow with a swing of his head.

No wife of the lord Ku may become a free female. Death before dishonour. He clicked it to her softly. *I am sorry.* The vira males came forward to surround Devi.

Witness the fate, clicked the lord Ku to the pod, and Ea was not the only one to hear the crack in his voice, *of the defiant female who tries to lead, endangering the whole pod.*

The vira commanders began to thrash Devi with their swinging heads and tailstocks. The force of the blows went through the water into the bodies of all the co-wives, as it was intended. Far away they could all hear Chit screaming.

STOP! Ea heard her own buzz in Tursiops speech and came forward. *It was me!*

The lord Ku signalled to pause the beating. Devi rushed to surface, choking and gulping air.

Ea went in front of the lord Ku. *I needed more sarpa. I will not live like this any more.* It was such a relief to say the truth. In the vira ranks, ready to be called to beat, she recognised the three young males who had captured her. *Do not touch her again,* she buzzed loudly in Tursiops. *You, who left your brother, son of Split, to die in the Sea of Tamas. My lord Ku, they raped me and then gave me to you as a gift, so they are liars as well as thieves.*

The three protested but were silenced by a look from the lord Ku. He came forward to Ea, then swung his own huge head against hers. Dimly, she heard Chit cry out again as if it were done to him.

You dare insult the vira, to set male against male? Ignorant spiral, know this: sarpa is not for the fear of weak females. It is for when the demons roar.

Through her pain Ea managed to answer him.

I have my own demons and they also roar.

He hit her again. *There. Now you hear them less.* Then he turned again to the pod.

Discipline is our strength against the ocean demons. If we have no sarpa, we will eat bloodworm. And before the Great Spawning Moon we will have the vira games, to renew our alliances. All those who would be tested to join will have their chance. After that, we will deal with all the females and restore good order.

At this, the pod whistled and squawked in excitement, their mob-lust to see Ea and the proud First Harem humiliated forgotten at the prospect of this spectacle.

The First Harem went back to their bay. Devi still shook from her ordeal. No one spoke. Ea rested at the surface, her head in pain but her mind clear. She felt her mother's energy in the water. Like the kelp, the poison hidden in her memory had burst. The flashes of her dreams came together, and she remembered. She had swum out and tried to use Exodus to rid herself of the Remora. Her mother had rushed to save her with her own life. The red bloom in the water. Ea cried out in shame and grief. She did not deserve to live.

You do. The silent voice came from Devi. *You protected all of us.*

But Ea cried for her mother like a little calf. The co-wives rushed to surround her, to press their bodies against her in comfort. The water softened and Ea felt the love, not just the care of her co-wives but something stronger and still more beautiful. She felt her mother's presence. As if the sun had come out. The water was shining and Ea felt so strongly surrounded with love and protection that she knew without doubt her mother was with her. She was the ocean around her. Ea felt herself relax and, for a moment, she was not confined to her tiny struggling self. And then the feeling surged away like a wave, and she was back in her body, pressing against the co-wives, grateful they were there. She felt Devi beside her, and their fins touched. The group of females barely moved, not understanding this beautiful feeling but not wanting it to end either.

Ea pressed herself against Devi's side and Devi understood. Slowly, they synchronised their breathing. Even in her battered state, Devi's was stronger but too fast to go deep, but gradually they found the pace. Together they sank into the right brain left eye, then switched over, left brain right eye. The co-wives made pairs together, then their pairs joined, Ea and Devi in the centre. From above, their long sleeping bodies looked like the silver petals of a flower floating in the shade of the First Harem's bay, theirs but for a short time more.

28

Transitions

The Wrasse felt the ripening of the Spawning Moon inside his own body. Flushes of heat and pleasure alternated with sudden moods of rage or euphoria. He was also unnerved by the fact that he who had adored clams more than any other food, and now had six giant specimens at his mercy, could not bring himself to eat a single one. They mattered more as companions, and each time he visited them he became more sensitised to their subtle habits.

He began to feel the way they pulled water toward them, so that as they fluttered and pulsed their mantles, he understood they were feeding. On what, he could not see, but he felt their hunger, their satisfaction, and also . . . their sexual excitement. Being near the clams became an arousing experience for him as the clams sucked threads of chemicals from the water, and released new compounds of their own. The Wrasse began to revel in novel bodily sensations. The tingling increased, and he had the crazy idea that the clams were making him change. Each time he looked at them, he saw new details in their mantles, as if his vision grew sharper. One day he noticed a delicate iridescent membrane that was a second skin. On another, he saw the dark eye spots dilate and gaze at him with intelligence. And every day, more little coloured eggs or moult adhered to the great shells so that, in time, the Wrasse imagined their grey carapaces would become completely adorned.

He could now distinguish between them, admire the different rhythms locked in the undulations of their shells, almost feel the thicknesses of their mantles and predict which clams would suddenly ruche theirs at the edges. Sometimes they all seemed to relax and let their mantles out, and then the Wrasse felt the subtlest current, to which he had previously been oblivious. This madness was relief. He knew who he was, because despite the way he could literally taste their delicious mucal secretions, the clams had transcended in his mind from food source to independent life forms. They had chosen his territory, because he was, once again, a protector.

The highlight of his day was descending for a visit when the overhead sun fell on their ledge and lit the water column into a rippling prism. Then he could watch them feeding in full sunlight. They opened their shells and let their mantles drift and flutter. Their slow choreography soothed him and, ever sensitive to colour, he felt involuntary flushes of excitement in his own body as he noticed a depth of pigment in a fold or frill of flesh, and new details of their beauty. It was as if they were revealing their hidden divine nature – and he too felt himself splitting. Sometimes he felt joined to them in some impossible communion, yet at others he knew the predator still lurked in his own nature, waiting to overwhelm the protector. The clams seemed aware of his struggle, sometimes pulling themselves in and closing their shells with an audible pop of displeasure. But if the Wrasse watched them in a calm state, they responded by showing themselves. He understood that they communicated in some silent but totally intelligible way. He felt they saw him through the eye spots in their mantles, far more clearly than did the Fugu.

The Wrasse abandoned himself to the spiritual yet erotic pleasure of his relationship with the clams, and began to live for the midday visits. From considering them his property, he now began to feel that he was theirs, and their safety his job. He became sensitised to his own shadow, and took care not to let it fall on them and spoil their basking time. Each day he had a different favourite and even imagined they undulated their mantles, competing to attract his whirring fins to stir more water over them. They pulsed their colours and the Wrasse hung there fluttering his fins like a female, his huge sensitive eyes drinking in their mesmerising displays. He loved the deep pink one, whose veins ran purple and blue, and whose multiple dark spotted eyes contracted and dilated almost flirtatiously, so that it was very much like a conversation when he spent time with – her, or him, or them.

The Wrasse felt a pang of desire, and fear. Like coral, the clams were hermaphrodites. They could mate with themselves, but yet they wished to mate together, or else why would they have come together in this group? Each night he was aware the moon was waxing, and soon it was the anniversary of the great trauma and disaster, the festival of sex. These clams were surely going to take part.

The Wrasse stared at the darkening muscular siphons, retracting into the shells now that the clams had finished feeding. Then he felt his body touched by six warm jets of water, as they blew up at him, as if teasing him. At that thought, he felt a quickening in his body. It was a thrillingly new kind of sexual arousal, mixing that of a lordmale for his ladies with the fertile languor of the females. Without meaning to, he started to dance and flutter like a female, alternating with the muscular movements of a dominant male. He glanced upward, but the Fugu was not there to mock.

He gazed at another clam, the deeper blue one that opened most widely, and now – the Wrasse saw the pale rippling nacreous gleam within its flesh – a pearl! A long irregular pale grey pearl nestled inside the orange and white mantled clam. The sun moved and the clams exhaled again. Their filigree lines and patterns were brighter and, as they began to close their mouths, the Wrasse saw something else. The whole of the ledge on which they clustered was covered in more of the fine gold filaments, denser around each of their anchoring places. It caught the light and now, as he looked, he saw it all over the pinnacles, where other smaller clams gathered in the shadows. The outside of the pinnacles was still black, but secretly inside, a gold lace grew around the clams.

Excited, the Wrasse realised more of them were arriving here from all over the ocean, carried on a current he had never noticed. They had drifted or swum through unknown waters to reach the pinnacles, called by the chemical signals of his own clams. The water was charging with erotic energy and they were waiting for the moon. They were going to start the festival of sex from these pinnacles. What would happen if he joined in?

The Wrasse came shooting up the water column, heart thrumming as if he had been chased. If the orange triggerfish had appeared now, he would have fled like a female. His gills whirred so fast that the Fugu rushed over to her preferred alcove and prepared to inflate at whatever threat was near. The Wrasse struggled for calm. The Fugu was staring. She looked around, and saw no threat. She calmed herself and inspected the Wrasse.

I have something of great importance to share. It concerns the Spawning Moon, which is almost here, in case you're even aware of anything but your bivalve friends. Who, by the way, are having a very peculiar effect on you. You'd better get your change over with fast, or no one will know how to spawn with you.

The Wrasse forced himself to pay attention, through the fine gold filaments of byssus silk dancing across his vision. He felt it drifting from his own fin tips and did not know if it was really there or not, if he was the centre of a great golden aura that the pinnacles were turning from black to gold as clams of all races wrapped them in their erotic decoration—

Stop! The Fugu had come right in front of his face. *Stop! I don't like it! You're waving your tail like a female, your colours are pulsing – are you sick? Are you going to spawn early? Please do not, it'll throw everyone out and it will be extremely selfish – I haven't even seen anyone you could do it with—*

Nor have I. He could not spawn with clams. He was sick and perverse to even have the idea. But even he could hear the new tone in his voice.

Well, I have the opposite problem, and it is extremely important and moon sensitive. Are you listening? Your voice is changing, your face is changing – what's happening?

The Wrasse convulsed. Its fins shook and pulses of heat ran through its body. When it spoke, it knew its voice was different. The Change had come.

The Fugu inflated in shock. Before her was a transcendently beautiful hermaphrodite fish, with a powerful lordmale head, but an exquisitely feminine face, and whose scales were all the colours of tropical reef.

Don't be afraid, said the Wrasse, and its voice vibrated the water like music. It felt huge and peaceful and free. *I will help you*, it said.

While some of the minute colourful moult fragments that the Wrasse thought were dead eggs made their way on the current to the pinnacles and attached to the shells of the giant clams, larger pieces drifted in the ocean from many directions, and added to the Sea of Tamas. It grew by the day, by the motion of each tide, yet it remained an inert drifting thing, a negative sea within the ocean. It gathered its great amorphous body piece by piece of plastic, and it made peculiar sounds as it crushed and released, spreading out on the surface, and down to the depths. Despite the vibrations and rumblings in the ocean around it, those dead skins, plaques, carbuncles and inorganic lesions that gave it form absorbed sound so that, as Google entered its treacherous reaches, he wondered at this new place.

The acoustic route the old Rorqual had thrown out for him had vanished into this morass. Google was not frightened; he had encountered these substances many times in his life, and much of his early world was made of it. Yet there had been form and order and here was chaos. Chaos and the atonal dissonance. But surely it was a sign of anthrops.

Google looked for a way to go around this place, but like Ea and her captors, he found this sea had closed around him. Each way he went was plastic, but when his wild self panicked, his anthrops-trained brain instantly reasserted control. He recalled the images of a training toy, a float, a pontoon. He knew it would hurt but he tried to use his sonar. The dull pain of feedback dazed him. All he got were distortions of the bizarre environment.

The only time Google had felt fear was when he was alone in the ocean before he met the Rorqual, and that was because he was failing to Find Base. When the Rorqual sounded and left him alone again, Google felt the protective caul of love being pulled away. Since then he had acclimatised to being alone and swam on through the bumping drifts of plastic. He was not frightened because this substance was familiar, but the water had an alien atmosphere and his raw skin hated the random abrasions of the debris. His cetacean impulses made him want to panic, but his military training held him steady.

Huge pieces of plastic rubbed against each other with dismal sounds, but there was no wind. Google concentrated, and detected the smallest trace of a current. It was the only live motion, except for himself. He nosed around to find where it was coming from. This was difficult because he could barely move in this ever-thickening water that was sharp instead of soft, blocked instead of clear. Google hated confusion, which caused slowness and the failure of tasks, and if this was the Workplace and he was trying to Find Base, he would think back through his recent actions to locate where he had gone wrong. Then he would correct his course. But when he tried to think back, all he remembered was how the whale had left him.

Then think about that. The whale had imitated the sound of ships, that was why he had found him – Google could not recall much except waking up from a very deep sleep, and being able to speak. Then the whale had sung to him. Google stayed shallow so that he could breathe and concentrate. He was always the best learner in his cadre of military dolphins, and now he put his mental discipline to use for himself. The haunting sonic patterns were there in his memory . . . and now he understood.

The Sea of Tamas

Death and ghosts and nets

Keep moving, keep moving—

Google found the current and stopped. Here were hundreds of swaying corpses in the nets. Countless rotting fish of all sizes. Sea birds. A decomposing whale calf, and its mother.

Google struggled to keep his military mind as, twisted in the netting below him, he saw a bottlenose dolphin. He did not hesitate, he went down to see his colleague. But it was no one he recognised, though a male of the right age and size. The striped scars on his face were still clearly visible, and his eyes were only just clouding, so he had not been dead for long. Google stared. At Base they trained them with mirrors, and for a moment he felt he was seeing his dead self.

Keep moving, keep moving! wailed the Rorqual in his mind, and Google felt his spine ripple with fear. This water was deadly. He must get out alive. He stared at his dead image one more time. His people had passed this way, and he would find them.

The Wrasse followed the Fugu out of the area of the pinnacles to a nearby shallow seamount, notable only by its dullness. It was bare of interesting forage fish or coral and had very little seaweed at its circumference, but the chattering Fugu presented it with a flourish of her fins.

On the shallow saucer shape of its top was a thick deposit of sand, protected by the higher sides. In the sand, like an odd pair of eyes, two different circular designs looked up – and by each, the Wrasse saw the artists emerge from their camouflage. They were two male fugu, each fluttering possessively over his creation, and staring intently at the female above.

I just can't decide, the Fugu said, in a sweet tone totally unlike the hectoring voice she used to nag the Wrasse into paying attention to her. *They're both beautiful, but I can only spawn over one. Don't stare at my friend like that*, she called down to her swains, *a lot of people are sexually confused these days. It's happening everywhere.*

The Wrasse wanted to laugh, but knew the water disturbance of its massive body would spoil the fragile designs. The Fugu went down and swam to and fro over them, flirting with both males.

The Wrasse had never felt more alive. It was newly sensitised to the entire ocean, tasting the rising sexual charge of the water itself, overwhelmed with a tidal gratitude for all the beauty that rushed upon its heart, the memory of love and all the people—

Spasms ran down its sides as its electroreceptors whorled with energy. Its face pulsed with pain for a moment and then it felt the racing tingle as new lines and dots emerged on its skin. It loved how its fins rose, shuddered and then lay calm again. *Let it happen.*

All three fugu below stared up, ready to void their toxins if required.

Spawn together, said the Wrasse, in its beautiful new voice.

This was how it felt to be released from mental struggle, as spacious as the ocean. The clams had given this gift, the Wrasse knew without needing to understand how. With their soft and flawless intuition, they had sensed the Change was coming, and each time the Wrasse had swum down to their hypnotic sensual beauty advanced it a little more. The pulsing, the pain, the sense of exaltation – the Wrasse felt it was the last of its kind in the whole ocean, but deep in its body a new energy was taking form. It was going to spawn, with the whole ocean. It would do it when the clams began. And then the vent would take it, and it would die in bliss.

The Wrasse loved this outrageous, beautiful, depraved, exalted thought. It would just give whatever came, sperm or eggs or both; it no longer had any sense of itself as male or female, and then it knew it had become both. These strange waters of the pinnacles had changed it and there would be no other mate, no lordmale, no harem. Only the ocean to rejoin, and even as the Wrasse felt the mighty power of sex lighting up each scale and shivering every muscle, it knew that would be the end. It was ready. But the time was yet to come, and meanwhile below, there was a hoarse chirping in the water. The Wrasse remembered the Fugu.

Together? she shrieked up at the Wrasse, exasperation in her tone. *Is that allowed?*

Everything is allowed. The Wrasse whirled around the seamount without disturbing the delicate courting displays. It loved how the slightest inclination of thought sent it gracefully and powerfully where it wanted. It felt the anxious energy of the three fish pulling at it to give them attention. The Wrasse felt kindness in its heart and gazed on the displays.

One was minimal and hypnotic. The other design was highly detailed with precise indentations. Both artists had found tiny fragments of coral and shell, and placed these for best effect. The Wrasse felt love for their actions to find each other and go on with life. Never had it loved life more, as it was coming to an end. Never had it considered that this intense spiritual, sexual, oceanic desire was also death. And to think it learned this from those holy hermaphrodite clams. It even felt love for the trigger fish.

A long shadow fell across the seamount from above and all three fugu inflated. Silent and alone, a big male bottlenose dolphin stared down at them.

The Wrasse instinctively put its body between the three small fish and their sand art. As a male he would have jutted his fins in aggressive display, as a female she would have fled, but now there was no urge to defend or attack, only to shield the precious mating displays from disturbance. From nearby came an unpleasant piercing sound – the three fugu were shrieking at the filthy predator to go away.

The dolphin looked down with bewilderment at the sound, then back to the Wrasse. The Wrasse gazed up at the dolphin, wondering if it would attack. The dolphin gazed back, equally confused. Then it spoke, or rather, it sang.

My people! it called out in Old Pelagic. The shallow-living reef dwellers like the fugu did not know this click, but the long-wandering Wrasse had travelled through the vast, and recognised it. Had the dolphin spoken the rough Tursiops dialect, the Wrasse might still have felt a threat, but instead it rose up, fearless and peaceful. This dolphin was huge and strong but bore terrible wounds, and though a mature male Tursiops, the look in its eyes was open in wonder at the sight of the Wrasse. There was something so young in this dolphin's eyes, despite the pain it must surely bear, that the Wrasse instinctively connected to it. It had never done this before, and it was a new kind of shock. Fish and dolphin looked at each other, feeling the energy of the other.

My people? asked the dolphin. *Keep moving, survive?*

The Wrasse heard the exhaustion in its click. The dolphin was asking for help, but all the Wrasse could think of was the swelling moon, the rising shimmer in the water, the ripples of bliss in its mind.

Sex, said the Wrasse, in what it knew of Old Pelagic, *my people, yes.* This was not good enough, but it was hard to think of anything else. It wanted to be with the clams – and then the memory came, of those three male Tursiops, travelling past with the foreign female, whose sadness trailed behind her. The Wrasse did not know how long ago that was, but gestured in the direction of the Tursiops homewater. The dolphin understood. It clicked or chirped or buzzed, it set the water vibrating with its sound, then set off at speed.

The Wrasse felt a physical rush in its body. Connection with a dolphin. Connection with the clams, with the fugu. With the whole ocean, filling with desire and movement and risk, everyone searching for their people, the waters gathering energy.

My people, the Wrasse cried out into the ocean in its new voice, *my people!* Below, the three fugu gazed in wonder at the great and beautiful fish in its sorrow.

29

Vira Games

The death of the sarpa shoal revealed the scale of corruption in the pod. It was an open secret that the First Wife had unfair privilege and had clearly abused it, but many of the vira had also been in the habit of taking more than their ration. In cackling denial, some people insisted on seeing the dead kelp grove for themselves. At the sight of the once towering fronds now slumped in decomposing piles on the seabed, they became enraged. Patches of yellow mud showed the streaky red casts of bloodworms, and clumps broke apart into thousands of tiny threads of them. Other people were so desperate for sarpa that they dived to poke the slimy heaps with their rostra, only agitating the soft, ill-smelling mass and further fouling the water.

There surely must be more sarpa shoals out in the vast, but this shoal had been so prolific and so easily retained in the grove that no one had ever thought to search for more. Sarpa was always there when they needed it so they had never thought to tend the kelp grove.

Now the mass addiction was out in the open, it was dreadful. Tension quickly became physical and nips, rakings, head-butting all increased. Calves were beaten for the smallest infraction, and the thought went through the raw consciousness of the pod that now they would also have to hunt without the reassuring mental cocoon of sarpa.

Within a day, the residual chemical levels from eating sarpa broke down. The dulled and bludgeoned neural pathways of the Tursiops flared back to sensitivity, and though the ocean demons were not roaring, the pod once again became aware of all the acoustic assaults in the ocean. To cover that, they raised their own noise, chattering louder to mask their fear and all other sounds, until the whole pod buzzed and chirped in compulsive gossip, slander, laughter and rage.

Sheltering in the First Harem – which was in full click and whistle – along with the rest of the pod, Ea did it too. The normal rule that females were silent so that the vira could hear themselves communicate more easily was now as dead as the sarpa grove. Ea yelped and squawked, as guttural as any Tursiops, but she had the distinct sensation she was watching from somewhere else. It was similar to the state she had put herself in when the lord Ku first raped her, but yet not like it, because she remained conscious. Part of her was still in the kelp grove, hearing the voice in her own head that told her to go up for breath, not to eat the fish. The voice that was not her mother's, but her own.

When Devi had eaten and suffered agonising pain, Ea had seen the terror in her eyes, but she had also heard Devi on the hunt, and been able to speak with her without sound. The Tursiops females did not bond with each other, and yet – she felt it, just as she had felt fear of the co-wives on her arrival. If it was possible with Devi, it was possible with all.

The pod whistled and whooped itself into a state of hysterical exuberance, and when the young males took up the chant of

Tursi-ops! the formless chatter became a heavy pulse through the water. The co-wives joined in but Ea could not. In the midst of the chant of *Tursi-ops!* Ea sang out into the din, *Longi!* in that dialect she had not used for so long.

Longi . . . It was the sound of their silver bodies leaving the water and the crystal arc of drops in the air, *Longi* . . . a beautiful resonance beyond the reach of the mob.

Ea called it out against the din, and felt the vibration of the sound in the ocean of her own blood. For a moment she was in the turquoise translucence of her old homewater, swimming in the cool smooth weave of the currents. So much knowledge and beauty, the different colours and feelings of the reef with its great coral pavilions and plazas, and the constant music of the copepods, the different fish-song – and her peaceful beautiful people she had defiled with her behaviour—

No, Ea, her mother's calm voice spoke in her mind, *you are still beloved, your spirit is always pure, and you know the way to feel it. Never be lonely, my daughter, you can always find me . . .*

Where? Ea felt physical pain in her heart. Her mother was not there, she died in a cloud of blood. She was just imagining it.

TURSI-OPS! TURSI-OPS!! The deafening chant broke into loud whistling and cheering in the pod, and then they were on the move. At last it was time for the vira games.

The male alliances assembled just beyond the Edge, raising a huge noise to show their strength to the ocean demons and any sharks in the vicinity. They whistled and buzzed, they leaped and body-slammed into the water, each group showing off its strength and aggression. Each alliance was followed by aspirant males, who would fight but who would not be defended, unlike the ordained members. The combat would continue in the near vast until a new dominance hierarchy had been established, then the alliances would return to the homewater. Braving the perils of the vast was an essential part of the victory, because the alliances existed for the security of the whole pod, not just the prestige and privilege of the winning vira.

The harems jostled for the front, aware their fortunes were tied to the outcome of the games. Out in the gathered ranks waiting to fight, Chit was rearing and cackling in his father's First Alliance. Devi cried out as she saw her son in with the great males at last, and the sound of his high calf-like voice carried through the louder whistles of the males.

The combatants began to clap their jaws at each other. Again came the breaching, higher and closer this time, hurling heavy slams of water down against their rivals as they fell, trying to destabilise them. They reared up to show their great size, and then they closed on each other. The spectators were now allowed to rush forward over the Edge, shrilling with excitement. Ea felt it too, and when someone barged her, she lashed her tailstock like everyone else. She was in the mob, in the megapod, completely focused on the fortune of the First Alliance. The lord Ku wished to spare Devi, they all knew it. If his First Alliance won—

Ea glimpsed her erstwhile captors in the opposite alliance. Rage twisted her heart and she too screamed for them to get slammed, rammed, beaten down by the First. She hated herself for it even as she cried out beside Devi, still loyal to her lord, for victory for the First. When they saw Chit ram someone, Ea cheered with all her heart.

The fights between the alliances were closely matched and swirled out further into the vast. Spectators were not permitted to intervene, and Devi desperately raced around trying to see her son. The mass of fighting males rose to the surface and went down again, and the water was filled with bursts of enraged buzzing and pulse-bursts of pain. Spectators goaded on their favourites or cried out in protest but that was all they could do. Ea and Devi and the First Harem went out further as the combat between the First and Second Alliances, now the last to be settled, looked evenly matched and no less vicious than when it started. They kept moving further into the vast, until it was no longer safe for the onlookers. The scouts pushed them back into safer water.

At the sound of her son's scream of pain, Devi threw herself forward but was pushed back. Sonar was useless to see what was happening because the throng of bodies was still twisting and moiling, bursting to the surface in an indistinguishable mass, then disappearing for so long the spectators feared they had perished. No one had ever seen such savagery in the pod. And then from far away, the triumphant formation of dorsal fins rose up.

All the First Harem strained to see the tall crooked fin of the lord Ku. It was not there. Yet led by Lord Split the First Alliance came back in whistling and shrilling their victory, and after a shocked pause, the Tursiops pod cheered back.

Long live the First!

Behind them came the straggle of the badly beaten vira warriors of every alliance, and though Devi raced out again and again to search for her lord Ku and her son Chit, they were nowhere. The vira would not speak to her, only brought her back more roughly each time, until at last she returned of her own volition, to discover the cause.

Where is my lord? Where is my son? Devi shrieked at Split, but he did not deign to answer her. Instead the new leader turned to address the pod.

There were two tragedies in our noble games, he clicked. *One was old and infirm, one young and incompetent. We mourn them, and we move on in greater strength. Strength and Growth, Tursiops!*

After a moment, those vira closest to him understood, and repeated it. *STRENGTH AND GROWTH! TURSIOPS!*

Hesitantly, the pod picked up the click and began repeating it. The First Harem were clustering around Devi, all of them in shock, when Split signalled to the pod and buzzed harshly. After a brief moment of hesitation, all the vira males began to shove the females into one big group. Those who protested were swiftly dealt heavy tail-slaps and bites to get them moving. Ea and Devi and the rest of the First Harem were pushed in with the remainder of the females. Devi was still absorbing the news about the lord Ku and Chit, and barely seemed to notice.

When I am rested, clicked Split, *those spirals I want to keep, I will over-mark. Like this one*, and he took Ea by the right fin and ripped it. It was a small tear but the pain was agonising. *Quiet*, and he lashed his tail at her. *Good wives will be reallocated. Others, troublemakers, pretenders to power*, and he went to Devi, *will become peripherals. It is long overdue for some of you.*

All the females were pushed into the First Harem bay, with no space for the groups to stay apart. Knowing the old order was gone, the most dominant females rushed for the best places. Now that they could do it with impunity, many nipped and insulted Devi as they shoved by. Her co-wives did their best to protect her but Ea had swum to the edge of the bay to nurse her wounded fin. She knew there were Longi remedies for cuts, but her brain was thick with the sound in the water and the fear of what was going to happen to them. If she fled, Split would bring her back and treat her viciously. If she could even reach the Sea of Tamas she might die there, and she did not know how she could survive alone in the vast. She felt so much older than that person who had left the beautiful Longi pod. That Ea no longer existed. Pain in her fin reminded her that this Ea did, and suffered. A co-wife from another harem was near her, and raised her own fin to show the healed tear.

He is practised at it, she clicked to Ea. *Never so deep that we cannot hunt again, just enough to remind us.*

He does not deserve any female, said Ea. *No male of my people would ever hurt a female, or a calf, or another one of his pod.* The pain went through her heart again at the thought of her people. The scarred co-wife remained by her side.

Tell me of your people, please? Before they come to sort us? If we have no more sarpa—

You do not need sarpa! Ea buzzed it more sharply than she meant it and the co-wife drew back, frightened. Ea could feel the anger in the water, and the fear. She felt her heart beating fast and the tightness of the skin around her eyes. Other females had heard the click *sarpa* and were now repeating it, the timbre of their clicks rising to panic. Ea looked to Devi, but she was staring out into the vast and they knew she was looking for her son.

Stop! Ea clicked to them all. *This new vira is vicious, do you want them to come and shut us all up?* She looked around at them lying at the surface, erratic spray from their blowholes. They had no sense of their own power or their abilities. They waited at the back of the hunt, they accepted the orders of the vira command. They beat their beloved calves to shut them up. They were suspicious and vengeful and competitive with each other.

Tell me instead, Ea clicked, *how you came to this place that was once the homewater of my people. What happened? Why were you so cruel to us? Just because we were Longi?*

They buzzed in surprise. The harems were mixed up so they could not confer in private. Then, softly, they began to speak.

They could not remember any cruelty, but they were forced to cross the vast to come here. Black filth came one day, as if the demons had poured the waste of their bowels into the water, and then the homewater was gone. They moved all together, and once the pod was much larger than this, but many died on the way—

Like my people, said Ea. *You forced us from our home, it was beautiful and you made it filthy. I grew up knowing the story—*

Then many of the older females joined in, as quietly as they could manage, but they were agitated to hear this.

This place was beautiful and your people did not want us! We had nowhere else, we wandered and suffered—

But you made us wander and suffer, Ea told them.

Not US, said one of the older females, *it was the males. We would have lived with you—*

You wanted to be above us! Ea told them. *You thought Tursiops above Longi—*

And you think Longi above Tursiops! Admit it!

Sharks will take both of us, another harem wife said, *let us not crave being first there.*

Then the harem wives told Ea of their journey here and the attacks from sharks, of how valiant the Tursiops males were, how they killed sharks – could Ea's people do this? That was how the vira formed. The males were brutal but they protected them all.

Ea listened. Her people could do many things, but she had never heard of any sharks being killed. All they prided themselves on was spinning, and living in peace.

The Tursiops females went on. They had not wanted to leave their original homewater, which was better than this one, but when the black tide killed all the fish, the males sorted them into harems for their own protection – Ea should not laugh, it had saved them—

In my tribe, all the females chose their own lovers. There are no rules except kindness . . . and spinning.

Spinning! This was what they all wanted to know about; she had refused to do it for the lord Ku, what was the secret? She must tell them, while they could still speak freely. Why did her people spin?

To hear the music of the ocean, came her mother's voice and Ea spoke it as she heard it, as if for the first time. *Which is inside us all. We spin to hear it, to join with the ocean.*

The wives had never heard any music. Maybe if they could get more sarpa—

Ea felt their rising panic, and the sound of the grinding in the water, and the wind on the waves, and the splash and heave of their jostling bodies.

It is always there, said her mother's voice in her mind, or her heart; they were the same. *The ocean is always waiting for us. We are part of her, she is part of us.*

Ea heard Devi's choking sounds as she tried to grieve in silence, and she went to her side. She heard the slide of their skin and the frightened breathing of the females. The voices of the vira in another bay, carrying faint on the breeze. The crying of calves. There was no other music. But there was the hard painful beating of Devi's heart, and Ea felt it.

The hissing of the kelp is the music, Ea said, to try to calm her. *The throbbing of your blood when you dive. The wash of the tide. The screaming of the demons. That is all there is. That is the music of this ocean.* At last she knew it. *And I have always tried to block it out, and my people spin to take away the pain. Spinning is our sarpa.*

They gazed at her, not understanding. Then, from out in the vast came a high, faint familiar voice, calling out his baby whistle. Devi whirled around at her son's voice and her co-wives rushed with her. The males were already there, gathered in their defence formations at the supernatural sight coming into view.

His head unnaturally high in the water, the lord Ku emerged out of the haze of the vast, gliding toward them in a strange motion. Beside him, low and normal in the water, swam Chit. He whistled out to his mother and Devi called back, but a cordon of the new First Alliance of males blocked her from going out. Everyone near them noticed their silence, and how their tailstocks swung slowly in unison as they waited.

The mystery revealed itself as Chit and the lord Ku came nearer. The body of the deposed leader was borne on the head of another dolphin who kept him from drowning, as a mother might with her newborn calf. He was close to the pod before they could see the cape of burned skin on which the lord Ku's body rested. Some skin had healed shiny and silver and in other places the livid red lines were turning black, marking him like a tiger shark. By the manner of his approach, this huge stranger was as fearless.

30

The Stranger

Google had never heard so many dolphins gathered in one place. Their cries and whistles filled the air and the water and, on his back, the wounded lord Ku threw himself off his rescuer and swam forward eagerly. Google saw how the son – he could feel that relationship between Ku and Chit – rushed by his side, his fins down as if still expecting attack. He followed. Beneath the chatter and cries of the people, he could feel the grinding of distant ships. He was surely close to Base, of some kind.

At the sound of the females, Google hesitated. Females were rare in his world and he worked in all-male groups. Since he had been taken from his own mother when she rejected him, he had never been close to others. And now a big group of them were rushing forward to surround the old male. *Lord Ku! Lord Ku!* was their tender click as they caressed and greeted him. To his amazement and delight, Google understood these people. The way they spoke was not dissimilar to the crude dialect of Base – and another reason he felt happy. The grinding in the water and the presence of so many like him – Google had found his people and Base at the same time. He rushed to greet them.

At once a number of large males came forward to block him. Some of their faces bore identical rake marks, and all their bodies bore fight scars. Had they too been crammed in a tank? That was where the dominance struggles got vicious. But there was no sign of any of the structure of Base, no holding tanks, walkways or pontoons. Nor, despite the distant grind and rumble in the water, any signs of anthrops. Google stood up in the water on his tail, trying to see.

A buzz of astonishment went through the Tursiops, and Google came back down. It was not a move he liked, but he knew it amused anthrops. He had learned it young and gladly performed it, until he noticed that those people who did it well, as well as other meaningless behaviours, were taken away and did not return. Google did not want to be taken away from Base so he stopped doing it. But the trick was useful to see further, and what he saw amazed him. Hundreds upon hundreds of bottlenose dolphin backs, fins, faces, all in a big dirty cove backed by a plastic-strewn beach. Anthrops must surely be close by. When he came back down, he found himself surrounded by the marked males.

Where are your sleep tanks? It felt very different to speak the common click after Old Pelagic. It made him uneasy, as if he had two selves. Before he could try to speak the way the whale had taught him, they were answering him in common speech, an overwhelming racket of voices that blocked his ability to understand. So many dolphins all shouting at him, and for the first time in a long time, Google felt the missing jab in his fin, and remembered how the little sting took away this frightening feeling.

The thought of getting an injection made his neurons pulse with anticipation and his body flush with heat. In response to that change, the males immediately pointed their fins down and arched their backs. Google looked around to see what created this threat display, but saw nothing to alarm him. He did not understand their accelerated heartbeats and hard stares. Perhaps they had all been on difficult missions, even if their bodies were not as damaged as his. He had seen cetacean colleagues fall into deep depressive states, or become randomly and violently aggressive. It was normal. He wanted his injection badly, and held out his left pectoral fin to show them the hundreds of puncture marks.

Where do you get it? Holding his fin out like that stimulated the muscle-memory and redoubled his craving for drugs. He had not thought of the drugs when he was with the Rorqual, but feeling the fear and tension of hundreds of people in the water was new and very disturbing. While he was moving, while he had a mission, he could outswim terror, but these people were bringing it to him. With a shock, he remembered the male dolphin drowned in the nets of that sickened sea. He had left it behind, but he carried the dead in his mind.

Get what? Split swam up to Google and raised his own deeply torn and sealed pectoral fin. *An injury like this?*

You gave noble service, brother. Google respected all colleagues at Base, though the ones who were injured were taken away and did not return. His brain burned as he tried to make sense of this place. All these colleagues, yet so many females, and no tanks. But yet the common click—

Base! Google buzzed in despair. *Where is Base?*

Base? Split repeated the unfamiliar click.

Live my people, Base! Google could barely control his frustration at not being able to explain what Base was. He pushed down the thought he did not know. It was a tank, it was pontoons, it was the metal grille that opened into Work. But all this was Work, so much more than he ever knew. Nothing made sense any more. He became aware he was twisting in the water in his anxiety, and that the large male with the deeply ripped fin watched him closely.

You mean your homewater. Like this, where your people live?

Homewater. Google added the click to his lexicon. *Yes. Homewater.*

You are here, Split told him. *You are a Tursiops, and so I am your leader.*

Leader, Google repeated, to learn it. *Homewater. Here.* He had learned a little from the peculiar clicking of Chit, who never left his side while his wounded father was borne aloft, but the young male spoke in his own peculiar way. Google could not see him any more, nor Ku. *Will the old one be treated?*

Split burst out in a harsh cackle, as did many of the males. *He will.*

I will go to where they do that, said Google. *I need my—* and he held up his fin again. He felt tense and strung out and did not know if it were these people or his own brain. *I have to get some more – of the thing that takes away the pain—*

All our sarpa is gone, if that is what you mean, Split said. *The fault of the one you brought back. You should have left him where you found him.*

Sarpa. Now Google had the click for it. *I need sarpa*, and again he held up his fin.

At this, all those who could hear began laughing, and the tension broke.

An odd way to take it, said Split, mentally measuring Google's size, weight and fitness against his own. *We will take you for bloodworm, when we know more about you.*

Now it was Google's turn to laugh, and he did it in the same style as these people, so they would understand he was amused. *Where are the anthrops?* It was good to be with dolphin colleagues again, but he wanted the sting, the sarpa, whatever they called it here. For a moment he saw his handler's young face in his mind, and his heart hurt. *Where do I find them?*

He wants to know where to find the anthrops! Split repeated it loudly, and after a few seconds hundreds of people were cackling harshly.

Anthrops! they repeated, and began to call it out mockingly. *Anthrops!*

Google felt the forbidden sensation of anger. Aggression at Base was punished by isolation, but each time he heard the mob's mocking click of *Anthrops! Anthrops!* He felt his heart-rate surge. He knew this pod enjoyed violence but he could not stop himself.

STOP! he buzzed at Split. The pod fell silent, but he felt their hostility sharpen.

Split remained composed.

We do not have many strangers here. And when they come, like you, they do not give orders. To the leader of the pod!

Google saw all the threat signals from the males. He had witnessed the fights at Base, always between those who wished to be shown the most respect. If the matter was not quickly settled, the anthrops removed the lesser of the combatants, who did not return. Google remained apart from all fracas, by the simple victory of giving way. The interesting work was with the anthrops, and so long as he had his injections, he did not care who fed first or claimed leadership. In Split, he recognised the type. Desperate for respect, willing to settle for being feared. Google remembered his tank tactics, and remained in a calm, though not submissive posture. Remove threat from the interaction.

You are the leader.

Yes! I am the lord Split, leader of the pod! Split whirled around so that all could see his dominance. The pod dutifully buzzed and clicked the refrain.

Lord Split, leader of the pod!

Lord Split, leader of the pod. Immediately Google clicked it, he felt the tension slacken in the water. The lord Split looked him over.

By your foreign click you have come far. What happened to you? Your wounds. Was it the demons?

Google did not know what to say. All he could think of was the face of his boy, and how he would not look at him. The weight of the new harness. He cried out and immediately stopped himself.

You must tell us, commanded Split. *Was it vira games as well?*

Vira . . . Google had heard Chit and Ku click it many times.

Warrior. Vira means warrior, you are a warrior. Your wounds, who did you fight?

Google understood, but could not answer. Never his dolphin colleagues, never the anthrops, and then he thought of his journey.

Fear, he said.

And you won. Split knew that many were looking at the more impressive wounds of this stranger. His own wound was old news, and this newcomer was younger as well as large. He seemed peaceful but he was powerful. He was a very great threat.

Completely unaware of Split's apprehension, Google was fully absorbed by the revelation of so many of his own kind. And the numbers of females he had glimpsed – he was gripped with the desire to see them again. The thought of them was physically arousing – and his body expressed it. This had only happened to him a few times, and he connected it with a lack of drugs. It was another disturbing effect of withdrawal. Those Tursiops close enough noticed Google's prominently aroused state, but did not laugh. It was a significant threat display, and they watched to see what Split would do.

Split did not betray his alarm. Sexual domination of male by male was a normal part of the Tursiops method of determining hierarchy – but it was at odds with the innocent eyes and calm demeanour of the stranger. He thought fast.

Stranger, you shall have a female; in fact you might even win yourself a harem, once you give account of yourself. Why do you ask for the anthrops? They only come when the demons have roared. Then they give us fish because we cannot hunt.

Demons. Google remembered this word from the Rorqual.

Picking up the grinding sound in the Tursiops homewater, he grunted in emulation. His sound was so coarse and frightening that he felt people flinch around him. He was only trying to make connections between what the whale said and what these people heard. *Demons* ... *Base* ... Once again, his frustration made him angry.

Split watched Google in his mental struggle. He used his cunning. *Demons made your wounds, didn't they, Stranger? Tell us how. Then I will give you a female, for the pain.*

The water. Google had no way to explain the flames on the surface, the way his harness melted and burned into his flesh. He only remembered the pain and how hard he swam but could not escape. He remembered the broken ship, and the sling on the side.

Google gasped for air at the surface and found himself encircled by big strong males, as if he wished to attack the lord Split. He knew that despite their size he had training to break free, but he wanted to connect with them. He relaxed so that they would not press against his painful skin. This leader Split said he would give him a female to heal the pain – Google badly wanted that. He must speak to them in a way they could understand.

In my pod ... in my vira ... we do things for anthrops. Like you.

The males broke out laughing again, an ugly sound to Google's ear. He pressed on. *They feed us every day – they give me this to make me sleep* – he turned his left pectoral fin in the usual way to receive injections, and remembered the click: *Sarpa. For the pain.*

Sarpa! came a few cries of recognition and craving. *Demons!*

Not demons! Google buzzed in frustration. *Anthrops Tursiops pod, together!*

Split had had enough.

Listen to me, Stranger. I think you were thrown out of your vira because you are sick. Tursiops and anthrops cannot be pod together! When the demons fighting makes us so sick that we can't hunt, then anthrops come to help us because they also hate the demons. You are strong, that much is clear, and there might be a place for you in my vira, if you can obey orders and believe the truth. Do you understand?

Google could not take in everything Split was saying. The anthrops, the demons, the sound in the water – the wounded old male and his son, so close to the pod . . .

Why was he left out there to die? The one called Ku.

Split showed his leadership.

Can everyone hear? The stranger asks: why was the lord Ku left to die? Because the vira games tell the truth: a leader who is old and sick and weak, who will not give up his place when it is time, cannot protect the pod! Only strength is safety!

TURSI-OPS! came back the cry from the pod. *TURSI-OPS!*

Split turned to Google. *Can you understand?*

Strength is Safety. Google knew Split loved to hear his own click. *Tursiops!*

This pleased Split so much he signalled his vira to move back from Google.

You are strong and learn fast, he clicked to him, conversationally. *There are things you can do to win your place here. First let me show you the reward of allegiance. Come.*

Google clicked in assent, his mind working furiously to try to understand what this pod believed. He was trying to remember what the Rorqual had told him but he could hear female voices. He could feel a different energy getting stronger in the water, and all thoughts of demons and rorquals and anthrops left his mind as, before him, he saw the huge assembled group of all the Tursiops females. Near the front was one who was different. She was smaller, and her black-lined eyes looked directly back at him.

All corralled together until the Sorting by the new First Alliance, the females fell silent at their approach. All wanted to see the grievously wounded young stranger who had brought back the wounded lord Ku and Chit, both of whom had taken many blows to shield each other. Unafraid and furious at what had happened, Devi kept them both within the stronghold of her loyal co-wives. Still more frightened of her than Split, they tended their failing lord. Chit came beside Ea, staring out at his rescuer. On his belly, the tenacious Remora was also badly damaged, but one eye still flickered with life.

When you have completed your initiation, Split explained, *you may choose a harem for yourself. That is a group of females to own. No more than six to begin with.*

To own? Google could not take his eyes from Ea, who held them.

No one may use them but you. Though you may lend and borrow.

Use them? The only things Google ever used were toys and tools.

Try not to damage them. Though sometimes it cannot be helped.

This one. Google went straight to Ea. *I will not hurt you.*

They looked at each other and as their energy met, Google felt a rush as when he got the sting in his fin. It was in his heart and his body, and for the first time in her life Ea got it too. It was thrilling, it was frightening, he chose her and she wanted it and she was completely panic-struck so she dived.

Immediately there was uproar, but Ea was not trying to escape. Her body knew what to do as Google dived and found her. Without trying or thinking, she began to twirl in the first instinctive motion of the primal dance, and to his astonishment, each movement of Ea's made Google follow as he had not known he could. Then the Tursiops crowd was down with them ogling their every move as they danced, closer and closer—

And then Ea felt herself barged away by vira males and brought up between them to the surface. She was furious as never before but the guards held her easily. Google was up alongside her, completely confused.

All but Ea. The lord Split approached her. *I am trying this little favourite for myself, when I have marked her again. You must devise your own mark; this is mine . . .*

He went to bite Ea's fin but she screeched and leaped from her captors high into the air, spinning as she fell. There was a moment's shock in the pod. Split covered it with his cackle, but as his vira went to catch her again, Google blocked them with his own body so that Ea could disappear back into the safety of the massed females.

Split came to him. *You do challenge my leadership.*

I did not mean to do that. I – could not help it. Google felt his own heart hammering in the great barrel of his body, not because of Split, but because of Ea. Those eyes with the long black lines around them – she saw him, she felt him, he felt her, no one had ever looked at him and seen him as she had, they had just begun to merge their energies when they were wrenched apart. He was hers, she was his. That was the truth.

As was the immediate danger, in the waves of anger emanating from Split.

I do not want to lead, Google clicked loudly, so the pod could hear. *Truly.*

All he wanted was to be with her again, because the feeling of her was better than the sting in his fin; he had never known there was better than that. She did not dull him down, she made his heart warm and huge and powerful like a sun inside him. He searched the female group with his eyes, but she had gone. The lord Split was taking him away, touching him with his fin as if they were friends, but the anger was still there.

That Longi spiral is mine. Do you understand?

Yes. What is a Longi spiral?

Split cackled. *The small one, Ea, she is a Longi, the weak tribe that everyone still wants to try, even you. But I might give her to you, after I have used her, if you complete the task you interrupted. It is for the good of the pod.*

I need to be with her. Google felt capable of anything for that reward.

Kill the cowardly lord Ku, who hides among the females.

Google stopped.

I do not kill. He knew that as surely as he instinctively knew to protect Ea. As surely as he knew to go to the rescue of the distress cries of Chit, supporting the old beaten body of his father, the sharks already on their way. Google had rammed two sharks and the rest had gone. That was part of his training and it made sense. What did not was when they asked him to ram divers with a spike on his harness. He had done it the first time, before he understood. He disliked the feeling and refused ever after.

No, he told Split.

NO? Split made a sound, and his alliance was around him. *Then you must leave us.*

But – I wish for Ea. Google longed for her. *She wishes for me, I know it.*

Split buzzed his displeasure. *Females wish to serve their lord and you are not her lord, I am.* Google faced Split. She danced for me, not you.

He did not know his fins were down, his back arched. Or that he made his clicks hard like Tursiops vira.

Split signalled his vira to move alongside him, so they all faced Google.

So, Stranger who can make the sound of demons, you will not kill one useless old burden to win her?

Why?

Because I am the leader of this pod and I say you will! Split forced himself in front of Google, pushing him back. *You were cast out of your pod, weren't you? You were made a peripheral, you were given to the demons for punishment, but you escaped. They will come searching for you, won't they? Or are you a demon yourself? Is that it? You are a demon in the form of a Tursiops come here to destroy us! That is why you want the Longi spiral because she is foul too! Demon, begone! Death if we see you again!*

The vira alliance moved on Google, clapping their jaws and beating the water. It was a sound the whole pod knew as alarm and they gathered again, taking up the chant in fear.

DEMON, BEGONE!

TURSI-OPS! TURSI-OPS!

Dazed by the hate and violence coming from them, Google was driven backwards by all the males. One forced through to his side – it was Chit, crying out for them all to stop, to leave him alone. Google could hear how wounded he still was, and feel his broken fin joint as he touched him in support.

Stay, he told Chit, in the commanding click of the vira. *Protect the females.*

Chit immediately dropped back, and the Tursiops jeered them both.

DEMON, BEGONE!

COWARD!

They struck at Chit as he retreated to the females. Unheeding the blows against his own body, Google waited to see him go. Then he turned back, and went again into the empty vast.

31

The Sorting

Junior vira males were the most feared because of their enthusiasm for carrying out orders, and Split set those to contain the females, now all mixed into one large group. The new leader would have first pick, then the most senior of his alliance, and so on. But first every commander had to relinquish his females, and every female, her role in the private feminine hierarchy. It was total social upheaval, but excitement about the stranger trumped everything. Whether or not they had actually seen him, everyone had an opinion.

Ea wanted to block it all out. To hear him discussed and speculated about was terrible. They were desecrating what had happened. The wounds of his body described over and over, her own name mentioned enviously, but what was his? The mystery made him all the more fascinating. All Ea knew was that he had reached out to her without even touching her, and she felt their spirits join as if they had been separated all her life, but at last reunited. The feeling grew stronger when they began to dance, and with him there was no fear, no doubt, only a great joy. Back in this mass of shrieking females, she had never felt more alone.

They were rousing themselves to a frenzy, using the stranger as the safe focus of all their frustrated desires – and terror at what the males would soon do to them. Why had Split not killed him, or the other way round?

The females laughed louder to cover up this dangerous utterance, then noticed how the young vira guards winced at their cacophony. No one could punish them for laughing, though they could punish these young guards for the violence that was coming to the harem, and in which they would certainly take part. By unspoken signal, the females kept laughing, rising to the sound of madness. But during this terrible noise, though there was jostling and shoving, no one nipped or tail-slapped. The harem structure was temporarily dismantled, and with it, their strict dominance ranking. When the lord Split began the Sorting, that would resume in surreptitious earnest, but for now, all were equally vulnerable.

At the front, mothers and kin were now berating the young vira guards who pretended to no longer recognise them. In the deafening clamour they were demanding to know their fate, and how long they must wait before the lord Split decided it. No one could bear the uncertainty, this whole situation was a terrible joke, who would answer them?

To get away from the worst of their laughter, Ea pushed and shoved her way back into the great mass of females, seeing new faces and feeling different energies. She tried to believe that if she kept moving, Split would forget about her and how she had publicly leaped to escape him. She also knew there would be no hiding, and felt bioluminescent with the attention. All the females knew the Sorting would begin with her, and that she would be painfully marked. This time there would be no protection.

She stopped in surprise. Blocking her way was a group of old scarred females. Devi was the oldest one she had ever seen in the Tursiops pod, and it was part of the harem's daily job to reassure her of her ageless beauty. Ea had joined in for her own survival and also because it was true, but she had never thought to wonder that all the females were of breeding age. These were definitely not. She realised she was looking at old peripherals.

We came when we heard, one clicked, and she could not distinguish which one had spoken. *This chaos is our chance to return. We wish to live in the pod again, under any terms.*

We are still female, one of them said to her, *no matter what else. Is that not an alliance?* With a start, Ea realised she had thought it to her. She felt laughter from them, a ripple in the water.

The old speech is not allowed here, but we peripherals have no rules except survival.

My mother spoke to me like that. Ea had the urge to go to the old female and press herself against her side.

Then your mother was wise, said the old one. *Would you come to me, little one, and let me hold you while I can? We had calves, once. We still have love to give.*

Ea went to her side, and the other old females pressed around her. She felt their sighs go through her body and felt their grief, but not the reason.

If your child is not whole, or weak, they thought to her, *they take them away. Unless you are like the great Devi and can keep him safe. It is why so many females do not breed. Have you not wondered?*

Ea thought about it now. There were few calves in the megapod, for the number of females. The population was heavily skewed to the male.

You clench your spiral, one said, *then expel what he puts there, when you are safe.* Ea laughed out loud. She had done this every single time, without even realising.

Clever child, one said.

She is no child, to do that, said another, and then they all laughed, in silence.

When they choose, we will be rejected, of course, the first one resumed. *But if a First Wife will let us in again, we will serve in any way.*

Ea felt them all hold tighter together and knew it was fear.

If she will not, then the guards will beat us back to the Edge. Where we are living tithe, for the Residents. Death comes to us all, so we try to be ready, if not willing. And hope it is quick.

Ea remembered now how Devi had threatened her with being sent to the Edge for the sharks. She had not believed it then, because to make anyone live as bait, or like the shoal of forage fish at the nursery, was unthinkable. Now she knew it was true, and felt a fierce love and respect for these old females. No Longi could tolerate such cruelty.

Break the pod. The message flashed in Ea's mind. This pod was already divided into male and female by Split's command. The Tursiops females were as strong, courageous and clever as the males, and even if the lord Ku was half dead, his First Wife was very much alive.

I must find Devi, Ea told them.

Out in the vast, Google did not travel beyond the clamour of the females. Split had not given an empty threat and Google had seen the vicious combat of the vira games, though he had not really understood, even when he had helped that son save his father. For colleagues to fight to the death was new and awful to him. He felt anger that the Rorqual had sent him here – he did not want these to be his people, and yet he knew they were the same.

It was death to return, he did believe that. But it was impossible to go on, without her. Google felt a completely new kind of confusion, as if his sonar kept returning her image to his mind, and her feeling to his heart. He felt rage at the thought of her being hurt, at himself for not knowing what to do, and at the grinding sound of ships that these barbaric people believed to be demons, and that were not the same sound as Base. He did not even want Base, he wanted Ea.

Google felt something coming for him and twisted around to fight, shooting out his sonar in instinctive response. But the stream of images showed nothing, and all he heard was the dull maddening grind in the water. He wondered if he should go back to challenge Split. He felt total and disinterested confidence he could win, and then those males would follow his orders. But here, as at Base, he had no interest in that.

Base. The thought made him uneasy. Something bad hovered in his mind just out of reach – and then memories attacked him. Google thrashed in empty water as his mind lost control and he saw it.

The boy's face, his anthrops, full of sadness, refusing to look, refusing to join—

That feeling. Google felt it in his heart again now as strong and sharp as a bite – he breached at the shock of it, and he heard the Rorqual's voice in his mind as well:

Anthrops do not love us! You are mad!

Google came slamming down alone, the boy's face in his memory, they were kin, he felt his left pectoral fin rising as if to get the sting.

Sarpa – he breached again and felt the phantom rush in his veins of the little pricks and then the tide of relief – *sarpa those people call it and theirs has gone as well.*

He could feel his heart pumping so hard his burned skin throbbed a second shape into the water, hot and searing, and he saw it again, *flaming water.* Each time he came up for air, it ate him alive – and when he went down the explosions beat his skull.

Google lay at the surface, his blowhole gasping, each wave a memory worse than any injury. And the worst one was the boy's face, as he had fastened him into the heavy holster, and sent him out to die.

Google screamed, and the sound had form. *EA*, he cried out in agony, for the one who could heal his pain, *EA* . . .

In the Tursiops pod the females were now clicking and whistling for Split so loudly, that the new leader was seduced by his sudden popularity. He had checked on his deposed brother and decided to quietly let him die of his wounds. It was unfair to ask any of his new commandants to hasten his end, and as they had recently witnessed a refusal, Split would not risk a mutiny. In any case the once-lord Ku would not live much longer. Then his pathetic son who clung to the females would make a valuable peripheral, or disposable sparring partner for a junior vira.

Strength and Growth! Tursi-ops!

Split listened to the warlike chanting of the vira. They were excited by the prospect of the Sorting, and Split decided that under his regime, the Tursiops would project more power and colonise a new homewater atoll. They were used to the ocean demons and their language was sufficiently contracted to communicate the basics at distance; all that had been lacking was Ku's will. But Split was different. He would cleanse the pod of sickness, sending all who ailed to the Edge. There would be no insubordination from calf, spiral or vira. The Tursiops would take over the ocean.

Lord Split! Lord Split! So gratifying to hear his name being chanted by all the females. They were craven of course, rightly fearful, but it was still pleasant. Split had always resented Ku because even though there was nothing between them, Ku had the hearts of the people. He was just as brutal as Split, yet the people still preferred him. Split had fewer lesions, was just as fine a male specimen – but he knew what it was. He liked to kill those who angered him. It did not matter if it were a calf, a disobedient vira trainee or a high-spirited female who tried to get away. When his anger overcame him, he acted on impulse. The lord Ku always acted judiciously, even when harsh. Split decided he would now do likewise. Beginning with selecting his harem. They would all be marked, and properly. An enjoyable task.

Split mistrusted the eagerness of the females. When he arrived for the Sorting, they overpowered the vira guards and surrounded him, each one clamouring with flapping slapping fins that he would choose her. He had never seen them in this state, blowholes sending up rude masculine jets of vapour from their overheated jostling bodies, clicks high and screeching his name – was there a tinge of anger in it? He wanted to find Ea; his intention was to begin with her, then cast out the upstart male in female form that was Devi, have her beaten and taken to the Edge – but it was impossible to find them in this roiling mêlée.

Split and the vira males stared at the sight. The females were crazed, but there were too many of them to try to instil discipline in the usual way. As if the females discerned this, their noise rose. They were all clicking and whistling and buzzing the same sound.

Split! SPLIT!

He noted that they did not bother to call him lord. Lacking all feminine decorum, they rolled in the water to show their spirals, they slapped like young males playing. They blew vulgar plumes of spray. Split stared. Such insolence, all together. So they had organised themselves. He ordered the vira to pull out the nearest one – and to his disgust she was large and old and scarred. A hideous peripheral among the younger acceptable females. She looked back at him calmly. She had known Split when he was young, back in the Oldwater. Refusing to recognise her, he struck her with a sideways blow of his head. She grunted and fell back. To his astonishment, another aged female immediately took her place, and looked calmly back at him. Split hit her as he had done the first one, a sense of unease disrupting his normal pleasure at violence. He could see others waiting – they had all gone mad so that was another problem for him to deal with. If he beat each one of them himself, he would become ridiculous. He would instruct his vira to mete out discipline later.

He was aware that the day was waning, and the Sorting was not going according to plan. Better to postpone it and do it properly, without the bizarre interruption of those disgusting old females. But first he would lead the hunt. A pod with a full belly was the first solution to disorder. The second was to bring the females to order. Examples would be made, and this mass disrespect was surely Devi's doing. Split looked forward to finding her and fulfilling his thwarted wish to beat her to death. And the Longi spiral too, she was always going to be trouble. When he had finished with her, he would give her to his most loyal vira. After all that, the Residents were in for a feast. Split hoped the sharks would understand it was because of his new leadership.

When he gave the order for the hunt, instead of the usual cheers, there was a strange little pause. And when the cheers did start, they were weak. Even the vira seemed uncertain, and the females fell totally silent. Despite everything that was going on, everyone knew as surely as the functions of their own bodies that the moon was rising and tonight it would be full. No one hunted on the Spawning Moon, not even the unbelieving Tursiops.

Superstition from the old days! Split announced. *And a full belly for the new ones! This pod will hunt, and anyone fit enough who refuses will be severely punished. Strength and Growth!*

Strength and Growth, buzzed back the vira, and then the pod echoed it, though not as enthusiastically as Split would have liked. Behind him, the young vira guards noticed how the females were now as quiet as they had been boisterous. The lord Split had put the fear into them, that was surely the reason.

Out in the vast, Google heard the Tursiops hunting chant, but no female voices. He felt Ea's gaze, he felt her in his heart. Confusion was gone. He had a new mission.

32

Spawning

At last, at last. Below the huge glowing moon the ocean was succulent with sex. In cleaner waters the coral swelled and pulsed their colours, the signal to the great branching populations of fish that the moment was drawing near. Even those last starving survivors on derelict reefs were ready to obey the law and use their last energy to join in. From near and far, solitary individuals, small herds and immense shoals converged on the traditional currents, and boisterously navigated those places of disruption. For this one full moon night of the year, they were fearless. Spawning was sex and joy and the sacred explosion of life.

At the seamount, the tumescent male fugu had resolved their rivalry by joining mandalas, which now looked up from the sandy seabed like two eyes. The Fugu herself circled and wove above them, dancing her excitement and anticipation. At the pinnacles, the fluttering mantles of the clams were fully extruded. In tender iridescent waves of flesh they stroked each other where they could.

Above the clams, the sexually transcendent Wrasse, who had neither killed nor grazed for two nights, fed on the energy of the water and the beauty of the extraordinary molluscs. They were sensation and intuition, and the more the Wrasse studied them and felt their alien intelligence, the more the boundaries dissolved.

To everything. On first arrival at the pinnacles, the Wrasse had felt mental jolts as past and present collided. Now they blended so that while traversing one side of the pinnacles they would be intensely interested in the minuscule, vivid and tenacious growth of a new algae. The new life form would stay in the Wrasse's mind and, by the other side of the spires, would be part of a memory of a different place where it grew in abundance as food for the females to graze, where beautiful voices chimed in the water and where fins whirred for pleasure and flirtation.

And now this moon, the same moon as shone on that long ago aggregate, whose anniversary was this night. The water filled with the graceful ghosts of dancing females and the single majesty of the lordmale. The Wrasse was surrounded by memories, drifting and whirling playfully through the pinnacles. The Wrasse's gills drew in all the erotic hormonal delights of this night's water, and became everyone here in memory: herself and all the ladies, himself the lordmale, the whole entire tribe. The Wrasse felt oceanic desire, to share every lustful pulse and synapse, to spawn with everyone.

Something drew the attention and the Wrasse returned to the present: it was the clams, gathering their energy, their colours rising under the strong moonlight. Along their flowing mantles their dark whorled eyes gazed back at the Wrasse, and offered their invitation. They were about to spawn. There was time to join them.

The whole being of the Wrasse flushed with terror and joy. The feeling was there. Spawning from this body that was both male and female could happen. But there was something else beyond that, and the Wrasse intuited it more clearly than anything else.

The ocean gathered itself for the great act of life, but there was a balance to be made. The Wrasse felt the peace of its own truth. It no longer wished to remain a separate being, always craving or fearing, always alone. It wished to cross the threshold and join the vast.

Below, the clams tasted the pulsing chemical response from the great body of the fish, whose huge eyes remained fixed on them. Their own signal changed in response, joining to the Wrasse's. Then the Wrasse ascended, feeling the size of a copepod, the size of a whale, understanding it would follow their lead.

In the Tursiops homewater, arguments broke out. Unlike the Longi they were not a superstitious people, but everyone knew the old prohibition against hunting on the Spawning Moon. Even the Residents refrained from taking on this one night of the year, it was too easy.

Easy? That's what we want! Many in the pod were emotionally exhausted by the stress of the vira games, the anxiety of the change of leadership, the death of the sarpa grove.

Easy! the click spread through the pod. *Easy!* they were begging.

As a Longi, Ea felt the sacrilege keenly – but something more powerful was at work inside her, deeper than any rule. Life with the Tursiops had stripped her of so much of her identity, but also brought her in touch with her true instincts. The pod clamoured to hunt, but Ea's hunger was to see him again. The stranger, who was anything but, and who knew her without words. His burned and fearsome body was beautiful to her, and when they shared their energy, it felt like flying. Ea wanted him, body and soul. Silently she called to him, willing that he had not left the waters.

Easy! she clicked aloud in her new language, joining her desire to the pod. Let them hunt, let them help fulfill her own need. *Easy!* she chanted, pushing down the Longi in her.

*

With the females still combined and segregated from the males, to emphasise his victory over his rival, the new leader of the pod, the lord Split, ordered the deposed lord Ku and his son to be kept back with the peripherals. The humiliation mattered. He had given strict instruction Devi was to be kept away from both, but she was a respected hunter and the pod was hungry. First he had thought to make her an outcast, but perhaps if she were suitably terrorised, she might have more use as an enforcer of discipline to the females. The problem would then be selecting as able a female to be his First Wife. Perhaps he would pick and choose from a different harem each moon. He liked the idea of all the females competing for his favour.

Split listened to the chants from the pod. *Easy!* and *Tursi-ops!* The pod needed simple messages to follow. He gave the command to muster for the hunt.

Over the white ruins of the drop-off swam the gleaming Tursiops pod, silver muscle threading the waves. They felt the pull of the great white moon and in their hubris that they hunted in the face of superstition and empty ritual, they chanted their name – *Tursi-ops! Tursi-ops!* – as if daring the sharks of the vast to challenge their strength and number. The new vira alliances were invigorated by the combat of the games and consequent release of tension, and they whistled louder than before. And then they passed over the gathering point and fell silent as they entered the hunting grounds.

The order was still the same: the males at the front and the females behind. The new difference was that Split had not bothered to post scouts on the perimeter of the pod, and also that the females no longer swam in discrete harem groups that maintained a cold, dismissive distance from each other. They now formed the greatest single group.

*

Ea and Devi swam as a pair, those of the old First Harem now acting as the vira did in their alliances. They were ready to follow the lead, and all around them the females organised themselves into similar groups, waiting for instruction. Instead of wasting it on gossip and slander, they used their ability to communicate in silence, to hear hunting instruction from Devi. She ordered constant rotation out from the middle as they travelled, so that no single group bore the risk of the perimeter and the vigilance was shared.

They passed over great patches of courting waters, where the fish they might normally have preyed on were gathering in huge numbers. Ea tried not to feel bad as she saw that the fish were unafraid; they sang in great rambling harmonies that spread as groups merged together and the moon rose. Up ahead the female group heard some undisciplined male clicks of excitement for *squid! squid!* but they understood Devi wished them to remain silent. As it came to Ea's turn to take the perimeter, the group accelerated and veered away from the direction of the males. Devi had learned the Longi way of hunting, and Ea felt her conscience strain. She had taught them how to take as many fish as they wanted, even on the holiest night of the year when it was prohibited.

The moon pulsed light across the ocean, down into the water, and the fishes sang it back. Ea slowed, full of conflict. Devi and the females would find the spawning squid who would not be hiding. No spawning fish were hiding, they were showing themselves, they were travelling bright and joyful to the carnival of sex at all their ancestral ocean grounds, which even the Longi did not pretend to understand – only to respect. Ea felt the pod travelling on without her; she was sensitised to the particular wake of the Tursiops at all their paces, and now she felt them going deeper. She turned away, she would not do it. She was still a Longi.

Trusting that at least the Residents would not be trespassing against the ocean's law by hunting at this time, Ea relaxed a little and decided to watch. The ocean flexed and shimmered around her, translucent rivers and waves moved in the deep. She felt no fear, but delight at the tiny percussions of stones on the seabed as creatures moved. Bubbles were rising from hidden places, the moment was coming. But even as she absorbed the beauty and wonder of what was happening, the pain of loneliness came upon her. There was no respite, because she carried it inside her. She wished she had stayed and profaned with the pod.

The noisy hunting Tursiops had made it easy for Google to track them, but then he felt something change. The pod was going on ahead but he fell back, aware of a faint signal. It was tiny, then louder. He paused, trying to locate it. It came from inside, it was the beating of his own heart. If he turned, it grew stronger. He let his body lead him.

The ocean and moon drew breath. Ea and Google found each other.

Ea felt the shock of his great dark presence in the water but instantly knew him. Neither spoke, but took breath and then descended into the dark translucence, amidst the fearless, crazily singing herds of fish, flashing their colours and spreading their fins.

They swam together and followed glowing river lines visible on this night alone. They felt the energy of their own bodies merging so that they knew as one to ascend, ascend, *breach!* and then fall, a caul of moonlit bubbles around them both. They curved round to see the soft incandescence of the endless world beneath the moon.

They fell together pulling moonlight in their bubbles, they curved around each other and spiralled down, they came up in fast ascent. They leaped together and spun, they saw the silver twisting arc they made before they fell at the same moment. They went down and stayed together.

Google did not push himself on Ea, but she swam against him and made him understand what at last she wanted, and chose for herself.

The moon reached her zenith. At the pinnacles, suspended above the clams, the Wrasse felt the wave of energy coming from all directions. It kept its huge beautiful eyes on rippling mantles as they grew brighter – and then pale glittering jets of sperm plumed up. The Wrasse felt the caress of it over its own dazzling body, changing to a rush of ecstasy as now came the heavier burst of eggs, the mantles fully extruded and cycling through all their colours. The Wrasse felt its own body begin to shake.

At the same time on living reefs, coral burst forth in streams and clouds of eggs and sperm, and all over the ocean, fish whirled in living columns of lust. Roaring males rushed through crowds of singing females, releasing themselves in tides of pleasure. Waves of orgasmic chemicals surged into the ocean as sperm found egg and joined together.

Ea and Google stayed together in communion, rising and twirling in unison to breathe and then descend, glowing with the energy of the spawning ocean. For the first time in their lives, both were at peace.

As their primal dance began to subside, Ea's separate thought returned. The Tursiops were wrong to hunt on this sacred night. Sensing her anxiety, Google moved to reassure her. And as he did, somewhere in him twitched awareness of a sound he disliked. But Ea's movement against him took all thought and gave him bliss, and the sound was gone.

They stayed together, astonished at the rapid sinking of the moon, the way the fish began to disperse, how the light in the sky was changing. They wished to hold the moon where she was and remain in their grace – but dawn was coming. Distant bawdy whistles carried through the water that Ea recognised as the Tursiops' sign of a good hunt. Side by side at the surface she and Google listened, the unsettling thought of Split and his vira piercing their happiness.

Quick, while we can! Ea pulled away from Google, curving out back toward the vast to avoid the incoming pod. He followed, curving around the outside of her.

I will come with you.

No – they will kill you. You're strong but there are too many of them. Ea's dread was mixed with their joy that they were communicating in silence. He knew how.

Then we must go, now – we will go to my people—

The calls of the Tursiops females were louder, whistling out Ea's name, Devi's the strongest of all. But Ea did not hear anger, only desperate fear that she was lost, or worse.

But these are your people—

NO! I am a Longi! Ea cried it aloud to make him understand.

At once they heard a harsh male whoop in response, and knew they had been spotted by the sonar of an outlying vira. There were ratcheting buzzes in response.

I beg you, go now, she said to him, *I will find you on the next hunt.*

I will wait for you, Ea. I will be there.

They heard the squawks of triumph as the vira located them.

GO! and she sped away from Google as fast as she could, directly toward the vira and whistling out Devi's name and the call signal of the First Harem.

Out ahead and already searching and calling for Ea, Devi and the co-wives heard her and understood her call for help. They raced to reach her before the vira.

She was lost, she was lost, she is found, she is found! cried out all the co-wives, making a protective circle around Ea just before the vira reached her.

She is stupid as well as wilful! Split broke through. Ea heard how his full belly changed his voice. All the vira would be slower. She must give her lover time.

My lord is right, she clicked. *I am slow and stupid.*

Stupid, agreed Devi. *Should I beat her, lord Split?* But Ea knew she feigned anger.

That will be my pleasure, but first I will rest. He came close to Ea, and she dreaded that he would examine her intimately. She drew in her spiral so that all the joy of the night was deep inside her.

She bragged of hunting but she lied! Weak, vain and stupid.

I will go to the Edge, my lord, Ea said. Split whirled around and slammed his fluke down across the top of her head, stunning her. With great difficulty Ea held in her cry, lest Google hear her and return.

Insolent spiral, Split buzzed into her face. *Trying to escape before I've used you? For that, when I have finished, you will pleasure every vira that wants you. Devi, if you value your son's life, you will safeguard her for that use.* Then Split circled round, calling out to the vira to give account of the pod.

All here, Lord Split! the vira called back, loud and raucous from the best hunt of their lives, bellies full and pride bursting like the coral. *Strength and Growth! Tursi-ops!*

Split's blow to Ea's head was heavy, but she was stronger now, like a Tursiops female. She swam back with Devi and the co-wives of the First Harem, and many other females that now chose to stay together heedless of former rank.

You were with him, Devi said to her quietly. *I know, because you shine.*

Ea did not answer. Chit was Devi's son, there was nothing she would not do to save him, no one she would not sacrifice.

I know love, Devi clicked quietly to Ea. *My lord Ku and I love each other, that is why he beats me, to show I have no hold on him. He only proves I do.*

Your lord cannot beat anyone any more. Once Ea would never have dared speak to the great Devi like this. Now she pitied her. *How was the hunt?* she asked, though she already knew it had gone well, because the whole Tursiops pod swam with weighty good cheer that was the same as in the Longi pod after a successful foray. Anything to distract from her lover. Ea had not even asked his name.

Let them tell you. Devi clicked, and at once the females surrounded Ea, eager to tell her their triumphs and tactics. Bright-bellied with squid and new confidence, they could now hunt like a Longi – Devi had taught them! They could speak without sound – Devi had showed them this too – the males did not know and they were going to keep it secret, so that they could protect each other from Split. They would continue to demand he mate with each of them, they would play-fight with each other to be his, so that there was no need to mark them, they would not be divided into harems . . .

Ea listened, but felt dread for them all. The males were too brutal, and no matter how much the females had learned about hunting and silent speech, like Devi they would never put their calves at risk. Nor could they withstand too many beatings. Ea felt the throb in her own head and misery at her mistake in returning. But Google would surely have been murdered if he had not left; they might both have been killed. At least this way, she told herself, if she could endure what Split would do to her in this next day – and if she could pretend to enjoy it and convince him she could be his new Devi . . . then she could survive long enough to escape. She could at least prevent him giving her to the vira, and take her mind to the moray wall when he raped her.

The moray wall. Ea had not thought of it for so long. She had only been gone for two moons, yet she felt so much older. To survive what she knew was coming, she would think of the moray faces, and the haunting song of that long-ago whale, and even here in this filthy water, remember how much her mother had loved her. Whatever Split did to her, she would be stronger, she would insist she go out on the hunt, and be reunited with her love. He was her true home and the next time they met, they would never part again.

A shudder of warning went through the pod, and Ea understood. Sharks were rising, because if this was not a holy night and the Tursiops had broken the hunting amnesty of the Spawning Moon, then so would they. Dawn was close and they were coming. Ea hurried to remain in the female group as they caught up with the males, because at this moment, to be big and brutal was protection. The noisy rabble hurried over the white coral ridge of the drop-off, heading for home.

33

Godaboves

Google knew Ea was right. The Tursiops males would have killed him if they had found them together, perhaps her too. He knew what they were like, those vicious games and how they left two of their own for dead. But as he heard the pod moving back toward the homewater, all he felt was pain and guilt that he had left Ea unprotected.

Something in the water made him instinctively move away in a course with changes of direction. He felt the fast muscular flashes as a mixed group of sharks came into the water. Some shot up from the depths to take lingering fish revellers near the surface, those too exhausted to go any further, their mission fulfilled. Tasting fish blood mixing with the milt, Google was glad Ea was not with him and used his sonar to check his own safety. There were several of the dark graceful shapes nearby, but they moved strangely. Something was wrong.

Wary but unafraid, Google's military training came back

to him and he descended to evaluate the situation. Some of the sharks were listing, lurching, struggling to keep their line. He flung himself aside as a tiger shark loomed out of the dappled light and went past him, blood trailing from its severed dorsal fin. Its electropulse stammered its pain.

Google swam away from the blood. This was a completely new scenario, never before encountered in the Workplace. The ocean reassembled in his brain. Were these wounded sharks tricks to distract him from his mission to wait for Ea? Distractions were often used in the immediate run-up to tests.

Re-evaluate. Re-focus.

Google struggled to make sense of what his sonar showed him. Some sharks hunting at the surface, yet others, listing and sinking, missing their dorsal fins. He saw another one stagger by, its jaws missing all the teeth, as if its whole mouth had been pulled out. Did they prey on each other? As Google took another sonic image, he heard a tiny sound he recognised.

The clink of metal against metal. Small but reverberant in the water. The way it was suddenly deadened told him the sound was an accident. He was used to stealth in his training. Instantly he knew something was hiding.

Mindful of the sharks, Google quietly travelled in the direction of that tiny little metal sound. All he knew for certain was that his mission was to wait for Ea, whom he felt in his heart and who gave him joy. But that sound worried him, and so did the sharks without their fins. Google heard it again, very faint and from another direction. Metal clinking. A chain.

The sound has moved. No – there are two sources.

Google listened again, with all his training.

BOATS. Nearby.

Google swam quietly below the surface, no longer hoping they were Base. Every natural instinct warned him to remain concealed, and coming up behind the line of boats, Google recognised the military manouevre. The sun was behind them to dazzle the target boats they attacked – but yet there were no target boats. Now he recognised they were close to the homewater. He stood on his tailstock to see. It was a shock to see anthrops again after all this time. They were so ugly – he had not realised. Google recognised their hunting tension. They were waiting for the Tursiops pod.

His vision beat white for a moment. His anthrops who had sent him to his death. What the Rorqual had said. Google felt his heart break and rage charge his blood at the betrayal. But first, his mission. He had to change it – he could not wait for Ea, he must protect her now. Everything before was a lie: she was his only truth.

The Tursiops pod, males and females, were over the drop-off and almost into their homewater when they heard the boat engines start up behind them, three on each side. The pod slowed and turned to see; feeding time now? Godaboves only came after the demons had roared, and never this close into the homewater. The pod had eaten freshly and well, they did not want to perform for fish, they wanted to get into their bays and sleep. For males and females alike, there was still the vexed issue of the Sorting, but that could wait until later. Everyone needed to rest; the godaboves should come another time.

The godaboves clearly did not understand because they spread out in a semi-circle and kept advancing. At the back, unprotected by any vira, the females were the closest to see that there were two or three anthrops, godaboves, in each one. They did not hold up their usual buckets, but instead held long poles. On a signal, they put them into the water and began to beat on the poles with stones.

The agonising demonic sounds shot through the water from

every direction, piercing the dolphins' sonar melons and blocking all thought. The mass of people convulsed in panic, fleeing into each other, crying out, shoving and gradually being forced back into the homewater, into the big bay with the high sides that was closest. How could demons be here now? Why did the godaboves not stop them? Everyone was shrieking for someone to do something and what was happening?

Furious and in great pain, Split pushed forward with some of his biggest vira. This was his chance to show his ultimate authority, and command the godaboves to stop the demons. If they were here together, they must end it! Kill the demons and show their bodies! First, he had to fight the press of frightened females who were no longer able to hear Devi above their panic and pain, because the demons were among them yet they still could not see them.

Split rose up on his tailstock to show the anthrops his majesty – and they cut him across the head with one machete, then another. He fell back spouting blood, but before he could struggle away, they lashed him by the fin to the boat.

The demons – the shrieked click rushed through the pod – *the demons are the godaboves!* The terror they had held off with sarpa, with fear, with hope, broke through to all of them. Demons and godaboves were the same. *DEMONS!* they screamed at each other, struggling to get away. *Godaboves are the demons!* they shrieked, splashing and cramming into the homewater as the boats revved their engines to panic them tighter, and Devi and Ea struggled to turn them round.

Google came up in the screaming mass of females that were the first in the line of terror. Those who were not blind with panic could see the faces of the anthrops, no longer smiling but turning hard black-lensed eyes on them, more terrifying than any shark. They were pointing out different people in the water and all the while beating on the metal poles so that, as the boats got closer, the sound became physical jagged pain in their heads. The people stopped thinking or hearing in their struggle to get away – which drove them tighter together.

An oily stink spread in the water as the grinding boats came closer. Closest to the shore, calves that were too young for the hunt shrieked in fear and their mothers shrieked back, unable to get to them as the furious screeching males ploughed forward to get rid of this threat. Ea saw the striped and silver-raw back of her lover and cried out, trying to get to him. He heard her and whirled around to stop her coming closer, and by his side she saw something else happening.

All the boats were facing into the lagoon, but behind them, one was laying out a long membrane across its mouth that dropped down into the water. Ea remembered the Sea of Tamas, and the veils of death made of the same stuff as this membrane. Google told her to wait and dived down but she could not, she had to follow him – but he was heading straight for the oncoming boats, the source of the agonising pain in her head. Following him, she saw the wooden undersides lit by the slant morning sun, and their black and white paint.

The underbellies of the circling mantas, the message. Black and white, black and white – *Break the pod*—

This was the horror they had meant, this was why it had terrified her. It was happening now, this was the moment to do it, but how?

Ea burst to the surface to find Devi – as Google exploded from the water in a massive breach – hurling his body to land on the standing anthrops spooling out the net.

Google slid off the boat and went under again, and all the anthrops started shouting to one another and taking out metal spears and big gleaming machetes. Without waiting for another attack, they pushed the boats into the mass of people and began to stab and strike at the dolphins, while behind, the fallen man rose to his feet and continued to lay the net.

Blood spurted and people screamed, but Ea could hear Devi's terrifying whistle that summoned her females to attention, trying to stop their headlong rush into the trap. Ea slammed up beside her and Devi heard her. As Ea screamed to her what they must do – *break the pod! make them separate, make them spread out!* – they saw Google hurling himself in another breach onto a boat, making a gap in the line of terror. Ea and Devi understood – Google was opening the way for the pod, if they could turn its panicked rush away from the trap of the homewater.

Take the gap! Ea screamed, trying to get behind the plunging terrified people, instinctively holding together as the anthrops wanted. The line of boats kept moving in, but Google kept breaching and knocking at them, diving under to miss their spears. Some of the males began to understand and started to copy him, but they did not have his training and were slain even as they succeeded for a moment in breaking the line.

Ea glimpsed the vast through the black and white wooden hulls, but then it was gone in the slamming blowing mass of Tursiops bodies. She dived aside as a spear flashed down beside her and missed her. It was too dangerous to look for Google – she saw a spear go through the face of one of her co-wives from the First Harem, her blood spurting high into the air. The man struggled to pull the spear out and the female shrieked in agony, pink spray bursting from her blowhole.

Devi was beside Ea, using her great tailstock to beat aside the nose of a boat. They were getting closer to the gap and Ea pointed Devi at it and knew she understood – and then the First Wife disappeared back under to try to push the mass of people out.

It was no good. The terror and blood were too much and no one could hear them – all except for Chit, coming forward singing loudly, *Take the gap! Take the gap!* The marvel of his speech and action combined got people's attention even in their fear, and he turned them. Behind him was his wounded father the lord Ku, close to death, but behind whom some people still cowered. The lord Ku put himself in front of them and held out his fins in protection, while he watched his son plunge forward to the front line, where Google once again breached onto a boat. The metal flashed above him as the boat went over, and Chit screamed in triumph and heaved forward to join his beloved stranger.

Other vira and males saw and drew courage, diving and breaching themselves suicidally onto the boats, where now the anthrops were ready for them with spears and machetes, but the line of boats was broken, and gaps were opening. The anthrops revved their engines harder to fill the water with the terrifying sounds as they worked to close the line.

Ea and Devi were driving forward as many people as they could, biting and striking them to move out, until they could see what they had to do. The boats were pressing closer and Chit whistled at any vira who could hear him, to press their bodies against the boats to let the females and the calves out through the gap while they could still flee. Somewhere nearby, Ea heard Google's voice giving the orders and Chit was relaying them – there was no time to wonder how, because she was forcing through all the people she could, striking them to stop their panic and keep the momentum of the escape.

Break the pod, break the pod – at last she understood: if the people kept their heads and spread out they could make a gap, there were too many to all be chased down – but they could not help themselves, they clung together to protect each other. Ea saw the crowd of people driven back to the fatal beach, on which terrifying two-legged figures with machetes and nets stood waiting in the shallows.

Take the gap, break the pod! Ea screamed, but it was too late. Some of the brave were going, but just as many could not think or move. The calves were paralysed by fear and refusing to leave their wounded mothers, and males Ea thought barbarian brutes now threw themselves in the way of the females to protect them. She saw the anthrops pointing at the calves and readying the nets – and the old peripherals coming forward and intentionally entangling themselves to save others. Ea rounded up the calves and was pushing them toward the closing gap, when the boats started up again.

Chit was behind the mass of people pushing them forward, but the boats were faster and soon they would all be trapped. Ea kept forcing forward, screaming at the calves to go – when suddenly there was a terrible cry of rage and pain from a Tursiops male – and then, a shouting from the anthrops, and one of the two boats about to close the gap faltered, and the noise of its engine changed.

The cry had come from Google. Unable to stop the boat in any other way, he had deliberately pushed his own tail fluke into the propeller. Even as it tore the flesh from his body, the boat slowed. Google pulled with all his strength and dragged it aside, so that its own wake turned it facing out into the vast. They revved the engine and he screamed, they rained steel and savagery on his head and back, but Google did not stop swimming to pull the boat aside, making the gap wider.

Ea felt the pain in her own being; everyone screamed as they felt Google's agony and how the water churned red with his blood. Chit roared rage and pain and slammed his huge body against the nearest boat, then went under before they could strike him, and the vira males did the same, throwing themselves against the boats until they were struck down. But now the four remaining boats had the measure of this aggressive pod, and redoubled their savagery.

Bleeding and almost unconscious from the torture flashing up his spine from his mutilated tail, Google knew he was dying, but also that people flashed past him as they escaped out into the vast. He hung still so that the anthrops would stop striking him, not because he did not want to fight, but because he knew his broken tail stopped the boat, and because he burned to see Ea one more time. He had promised he would wait for her.

Ea was back in the last of the group that could still move, trying to get as many people as she could away from the lord Ku, who put his body in front of all those who sought his protection.

Go, he told Devi, who was trying to move him. *Go, my First Wife.*

Never. Devi put herself in front of her lord, and Ea saw her many wounds. *Your loyal Devi stays by your side.*

Please! Chit whirled around before them, trying to make them move.

My son, whistled the lord Ku, in the honorific he had never before used. *Protect our people. Go with them, they need you.*

Go, beloved, Devi clicked to him, using his calf-name, private to them. *GO!*

And Chit turned away from his parents, and in his rush he caught up Ea on purpose, as the great male Tursiops could do to a small female, and he pushed her with him, until she too swam for her life toward the gap between the boats.

Ea did not need eyes or sound in the bloody din of the water; her heart found Google as he drowned in his own blood, his tail stripped of flesh but still holding the boat disabled. He felt her press against him, and her heartbeat. He wanted her to go while she still could.

I waited, he said.

Come home, Ea told him. She felt his last heartbeat. Then she fled.

Behind her the water ran red.

34

Exodus II

The prevailing current took what remained of the pod toward the pinnacles. There was no leader, but Chit found more energy, and moved around to keep the stunned straggle as close together as possible. Ea swam on, telling herself Google was with her, even though she knew what had happened. His final heartbeat made her own heart bigger, and her blood pumped with a roaring sound in her sonar, as if she fought through a storm. The females gathered close around her, she could feel that, and she automatically reached out to comfort and be comforted by their nearness. The calves were kept together, the females did that automatically as well. There were a few males with them, swimming in total silence.

They all kept to the surface. There was the occasional grunt or moan of pain, but they swam on because to slow down and let their wounds flow would bring new disaster. The sulphuric filaments in the water stung in a way that felt right, and they let the current carry them closer to the pinnacles.

Deep in the spires of the vent, the Wrasse felt their arrival by the darkening of the watersky and by the turbulence stirring its own great colourful mortal form. Its spirit danced and fluttered in readiness to separate, but the Wrasse remained in untroubled bliss. Somewhere in its newly spacious mind, it noted the strange silence of this pod – surely not the Tursiops. Even the Fugu at her seamount wondered at the sight of so many silent dolphins gathering overhead. Their movements stirred the water so much that the mandalas blew away, but by then they had fulfilled their purpose and all three fugu had spawned together.

The dolphins gathered around the pinnacles and slowly circled, grateful for the rest. Eating was the last thing on their shattered minds, but the warm sulphuric water of the vent stung and cleansed their wounds. One by one they passed through the place just below the surface where it was bearable. Then they turned and twisted, crying out as they felt the depth of the cuts in their flesh. Those with eye injuries – mainly the brave males who had breached against the boats – could not bear that pain, but Ea went through herself, feeling the lacerations on her head and back for the first time. She would be unrecognisably scarred now, but if she ever found her way home, she knew her Longi family would enfold her with love. And when she told them how the Tursiops had suffered, how the demons and the filth had made them frightened and brutal, they would have to understand and forgive. Ea would beg them, because now she too understood what it was to live in such conditions.

This was her plan, and as she felt the warm currents turn her in the pinnacles, she wondered if the Tursiops would come with her. If not, she would go alone. She had felt her lover die, she had seen unspeakable things. The vast held no more terrors. Ea heard people start to talk again, quietly and in nonsense, but clicking just to let each other know they were there. With a surge of love, she understood that the Tursiops used noise as the Longi used touch, just to remain connected.

The heat of the vent was soothing to her pain, but others were waiting. Turning her body for the last time, Ea looked up and saw the pale outline of the full moon, still high in the dawn sky. Sometimes the moon remained visible during the day – she had noticed it before. This time it seemed very important, but her brain was fogged with exhaustion and the adrenaline still charging through her nerves. Chit was going in next, and she saw the smashed but still living Remora clinging to his throat. Its one working eye was flickering, staring intently at her. Ea thought it was trying to connect with her, and she would not put it past the creature even in its wounded state to change its mind. It was amazing that it too had survived. As Chit rolled his big body in the water like a calf, though he was full grown and larger than Ea remembered, she saw all the slashes on his back, and the deep cut in his dorsal fin. Ku's son, yet with Split's wound. He was the right leader.

She heard the Remora's voice as Chit spun around. It had the timbre that was hard to forget, when it had been stuck to your own head. *Release me, please! I've had enough!*

Ea! Come and look! This time it was Chit's voice, and he was calling her to him. Ea went back, and saw what he was looking at. The midday sun shone down directly into the pinnacles, lighting up the water in a twisting prism of blues down to darkness. Far below on a ledge, supported on a bed of giant clams with curious coloured moult on their shells, was the radiant body of the Wrasse. Ea gazed down at the wondrous fish with its huge humped head, its enormous kind and gentle dark eyes surrounded with a turquoise lace pattern. She had never seen a fish so beautiful, as if a whole reef lived within it. Its long fins trailed gold against the black rock, and though its body was at rest, its gills still fanned.

Please, begged the Remora to Chit, and Ea knew it had seen the gorgeous fish below. *No more, let me go. There's someone down there, I could get on, I know it, please – no more dolphins, I promise—*

Go, clicked Chit. The Remora sprung free. At once, it swam with all its battered strength down toward the great Wrasse, but the water was too hot. The Remora recoiled, twisted, then tried again, weaker each time.

Ea stared in wonder. *You wanted to keep it?*

While I was learning things from it. But after the vira games, when they beat us so badly, it started to talk nonsense.

They looked down at the Remora, still trying to get down to the Wrasse – and then it rolled on its side, and began to drift. Its body caught on a spire, and then the current pulled it away and it was gone. Ea looked down and saw the great Wrasse's gills slow down and stop. Its beautiful body grew brighter as it died. Then Chit's voice pulled her away.

We cannot stay here, he announced, and the new authority of his speech and demeanour seized the attention of all. *If Ea agrees, we will try to find the Longi homewater.*

Ea felt a flush of amazement. She had not spoken her thought to Chit, yet he knew it.

We will try, she clicked in Tursiops. The pod was so weak, they would have to cross the vast, bleeding and hungry. It would be hard to hunt, and then if they stumbled into the Sea of Tamas, they needed energy and courage for such a journey. Without it—

But there was a way, she knew it now. If she put all her trust in it. Ea turned and looked around at the confused and frightened people. Chit was going around drawing everyone in, he was touching people, he was speaking in the common click and the silent language, and as he passed through the people, they became his. They turned their bodies toward him, as they had done to his father. He was the same with males and females, the young and healthy and those old peripherals who had managed to get out.

A feeling shimmered through them and reached Ea that was so familiar yet out of place with the Tursiops – but they were doing it. Chit was emanating the energy of the Shriving Moil, and it began to happen. These Tursiops who had never done it in all the time she had been there were now rubbing against each other and blowing hard breaths of sorrow and pain up into the air, comforting and reassuring each other, raising their broken hearts.

Look up, Ea. The thought came in her mother's voice. Ea looked up and saw the palest ghost of the full moon. *The Spawning Moon lasts two nights. You can still do it.*

Her mother's voice was gone but Ea felt a new energy rising in her body. She wanted to move, she wanted to leap. She wanted to spin, but first she had to warn Chit, who was leading the pod from the pinnacles, heading out into the vast. But when she reached him—

Sea of Tamas, he clicked to her. *I know because the Remora told me. We will go south on an old whale path. If I can find one.* Then Chit cried out in sudden pain. *Oh my mother, oh my father, how could I leave you to die*—

Ea felt her own pain burst out of her. She did not know her lover's name because she had never asked, but she felt his heart beat inside hers. *Come home.* The feeling made her dive for the pressure, to hold her grief inside. She went down as deep as she could then turned on instinct and came powering up – and through the watersky in a huge breach.

She felt herself fly, and then spin. She did not try; a force far greater than her own lifted and twisted her so fast and high into the air that she felt herself disappear. The sky and ocean spun as one. Ea felt her lover spinning with her, she was light and strength and joy in motion – and then she fell.

It was the first time she had ever experienced it, that moment of complete abandon and despair that caused the reverberations she felt when others had done it. Now she was at the centre. She thought she would slam down into the water but at the instant of the blow, she felt the ocean open for her and wrap her in a cocoon of bubbles. Everything slowed. The ripples of her fall travelled out into the vast – and then at last, she heard it.

LOVE, the ocean sang into her blood as she rose back up to the surface to breathe, love was in the water, in her mind, in her memory, the ocean held it all. And Exodus was what she danced now, without trying, without fear. It was the dance of all who were loved and lost, of all the homes they left behind them, and the hope that kept them alive.

Ea did not hear the music as much as she became it, going down again and again; no longer tired or heartsore, but filling with more energy each time. He was with her each time, in every whirling spin of light and air.

Ea tired. She came up to rest, and saw other silver shapes, more solid and slower, diving then breaching with heavy and passionate falls. The Tursiops were learning to do it. More and more of them were starting to spin as they leaped. She watched in wonder, and then delight as she felt the water start to hold and synchronise them, and then she too rejoined them and Chit was leading them, spinning and breaching, and the pod was travelling again, under the pale outline of the daytime moon.

After a while the pod slowed, then stopped out in the vast. Ea watched people coming to rest after an extraordinary length of time spinning and breaching. They were physically tired and yet they felt the waves of new energy created by their spinning.

My mother! My father! Chit whistled out again, loud and strong as an adult, but the click of a calf. He was grieving, and other people took it up, calling the names of their beloveds who had been left behind, so that the whole pod was crying out the names of the lost, the fathers, the mothers, the children, all the children.

The senseless chatter of the Tursiops was no more. Instead, they were raising their voices in a great chorus of sadness and love that made the water shimmer. The souls of their loved ones lifted in the ocean and the Tursiops felt it and cried out together, a sound Ea had never heard them make.

Love! cried Chit. *Love!*

LOVE! Ea cried out with them, and the sound was the same as in Longi.

Love! came the distant cry, in the Longi click, and then the faintest series of falls. Familiar, beautiful patterns.

LOVE! Ea cried back, and threw herself in an answering fall.

EA!! EA!! the cries came again, and she knew it was her people.

The Tursiops swam toward the Longi, Ea at the front and her heart bursting with joy – but as they drew closer to each other, she faltered. There were only a few Longi, and around them, like guards, were great black pilot whales, their feared cousins. Ea's body shot with fear, but the Longi kept calling out and advancing, and the Tursiops would not be stopped. Ea went on and saw to her astonishment that the pilots were part of the Longi pod – what was left of it.

She went to them in trepidation and they came forward. She knew by their eyes how much she had changed, but as they greeted her, she felt their loving hearts reaching out for her and for Chit behind her, and for all the Tursiops. The Tursiops came forward slowly, and the Longi went to them and caressed them, knowing without being told that they suffered so greatly. The Tursiops, to their shock, found the little Longi people were guarded by the young pilot whales, who waited for the signal before they relaxed. Then the Longi and the Tursiops and the pilots joined as one, and felt each other's comfort and strength.

Ea had never met any pilots, and found them strange and amazing and enormous. It was such a relief to speak the Longi dialect and yet she mixed it with Tursiops so those listening could understand – but the Longi could barely explain what had happened. Their homewater was no more, powerful devils were ripping the ocean apart and their screaming was killing pods of pilots, of humpbacks, of dolphins. There were nets of death where once was open water, there were great rents in the seabed. Death was everywhere, people were fleeing, the ocean was either full of refugees or terrifyingly empty.

The Tursiops said nothing. They had imagined a new sanctuary far away with the Longi, where they would live in harmony and plenty. The whole ocean was torn apart and they were all homeless.

Now the Longi gave vent to all their fears, and their shame that until they had heard the distant spins and falls, they had not even danced Exodus because it was too dangerous. But Ea had done it for them, she had kept the faith in life, in the ocean.

So strong and beautiful, Ea, they told her. *You always were.*

My mother— Ea could not say more.

Your mother has joined the ocean. She loves you. And Ea knew it was true.

Chit was staring out into the vast, seemingly unaware of the extraordinary merging going on around him. He stood up on his tail, and Ea saw how his torn dorsal fin was already starting to heal with a V of light in the centre.

Lord Chit, one of the young males clicked, and Ea saw it was one of her past captors, who had lost an eye in the battle in his courage to break the line of boats. He had been one of the best fighters, and had saved many people. Now he gave honour to Chit, and it was right. *What should we do?*

Before Chit could answer, they leaped in alarm as the pilot whales pointed themselves into the vast and cried out as one. The Tursiops and the Longi instinctively shrank together, but Chit alone went to the front of the pilots. Then everyone heard it.

From the vast came the great booming call of the humpback whale of her childhood, the rude, crude lonely old one whose song upset the adults – but now he was not alone. Many whale voices joined his chorus so that his song boomed and crashed, travelling across hundreds of miles of ocean, as rough and striking as ever before – and now the pilots called back in joy, their voices strained and broken.

Far away beyond the horizon, the old Rorqual boomed his song out through the vast, directing all who could hear him to *come now, come now to sanctuary, now while it is safe – come now, my people—*

He waited, then came the great chorus of whales of many tribes that were gathered with him, the tropical lateral bachelors who had faced the truth of his song and gone to find him, and the tiny whale of unknown tribe they gathered up into the fold, and the orphans and the bereaved of many species, all taking up the call of his song and booming it across the vast.

Sanctuary for the people,

Sanctuary here—

and then the Rorqual began a new verse, describing the currents, and the passage, and the time, and the distance, and the place of the sun, for he had learned to guide his people. All over the ocean of the world, the Rorqual song spread as others learned it and passed it on, so that it travelled the vast in a great overlapping round, changing in dialect and rhythm, but the message was the same. The old songs led to death, the new song was hard to sing, but led to safety.

The Rorqual could not hear the broken voices of the pilots, or the tiny calls of his little cetacean cousins, what was left of the Tursiops pod, and the Longi people. But they heard him, the straggling mixed and wounded pod of refugees that gathered up others as they went, shunning no one, feeding all where they could stop.

Hundreds of miles across the vast they travelled, Ea and Chit and all those who were left. The safety of one was the safety of all. They had no homewater, nor food but what was in their path. It was too dangerous to stop so they had no respite but their song, their stories, their love for each other and their courage.

Sanctuary for my people, sang the distant whales. The music of that ocean was a harsh and precious song, and sometimes the people were so exhausted they could only hear the one word of the chorus, but it was enough:

SANCTUARY

Acknowledgements

This novel required me to study several marine species. My full bibliography exceeds the space here, but a key source was *The Encyclopaedia of Marine Mammals (3rd ed)* edited by Bernd Würsig, JGM Thewissen and Kit M Kovacs. I'm indebted to them, to the work of Dr Sylvia Earle, and to the following scientists for further important material which shaped this story. In the interest of storytelling, I have taken poetic license in some places, and in others, filled out factual gaps with my imagination.

Bottlenose dolphins: are an intensively studied species with an abundance of excellent research material. But for those with particular interest in the astonishing facts of their use by various national militaries, see this from the U.S. Navy Marine Mammal Program: *https://www.niwcpacific.navy.mil/marine-mammal-program/*and do also read this: *https://hakaimagazine.com/features/the-great-dolphin-dilemma* by Lina Zeldovic

My gratitude to the ex-Navy SEAL, who on condition of anonymity, shared personal recollections of his work as a cetacean handler. Without his input, I would never have dared write Google's story.

Spinner dolphins: *Spinner dolphins in a remote Hawaiian atoll: social grouping and population structure* by Leszek Karczmarski, Bernd Würsig, Glenn Gailey, Keith W. Larson, Cynthia Vanderlip

Behavioral Ecology, Volume 16, Issue 4, July/August 2005, Pages 675–685

Mechanics Of Remora Removal By Dolphin Spinning (Marine Mammal Science, 23(3): 707–714 (July 2007). By Frank Fish, Daniel Wiehs & Anthony J Nicastro

Giant Clams: Dr Mei Lin Neo, of the National University of Singapore and 2021 Pew Marine Fellow of the Pew Charitable Trusts. Her website: *https://meilin5giantclam.wordpress.com* Be amazed.

Humpback whalesong: Dr. Jenny Allen, Honorary Research Fellow, Cetacean Ecology and Acoustics Laboratory, University of Queensland, *"Using self-organizing maps to classify humpback whale song units and quantify their similarity"* by Jenny A. Allen, Anita Murray, Michael J. Noad, and Rebecca A. Dunlop, and also Ellen C. Garland, University of St Andrews, UK.

Humphead, or Napoleon Wrasse: Professor Yvonne Sadovy de Mitcheson, University of Hong Kong. *https://www.biosch.hku.hk/ecology/ys.htm*

Remora fish: Professors C P Kenaley, A Stote, W B Ludt and P Chakrabarty for *Comparative Functional and Phylogenomic Analyses of Host Association in the Remoras (Echeneidae), a Family of Hitchhiking Fishes*, published in Integrative Organismal Biology, Volume 1, Issue 1, 2019

Films: ***Ocean Souls (dir. Philip Hamilton)*** is the place to start, an extraordinarily moving documentary with unimpeachable science. Available on Vimeo. ***Blackfish*** (dir. Gabriella Cowperthwaite, 2013), about the crime of orcas in captivity. ***Seaspiracy*** (dir. Ali Tabrizi, 2021), which will make you reconsider fish and how we treat them. Craig Foster's Oscar-winning ***My Octopus Teacher*** (Netflix 2020). ***The Cove***, also Oscar-winning (dir. Louie Psihoyos, 2009), investigating the 'harvesting' of dolphins in Japan. His organisation: The Oceanic Preservation Society. And a special thank you to the BBC Natural History Unit, for both series of ***Blue Planet***.

Social Media: Thank you to the numerous brave and beautiful ocean lovers, freedivers, film-makers, photographers, conservationists and activists who so generously share their work, and special thanks to Sophie Snowball for first curating my interest in sharks.

The family POD: Thanks and love to my agent Caroline Michel and her great team at Peters Fraser & Dunlop; and to my wonderful editor Olivia Hutchings and her inspiring team at Corsair Books: James Gurbutt, Zoe Hood, Emily Moran, and Phoebe Carney. Thank you too Tamsin Shelton, Tim Binding, and Kate Hamer.

Thanks and love too, to my dear friends and family who have supported me; especially to Adrian, my best companion on the long journey.

And for a lifetime of inspiration and his rallying call to action, thank you Sir David Attenborough.